From Prying Eyes

A Phoebe Braddock Romance

L. STARLA

Book design by L. Starla
Cover image by Enrique Meseguer from Pixabay
Editing by Felix Staica and Joshua Wake

ISBN-13 (paperback) 978-0-6488424-0-8
ISBN-13 (eBook) 978-0-6452783-1-6

Self-published.

Author's Note

This book contains coarse language, sex scenes, and sibling incest between consenting adults. Reader discretion is advised.

Epigraph

'I dedicate this novel to Heath and Jonah, who both taught me that love knows no boundaries.'
—P. Braddock.

Soundtrack

The characters in this story love music almost as much as their author. Some of these songs are referenced directly, while others fit the theme and mood of the story.

"Sex and Candy" by Marcy Playground
"Blow me Away" by Breaking Benjamin
"Fear" by Disturbed
"Smooth Criminal" by Alien Ant Farm
"Sinner" by Drowning Pool
"Short Skirt / Long Jacket" by Cake
"Stranger" by Goldfrapp
"All Mine" by Portishead
"I Put a Spell on You" Nina Simone
"Come Away with Me" Norah Jones
"Ain't It Funny" by Jennifer Lopez
"Hysteria" by Muse
"Synops" by Karnivool
"Passenger" by Deftones
"Mayonaise" by The Smashing Pumpkins
"Cry Little Sister" Marilyn Manson
"Roads" by Portishead
"Passing Bird" by Katatonia
'Sister Awake" by The Tea Party
"Taste in Men" by Placebo
"New Day" by Karnivool

Playlist available on Spotify.

Chapter One

The sound of a storm rumbling in the distance only enhanced Sophie's excitement and anxiety as she waited in the dark for her lover. She lay on her bed, dressed in a black satin slip. *What else could he teach me this time?* A sudden clap of thunder and the room lit up, then the sound of rain bucketing down. She chanced a brief look at the clock: 2AM already. He was late. She worried the weather had kept him away. *Should I remove the blindfold and attempt sleep?* A moment later, she heard someone opening her balcony door, the chill air touching her hot skin. Her heart skipped a beat before attempting to pound its way out of her rib cage. The door lock clicked, and the heat of the room intensified within seconds. He was upon her in a flash. Her mysterious stranger was with her at last. Her restricted sight enhanced her other senses. She could hear his fast, heavy breathing. She smelt his sandalwood cologne, which attempted to mask a more familiar scent she still couldn't place. Sophie

1

tasted his salty lips as they pressed against hers; felt the stubble on his cheeks scratch her skin. She welcomed the touch of his calloused fingers as they explored her body, starting from her face and gradually working their way down. As they reached their destination, her senses blurred, then…

She awoke with a start, dripping with sweat, heart beating. It was always the same whenever she dreamt of sex. She never climaxed. *Is this because I have never been touched down there?* She looked over to the spare mattress on the floor. *Where is Candice?* Then she noticed the cool breeze entering her room. The balcony door was slightly ajar. *Odd.* She never left it open except for a summer heatwave. But it was mid-autumn in Victoria, Australia.

Sliding out of bed, she stepped into her slippers and crossed the room to the balcony. When she put her hand to the cold steel frame of the glass door, she noticed faint voices travelling on the wind, coming from her brother's room. *Was that a girl with him?* She threw on her dressing gown and crept outside, quietly following the terracotta tiled path to Stefan's door. She shivered a little in the brisk air, with its strong fragrance of pine trees from their Mediterranean style garden.

When she reached his room, she peered through the gap in the thick Tuscan curtains. *What the feck?* He was lying naked on the bed with *her* straddling him. *How could* she *do this to me?*

She remembered what Candice said at Stefan's last gig: 'You know your brother's actually pretty hot.'

Sophie shrugged it off at the time. *Surely, Candice wouldn't break the code. But did she know the code?* A pang of jealousy gnawed at her while she watched them together. Stefan, her twin brother, had always been her best friend. Sophie often feared another girl coming between them, but he'd never found a girlfriend during their high school years. Candice was about to take his virginity. The first ever girl Sophie became close friends with was betraying her.

She should have left her vantage point and returned to bed, but Sophie was strangely intrigued by what was unfolding. At this point, it was literally the condom. Candice applied the rubber barrier with a deftness suggesting years of experience. Sophie was surprised by the considerable size of Stefan's erection. She'd seen him nude a few times since puberty, but it never looked like that!

My God, what's wrong with me? Why can't I look away? Sophie silently chided herself.

Candice was riding him, her hips thrusting with a force at odds with her fragile frame. Stefan's large, olive hands gripped her backside. They looked dark against her soft, pale skin. Candice applied a lot of makeup to her face to achieve the gothic pallor she wanted, yet the rest of her skin tone bore a close resemblance without cosmetics. Sophie had always admired her beauty; clearly, she wasn't alone!

They moved in a rhythmic unison; their breathing audible through the closed door. Hormones surged through Sophie's body. Subconsciously, she moved her left-hand to the moist area between her legs, slipped it inside her pyjama pants and thrummed the delicate skin with her fingers. When she caught herself plunging a finger deeper, she quickly withdrew, feeling ashamed. Mamma had always insisted masturbation was dirty and sinful, despite whatever else she heard.

The scene before her was coming to an end by this point. Candice groaned as she arched her back. Stefan gasped before screwing up his face, then Candice collapsed on him. Sophie quickly gathered her wits and dashed back to her room. Panting, she collapsed on her bed. She contemplated the private performance she'd witnessed. *Why am I aroused? Do I desire Candice? Surely it isn't because of my brother?*

℘℺

Sophie touched the delicate Venetian mask pendant on its gold chain briefly as she finished getting dressed the following morning. She remembered Carnevale five years ago when Stefan had gifted it to her. *Am I losing my dear, sweet brother?* Snapping herself out of her reverie, she put the necklace on. It was the only item of jewellery she wore, feeling more comfortable in jeans and t-shirts than anything feminine. She brushed her long, wavy, brown hair, and quickly spritzed herself with some white musk perfume. She was ready to face the day.

The inviting smell of freshly brewed espresso and toast greeted Sophie as she descended the stairs for breakfast, running her hands along the smooth, polished wood atop the wrought iron railing.

Her mamma, Francesca, looked up from her conversation with Candice, smiling warmly as she entered the casual dining area. 'Ciao Sofia.'

'Ciao Mamma.' Sophie moved in and kissed her on both cheeks, carefully balancing her steaming hot espresso in her right-hand. She took her seat at the table, then greeted Candice timidly with a forced smile, 'Um, morning Candice.'

Her friend replied with a nod and a mouth half full of food, 'Hey.'

Sophie applied some marmalade to her toast, then dug in, using her meal to avoid conversation.

Mamma suddenly looked at the clock and frowned. 'Where's Stefano? He's gonna be-a late.'

Sophie noticed Candice stifle a smile. Both her lips and Sophie's remained sealed.

They resumed eating in silence until Papà swept into the room in his designer suit, filling the

5

air with his overpowering citrus cologne and the rustling sound of papers. Attempting to close his overfull briefcase, he looked up and asked, 'Sofia, are you and your friend ready?'

'Sì, Papà—but Stefano?'

He glowered. 'Will have to catch the tram or drive himself.' Succeeding with the zip at last, he summoned them, 'Come.'

As if on cue, Stefan's dishevelled form stumbled through the door. Neither his short, undercut pompadour hair, nor his extended goatee had been groomed. He grinned at Candice briefly.

'*Stefano*!' Mamma cried. 'Why you make everyone late?'

'Sorry Mamma. Late night… studying.' He followed up with a kiss on Mamma's cheek, followed by Sophie's. 'Ciao Sofia.'

Papà scowled at him. 'Well I'm not waiting. You,' he pointed the leather case at Stefan, 'can find your own way. I'm already gonna be late for an important meeting.'

He poured the last of the coffee into his travel mug, then strode toward the garage. Sophie and Candice barely had time to grab their uni bags as they rushed after him.

℘ℛ

Sophie's ears were still ringing from the Italian opera that had blasted through the speakers of

Papà's Audi. She looked at Candice as they alighted the pavement. *Was that drive as painful for her as it was for me?* If so, Candice didn't show any obvious signs of displeasure.

Sophie shivered in the crisp air as they walked across the university campus, less enamoured by the hodgepodge of old gothic buildings and modern styles of architecture than usual. She tried to break the silence, 'So...d'ya get the reading done?'

Candice replied drily, 'Of course...I banged your brother last night by the way. Just thought you should know.'

Trying to act surprised, Sophie spun around to confront her friend, '*You did what?*'

Candice maintained her nonchalant composure. 'You heard me. I assume ya know what "banged" means?' She continued moving, urging Sophie forward again.

'Yes, but...' Sophie blinked in amazement.

The conversation was cut short once they reached the lecture hall. The drive from the Pacini family home in Toorak to the University of Melbourne during peak hour generally took between twenty to forty minutes. That morning the M1 was more congested than normal, making them late for Chemistry. After sneaking into the back row of the large, dimly lit auditorium, Sophie slumped into a chair and looked aghast at Candice. *How can she be so cool about this?* But Candice was too absorbed in their young Malaysian professor's talk on thermodynamics to notice.

ଯ୬ଓଷ

Dominic pranced across the North Lawn to meet the girls. He was in good spirits that day, likely due to the break in season. Cool weather meant clothing that had the dual effect of comfort and style. Embracing Sophie first, he exclaimed, 'Ciao bella!' Then they exchanged the customary kiss on the cheek. Turning to Candice he added, 'Hi Candice.' He didn't mind this strange goth who was following his bestie around, but it was hard to become close to someone as cold as the grave she'd apparently crawled out of.

Sophie commented, 'Hi Dom. Your accent's getting better. Those Italian classes are paying off.'

It was true that he had improved with the language since it became a university elective. During his high school years, most of his Italian vocab came from the bits he picked up around the Pacini household. He feigned insult in his reply: 'Thanks, Soph. I'll take that as a compliment.'

She pouted. 'I'm sorry, I didn't mean to imply…'

He cut her off. 'Nah, it's all good, really.' Pointing toward Union House, he continued, 'Shall we grab a bite? I'm famished.'

They made their way to a café for lunch. As they walked, he noticed Sophie glancing awkwardly at Candice a few times. *Have they been fighting?* They were lining up to order by this point and the delicious smell of pastries was making his stomach groan. Dominic, needing a distraction from hunger and unable to resist a good drama, inquired, 'Is something up with you two?'

It was Sophie who responded, 'Candice… took Stefan's V-card last night.'

Dominic couldn't believe his ears. 'Oh my God, Candice! You didn't, did you?'

Candice stared at him blankly. 'Yeh, but what's wrong with that?'

He was astounded as he cried, '*You broke the friendship code!*' Several startled students turned to look at him.

Candice asked, 'What's the "Friendship Code"?' She sounded so indifferent.

He sighed and rolled his eyes at her. 'Only like the most important unwritten rules of friendship *evah*.'

It was their turn to order. He promptly chose a goulash pie, fries, and a coffee. Once they were seated, he returned his attention to Candice. 'The "Friendship Code" says that we should never date or make moves on our friends' partners, ex-partners, or current crushes. It also says that we should ask permission before making moves on a friend's sibling.'

Candice gave him an incredulous eye. 'Sounds ridiculous to me. I can understand current partners or crushes, but the rest? Especially if you don't care about your exes anymore.'

A young man with blond, spiky hair and huge blue eyes delivered their food. He smiled at Dominic, which had him blushing slightly. They all dug in, giving them a moment of relative silence to think, amidst the din of the busy dining space.

Sophie sighed. 'I'm sorry Candice, but the thought of you with Stefan is weird.'

Dominic nodded with a mouth full of hot, juicy chunks of steak. After swallowing, he voiced his opinion. 'I agree. It's just too strange to talk about or even contemplate.'

Candice casually sipped her coffee then replied, 'Well don't think about it then. It's not like I was planning on telling you any details.'

Sick and angry with Candice, he didn't hide his disapproval when he asked, 'Does that mean you're just gonna go ahead and date Stefan anyway, despite Sophie's feelings?'

She answered in an amused tone, 'I never said anything about dating him. We had sex once. I can't promise it won't happen again, but I'm not interested in a committed relationship with him, or anyone else.'

Sophie seemed relieved then. 'I guess I can

deal with that.'

Dominic wasn't pacified so easily; Candice's behaviour was outrageous in his opinion, but Stefan was Sophie's brother, not his. If Sophie was content, there was little more he could do. His lunch hour was coming to an end anyway. He stood up to give his farewell hug to Sophie. 'See you at Ballroom tonight, Soph?'

'Yes, of course. There's no way Mamma would let me miss it with my debut approaching.'

'Awesome. See you there. I've gotta get to my CAD class now.' He stormed off towards the computer suite without so much as a 'See Ya' to Candice.

♾

'Ciao Derrick.' Sophie hoped her greeting didn't sound too enthusiastic. This was her favourite Friday class because of him, and she was relieved to be free of Candice. She sat down in the noisy lecture hall, pulling her *Biology of Cells and Organisms* notebook and pen from her bag.

'Ciao Sofia.' He smiled with a slight curl to his full lips and sparkle in his brown, deep-set eyes, sending flutters through Sophie's nervous system.

Is he flirting with me, or am I getting my hopes up again? They had been mates for as long as she could remember. But this tall, muscular hunk of a Venetian with his black, choppy hair and swooped fringe was among the elites at school and she'd only ever been an oddball. It was nice having him as a friend, but that was as far as it ever went.

She attempted her own coy smile. Suddenly overcome by the warmth in the room, she commented, 'Wow. I think they've overdone the heating in here.'

Derrick eyed her with fascination. 'Yeh, I guess they have.'

She stood up to remove a layer, sending her notebook flying into Derrick's lap and her pen to the floor. 'Shit! Sorry Derrick.' She quickly removed her grey knit jumper, then sat down.

Derrick was looking down at the open book in his lap with a grin. Sophie inspected the source of his amusement, then flushed. Her notes displayed a large diagram of the female reproductive system.

He looked back up into Sophie's eyes and his grin widened. 'Would you like to retrieve that, or should I *handle* it for you?'

This had to be flirting! Sophie decided to play along and smiled intently. 'Would you like to *handle* it for me?'

Derrick tittered. 'Certainly. But don't forget the pen. Should I grab *that* for you too?' He glanced down at the floor space by his foot.

The lecturer started talking at that moment and the chatter of the room hushed. Sophie leaned her head against Derrick's arm as she bent down for her pen, the tangy scent of his cologne invading her senses. She lingered a little, brushing her arm against the thick denim of his jeans as her fingers gripped their hard, plastic prize. He did not recoil at her touch. *This is a promising sign!*

With pen in hand, she gestured for her notebook. Derrick's index finger glided along the page, until it reached the section of the image marked 'Introitus,' then left it there a moment. He looked back into Sophie's eyes with a fierce intensity that made her own introitus quiver. *Is he testing me?* She refused to look away or betray her embarrassment. They remained locked in this holding pattern for a few minutes, then he ceded and returned the notebook.

Sophie tried to concentrate on the speaker up front, but his words washed over her. She was thinking about her neighbour and chanced the occasional look. It appeared that most glances went unnoticed, but he caught her once, halfway through the lecture. She hastily turned her gaze back to the front. When she looked back, his eyes were still fixed on her. He leered slightly before casually returning his attention to the lesson.

Sophie couldn't believe Derrick's conduct. *What had changed after all these years?* Her heart was pounding. *Should I try anything further?* She leaned in toward him slightly. He must have sensed her motive because he moved his arm across the back of her chair. *Oh my God! This is really happening!* She let her head rest against him. They remained in this sweet near-embrace for the remainder of the class.

When it was over, Derrick retrieved his arm and packed his bag. Sophie watched him hopefully.

Once finished, he spoke briefly, 'See ya in the prac on Monday.' He then stood up and left.

What the…? Was Derrick just teasing me? She packed her own belongings, then glumly made her way home.

Chapter Two

'It's time to Cha Cha Cha!' cried Cassandra, the dance instructor; her voice booming through the large dance hall.

Stefan groaned and bowed his head as 'Crazy in Love' fired up.

His next dance partner laughed as she moved into position. 'You never could stand Beyoncé, huh?'

He looked up and smiled at the familiar sound of his sister's voice. 'Well at least I have you for this one.' Sophie was the main reason he tolerated Mamma dragging them out to these lessons. He relished every opportunity to dance with her, to indulge his fantasies.

He extended his left arm so that his long, guitar playing fingers could wrap around the soft skin of her dainty right hand. He drew her closer as his right hand found purchase on her shoulder blade, her own left hand resting on his arm. A familiar passion surged through his body as he took in her sweet, musky aroma. They moved to the music. Stefan was vaguely aware of their teacher's counting, 'One, two, cha, cha, cha. Side, forward, replace, side together, side…' as his mind returned to last night. *Sex with Candice felt good and I like her, but she and I both knew she was a distraction, an outlet for my forbidden desires.*

Cassandra's voice bought him back to reality, chiding him, 'Pay attention Stefan! Your footwork is getting sloppy!'

Sophie grinned. 'You were thinking of Candice, weren't you? She told me what happened.'

Ah crap! He was hoping to keep his sexual activities a secret from Sophie. He didn't want her to think ill of him. 'Um maybe… kinda,' he admitted.

'It's okay. I think she's beautiful too.' Leaning in, she whispered, 'I don't mind if you want to imagine dancing with her right now.' She gave him a conspiratorial wink.

Little did she know! Oh God! He was getting a hard-on. He tried to focus on the steps to ease the tension, praying that Sophie didn't see or feel the bulge in his pants. As he led her into a rope spin, Stefan stumbled. *Damn it!* It was too difficult to concentrate. Time to employ the big guns. He brought the face to mind. The image that made him go soft every time. As Derrick's smirk and stupid hair appeared, he felt the yearning subside. He was finally able to voice a response: 'And you could imagine that I'm Derrick.'

Sophie's face went red as she spoke, 'I dunno, things might get too hot for TV, especially after the biology class I had with him today.'

Stefan knew all about Sophie's crush. Derrick's lack of reciprocation may have kept her single all this time, but it did little to buffer the pain. She still wanted Derrick, not him. It was absurd to think this way, his brain understood. Even if Sophie did want him, nothing could ever happen. But that didn't stop his heart, or his other longings.

Stefan was still curious though. 'Care to elaborate?' He broke their handhold and tried some arm styling.

Blushing again, she replied, 'Let's just say he was a flirtatious tease this afternoon. I'll fill you in on the details later.'

That bastard better not be leading her on! 'Are you sure he was flirting? Is there any chance you're misreading him again?' He grabbed both her hands then moved straight into some crossover breaks.

When they returned to the dance frame hold, Sophie answered, 'I dunno, Stefan, there was a lot of intense eye contact and he put his arm around me halfway through the lecture.' She paused for thought, then went on, 'But in the end, he just left without any follow-up.'

'Whatta jerk!' *Oops, did I say that aloud?*

Frowning, she asked, 'You think he's toying with me?'

'I dunno Sofia. If it was me, I wouldn't leave a girl I liked hanging. But he's an alpha. Their brains are wired differently.'

She shrugged, twirled through a spiral turn, then changed the subject. 'Has anyone asked you to the ball yet?'

He sniggered 'Nope, but I don't really wanna go. Not unless you're asking me?'

'It may come to that. I don't wanna go either, but Mamma's insisting this year, being my last chance before we turn eighteen. I just hate this whole stupid tradition of girls asking guys. I'm too nervous to ask Derrick.'

The music stopped and Sophie moved on. Elise was next and it was time to Rumba.

೫ೞ

'Ah Jesus Soph! How do you keep finding the energy sword?!' Luke cried.

Stefan chortled then briefly glanced at his *Halo 2* teammate. 'Nice work Soph! … Aw yeah, got me a shotgun. Here comes the deadly close combat duo.' He finished off Dominic, the last opponent threatening the objective and winning them the match.

Sophie dropped her controller and jumped up, exclaiming, 'Booyah!' Then high-fived Stefan.

'That's best of five, bitchas! Wanna try for seven?'

This was the Sophie he loved most, the one few people saw. She was in her element when hosting gaming nights. He took a moment to appreciate the view while she was standing. Her Pikachu t-shirt was a snug fit on her firm breasts and her blue denim jeans were flattering around the perfect curves of her hips and backside.

Dominic raised his hands, conceding defeat. 'Please, no more pain! Victory is yours!'

Luke, Stefan's best mate, rose from his armchair. 'I need a drink!'

Stefan agreed. It was Saturday night after all and he had spent the day working on his economics assignment. 'I'll grab us some beers. Who's in?'

He got a 'Hell yeah!' from Luke.

And a 'Yes please, though I'd prefer cider if you have any,' from Dominic.

Sophie followed him to the bar along the East wall of their gaming room. 'I'll help.'

When she leaned in front of him to grab the bottle opener, the sweet, musky smell of her perfume filled Stefan's nose. Being this close to her was intoxicating and he hadn't even started with the booze yet! He steadied himself with his left hand against the polished wood bench top. Without thinking, he put his right hand on Sophie's shoulder. She flinched.

Looking back at him, she asked, 'What,

Stefan?'

Shit! Think quick, you moron! 'Err... just appreciating how awesome my sister is.'

She turned to face him head on. 'Naw, you big softy. Come 'ere, you.'

He accepted her welcoming embrace. When he looked up, he noticed Luke was connecting his iPod to the stereo, filling the room with their favourite metal tunes. He caught his friend's eye and Luke shook his head in mock disapproval. He was thankful that Dominic was distracted by his Nintendo DS.

Stefan let go of Sophie as soon as the stirring between his legs started, before it grew into anything obvious.

When he returned to the couch with the beers, he handed one to Luke, then sat down. Sophie joined them with the ciders, giving one to Dominic and starting on her own.

'So how about a game of confessions?' Luke suggested, giving Stefan a sly grin.

'Yeah, sure. Sounds like fun,' Sophie replied.

Oh joy! Luke's gone and dug a nice big hole for me to fall into, Stefan thought.

'Count me in,' added Dominic.

Stefan sighed. 'Fine. But no dares.'

Luke asked, 'Who wants to start confessing?'

'I will,' volunteered Dominic. 'What's the first topic?'

Luke, flicking his long hair out of his face, answered, 'I say we chose the topics based on whatever song is playing.' He stopped to listen. It was 'Fear' by Disturbed. 'Okay, let's start with fears.'

Dominic took a large swig of his drink before speaking. 'I confess that I am most afraid of being insignificant.'

Sophie put a comforting hand on Dominic's arm. 'Wow Dom, that's full on. You will never be insignificant to the people whose lives you touch.'

Dominic smiled. 'Thanks Soph. You're a gem. I guess it's more that I don't want to lose my sense of self or be forced to conform, ya know?'

Stefan spoke up, 'I know what ya mean. We live in such a narrow-minded community. At least uni gives us a chance to express ourselves more than school ever did.' He looked intently at Sophie to prompt her. 'I think it's your turn to confess, Soph.'

She thought for a moment then looked directly at Stefan, 'I confess that I am most afraid of being separated from you, Stefan.'

Stefan sucked in an audible breath. Her words pierced the core of his being. 'Wow Sophia. That... that's mine too.'

She smiled. 'Makes sense. We are twins.'

'Naw, you guys are adorable!' It was Dominic. 'I wish my sister was half as sweet to me.'

When Luke caught Stefan's attention, he piped up, 'You definitely share a *special* bond.'

Shit! Has he worked out how I feel? He narrowed his gaze on Luke. 'So, what are you afraid of, Luke?'

'Oh, you know—the classics. Like poverty and illness. I find boredom hard to deal with too.' He skulled the rest of his beer, then stood up. 'Mind if I grab another?'

'Go for it,' Sophie replied. 'Can you grab more for all of us?'

'Sure.' Luke strolled over to the bar just as Alien Ant Farm's cover of 'Smooth Criminal' started up.

'So, I guess our next topic is crime,' announced Dominic.

Stefan chuckled. 'I can't believe you still have this shit on your playlist, Luke.'

Luke scoffed from across the room, 'So that wasn't Limp Bizkit I heard you playing the other day?' When the drinks were distributed, and he sat down again and started the round. 'I tried my first bong last weekend.'

'I thought you tried weed back in school?' Stefan inquired.

'Only as joints. This was different. It was at Chris' party, after you guys left.'

Chris was the bass player in their metal band and he'd just celebrated his eighteenth birthday.

Dominic was next. 'I'm not sure if my confession is valid now. It happened years ago, but I can't think of anything more recent.'

'Do go on,' Luke insisted.

'Well I did steal a pack of chewing gum once,' he admitted. 'It was in year eight and I was trying to impress Troy.'

Sophie giggled. 'You rebel!' It was a strange tone for her, likely due to the alcohol.

'Hey, miss judgey, this's supposed to be a safe space,' Dominic whined.

She pouted. 'I'm sorry Dom. I admire your law-abiding ways. I'm still pretty square myself. I think the most criminal thing I've done is speeding. I swear my feet are filled with lead when I get behind the wheel. I'm just glad I haven't been caught yet. How 'bout you, Stefan?'

He couldn't recall anything worth confessing. There was the time he stole two dollars from Mamma's purse in primary school, but that was about it. 'I really can't think of anything illegal that I've done.'

Luke ribbed him. 'Not that you've done *yet*, but I'm sure you've considered it.'

God damn! He must know. Sophie eyed him suspiciously. Stefan needed to proceed with caution. 'I'm sure we've all considered breaking the law before, but intent alone does not a crime make.'

'Amen to that,' Sophie declared. 'I still get

nightmares about the thought police after reading *1984*.'

Stefan shivered at the idea. His desires had been torturous ever since the onset of puberty, when the wet dreams started. He suspected it was wrong back then. Reading the Bible confirmed as much, but what he learnt in legal studies was the nail in the coffin. He even memorised the relevant section of legislation: 'A person must not take part in an act of sexual penetration with a person whom he or she knows to be his or her sister, half-sister, brother or half-brother.' (*Crimes Act 1958*).

He skulled the majority of his second beer and went for more.

Luke cheered him on, then followed suit. As they both opened their ale, Luke clinked his bottle with Stefan's. 'Cheers mate. Here's to our most law-abiding citizen.'

He sounded genuine and Stefan was relieved to move past the topic of his lecherous contemplation.

When Stefan returned to the couch, he assumed his favourite sitting position without thinking. Back against the corner of the L-shaped sofa, right leg bent against the backrest so that his foot was on the seat. His left foot remained on the floor.

Sophie snorted the moment Drowning Pool started singing 'Sinner' through the speakers, then fell back against Stefan's chest. She slapped his left thigh and squealed. 'Seven Deadly Sins! Come on Stefan, I know you are guilty of one of these!'

By God! The weight of her body pressed against his instantly ignited his passions. Rather than sitting back up, she remained against his lap. It was not unusual for them to cuddle on the couch like this when gaming or watching television, but the screen usually provided an essential distraction.

'Is that so?' Luke probed.

Stefan spoke candidly, 'I assume Sophie's referring to the night I had sex with Candice.' Beer sprayed from Luke's mouth into the air. 'Sorry Luke, I didn't have a chance to tell you about it before.'

'Holy shit man! You finally got laid! Congrats dude.'

'Thanks mate.' Stefan mumbled. He could tell that Luke wanted him to elaborate, but he wasn't keen to go into details with Sophie present.

It was Dominic who came to the rescue. 'I really don't want to hear the particulars. Your turn, Luke.'

'I've been guilty of all seven over the years, but I guess the most recent and frequent would be pride. I know I'm a good drummer and I feel smug every time I smash out a sick rhythm on the kit.'

'You ought to be proud of those skills man,' Stefan assured him. He was acutely conscious of

Sophie's arm. Her hand still on his thigh, the elbow pressed into his lap. *Is she aware of my raging boner?* He tried to control his breathing and heart-rate.

Dominic patted his pot belly as he spoke. 'Well I'm most guilty of gluttony. I tend to over-indulge in anything comforting, like chocolate, coffee, and clothing.'

'I can relate,' Sophie admitted, 'although not so much with the clothes. But I have a bigger confession to make for this one.' She drew more courage from her cider bottle, then continued. 'I didn't learn about Stefan and Candice after the fact... I saw it for myself... through the balcony window.' She sat up to look into Stefan's eyes. He briefly detected carnal need in her gaze. He was speechless. *Is it possible my feelings are mutual?*

'I was envious of her, Stefan. I've always feared the day you would get a girlfriend and stop spending much time with me.'

Stefan sensed that there was more she wasn't letting on, but he wasn't going to push it, especially with the others there. Their eyes remained locked together, both trying to read each other's minds.

'Well I think that's our cue to go, don't you Luke?' Dominic stood up and left the room.

'But...' Luke started, then sighed and followed Dominic downstairs.

They were suddenly alone. He desperately wanted to kiss her. *Stop it, you sick fuck!*

'Stefano? What's wrong?' She looked and sounded concerned.

He shook his head. 'I…uh…didn't know that's how you felt. I'm sorry Sofia.'

She leaned back in to embrace him. 'It's okay, Stefano. I don't want you to deprive yourself because of my petty jealousy. I'll get over it, I'm sure.'

His arms automatically enfolded her. Planting a gentle kiss on the crown of her head, he reassured her, 'Don't worry Sofia. I'm not gonna leave you.'

ജന

Stefan found Luke practising on the drums in the rumpus room, out the back of the Pacini property. The isolation of the building provided an ideal rehearsal space, as did the sound insulation. The rest of the band weren't due for another half hour, which was just as well. It was early afternoon and he was still recovering from their late night of gaming and drinking. He hadn't even been able to get up for church, much to Mamma's displeasure.

Luke looked up as he entered. He set the sticks aside to accept an espresso from Stefan. 'Thanks man… You look like shit.'

'Gee thanks. Maybe I overdid the coldies, although it didn't seem like much… I guess I haven't been sleeping well lately.'

'I can't think why,' Luke grinned knowingly.

Stefan sat down and imbibed some of the hot, heavily sweetened coffee he was nursing. He knew that Luke wasn't gonna let the issue rest. 'What the fuck is with you dude? You've been on my back about something. What is it?'

Still grinning, Luke replied, 'Come on man, we've been friends forever. You ought to know you can tell me anything. Perhaps you've been afraid to admit it to yourself.'

'Stop being so cryptic Luke. What the hell are you on about?' Stefan's heart was pounding. *What would Luke think of me if the truth came out?*

'I've come to recognise the way certain chicks affect you. One in particular. You want her bad, but you know you can't have her.'

Stefan set aside his empty cup then bent over to run his fingers through his hair. 'Am I that obvious?'

After a few minutes of silence, the reply came. 'Took me a while to read the signs, so no, I don't think so.'

Stefan looked up again. Luke's coffee was finished, and he was fiddling with the drumsticks. Stefan couldn't read his mien. 'I s'pose you think I'm a sick bastard.'

'Nah man, I don't see anything wrong with it. You guys make a cute couple… and a fuckin' deadly *Halo* team.'

Thank Christ! He found a sympathiser and someone to share his burden.

'Did anything happen last night?' Luke inquired.

Stefan's mind was instantly transported back to that tender moment with Sophie. The scent of her freshly washed hair, the warmth of her skin radiating through the soft, thin cotton of her t-shirt. He was completely undone by her. 'I just held her as we talked.'

Luke's expression was serious, a rare look for him. 'Does she want you?'

'I dunno. She hasn't said anything of the sort, but there have been times when her body language has hinted at the possibility. Doesn't matter though. I can't have her regardless.'

'Sorry man. I wish I knew what ya could do.'

The sound of voices approaching put an end to that topic of conversation.

Chapter Three

Sophie knocked on the door of the spare room, concerned that Dom hadn't emerged yet. She was answered with a 'Come in.' He was still wrapped up in the quilt. She perched on the edge of the bed and handed him some toast and a coffee.

He sat up to accept her offer. 'Thanks Soph. What time is it?'

She looked at her black digital watch, then looked out the window and noticed the sky was overcast and threatening rain. 'Eleven fifty. I just got back from church.'

'Already? Geez. I bet Mum was furious that I didn't show!'

'Your mum always looks furious, but she didn't say anything to me.'

He nodded, then devoured his toast before speaking again. 'How'd you shape up after last night?'

'Fine, but then I paced myself with the cider. You had a few more than me.'

'Damn that delicious nectar of the devil.' He looked at her, then asked, 'How'd your chat go with Stefan?'

'Huh?... Oh that. It went fine. He was very apologetic for what happened with Candice. Apparently, it was a spur of the moment thing. He has no interest in dating her.' Sophie thought back to her talk with Stefan. It was a strangely intimate experience. She remembered sensing something that she couldn't quite recognise.

Dom smiled. 'Good to know. You okay? You look spaced.'

'I'm okay… Just got a few things on my mind.'

'Such as?' he prompted her.

'Derrick for one. He's been acting strange.' She told him about his flirting.

When she finished, he jumped in, 'No way! That devious demon!' After another minute of consideration, he advised, 'You should ask him to the ball. Your crush must be obvious to him. It would be a good way to gauge how he really feels about you.'

'I dunno Dom, I really want to, but I'm afraid he'll say no, and I'll feel humiliated.'

He gave her a rueful look. 'Come on, *chica*, you won't know if you don't ask.'

Sophie sighed heavily. 'I know. I'll give it more thought, but I was also thinking of asking you to the ball.'

'Sorry hun, I'm taken already.'

'What? Really? Who?' This came as a surprise to her. They had always been each other's backup dates.

'Tegan asked me at our last ballroom lesson.' He smiled coyly.

'Oh wow. I had no idea you were into her.' Sophie avoided female company most of the time, but she had spoken to Tegan on occasion. 'She seems nice.'

'I wouldn't say that I'm into her exactly. We have become good friends lately though. She's studying design, so we have some classes in common at uni. I think she might be interested in being more than friends, but I honestly don't know what I want.' He paused to finish his coffee, then asked, 'So, what else has been on your mind?'

She blushed. 'Um… well… sex.'

Dom blushed. 'Anything more specific?'

'I've been having a lot of… naughty dreams lately. And unwholesome thoughts. I don't know what it means, or how to stop it.' Her mysterious stranger had been haunting her dreams every night that week and last night's dream had seemed more intense than normal.

'Why stop it? It sounds like you're turning into a woman,' he suggested.

Sophie frowned. 'But isn't lust sinful?'

'I dunno. It's not like I have any experience in the matter. I've never felt any strong desires for any of the girls I've met. I haven't even had a proper erection.'

'So, you've never masturbated?' she asked.

'Nope. The thought has always repulsed me.' He shifted awkwardly. 'Have you?'

'No, same reason really. What about wet dreams?' Sophie implored.

'Come to think of it, yes, I do get those, but I've never remembered the details.' He went quiet.

She realised that Dom was also denying himself any sexual pleasures. Sophie decided that maybe it was okay to explore her desires further. If it didn't hurt anyone else, what harm was there? 'I have an idea. Let's make a masturbation pact. I will give it a try sometime in the next week if you promise to do the same.'

It was Dom's turn to blush. 'Um… that's a pretty weird concept… but I guess I can give it a go.'

She smiled. 'Let's shake on it.' She offered her hand to Dom. He hesitated, but then complied.

'Just don't ask me to shake that hand next week.' He grinned as he poked her in the ribs.

She squealed. 'There's one more thing on my mind. I need your help with something, and we are going to need Candice for this too.'

☙❧

Shopping for clothes was not something Sophie usually considered fun, but that was the old her. The new Sophie was on a mission and she was enjoying her adventure through Melbourne Central. When they started, Sophie explained: 'I need a makeover. I want to look and feel sexy. Now Candice, I like the way you dress. And I think you look hot, but I don't think the whole goth look is right for me. I need help finding my own style.'

A few hours in, Sophie's basket was overflowing.

'This is cute, Soph,' Dom suggested, holding up a hot pink plaid skirt.

Candice shook her head. 'Too bright for my tastes.'

He snickered. 'Funeral wear was last year, Candice. Shall we move on?'

Sophie walked up to Dom and looked closely at the garment. It looked incredibly short. The old Sophie would have dismissed it instantly, but the new Sophie said, 'I'll try it on.' She added it to the pile of hot clothes and made her way to the fitting rooms.

She was pleasantly surprised by the ego boost she got from admiring her reflection in the new outfits. Slip dresses, pleated miniskirts, boob tubes, preppy pants, cardigans, and Juicy Couture sweatshirts all in a range of rich purples, pinks, reds, and blues. She avoided too much black, but there was one outfit she couldn't resist.

When she modelled the black top with mesh sides and matching skirt, even Candice was impressed. 'Gosh woman. Even I feel turned on seeing you in that and chicks don't normally do it for me.'

'Derrick won't be able to resist you in that outfit,' Dom agreed.

'Right, well that should be enough casual clothes. Now for some shoes, lingerie and makeup. Then the debutante dress.'

₧₧

After dumping the bags in the car, they found an exclusive designer label dress shop. The assistant approached them with a contemptuous look in her eye. 'I'm sorry, but I doubt we have anything to suit your budget here.'

Sophie was shocked by her behaviour. She'd been to plenty of posh stores with her parents before and never been treated like this.

Candice gave the woman a dagger stare. Putting on her best snooty voice, she spoke. 'Well Sophie, shall we return to Toorak and use your Daddy's credit card at a local boutique?'

Sophie suppressed her mirth and tried to play along. 'You know, I think that is a splendid idea. These people clearly don't want Pacini money.'

The assistant went pale. 'Did you say Pacini from Toorak?'

Sophie replied, 'Yes. I am Sofia Pacini. My parents are Roberto and Francesca. Do you know them?'

The woman gulped. 'Oh yes actually. I am sincerely sorry Sofia. I did not realise. Please, is there anything I can help you with?'

'I'm not sure she wants to shop here now,' Candice commented sardonically.

Several garments on the nearby rack caught Sophie's eye. 'It's okay Candice. I can see some dresses I like the look of. This place will do.' She turned to the snobby woman. 'I need a debutante dress.'

'Ah yes, of course. Did you want to go with the traditional white gown?'

'Um I guess so.'

She led Sophie to the fitting rooms and commenced taking her measurements. Apparently, this was the sort of shop where a dress was properly fitted and adjustments were made, so Sophie was instructed to return later in the week to pick up her dress.

80C3

'I need some sex advice,' Sophie told Candice, who

was in the middle of teaching Sophie how to apply liquid foundation. Their shopping trip had taken the whole afternoon and they returned half an hour ago. Dominic made himself scarce once the makeup stuff started. He claimed that he was required at home for dinner, but Sophie suspected he just felt out of place.

'What do ya need to know?' Candice didn't even show the slightest hint of embarrassment.

'How to masturbate properly. I've never tried it before and I'm curious.'

'Oh, is that all? Too easy.' She handed Sophie the makeup brush. 'Your turn.'

She struggled to apply the product evenly. 'Damn it! This is harder than it looks.'

Candice reassured her. 'It just takes practice. You'll get the hang of it… here….' She pressed her hands against Sophie's face to finish smoothing out the makeup. 'I promise that masturbation is much easier.' She picked up the powder and continued her demonstration. 'Do you have any sex toys yet?'

'Do you mean a vibrator?' Sophie blushed.

'Yeh. There's also the dildo and the clitoral massager. They all serve different functions.'

'Gosh, sounds complicated. But no, I don't have any… uh… toys. Perhaps you could… um… purchase some for me?'

'No problem. In the meantime, you can use your hand, but I find it harder to orgasm that way.

Not impossible though, if you have plenty of time and the right stimulus.'

Sophie had a bit more success with the powder and eye shadow. Watching Candice with the eyeliner, she asked, 'What do you mean by *stimulus*?'

'Either look at or think about something that turns you on. I normally use porn. You could probably start with a photo of Derrick.'

'Makes sense.' She picked up her liquid eyeliner and got to work. 'Shit!' She'd botched it bad. Her eyelid was completely black.

Candice smiled. 'Sorry, but this is the hardest part. You'll want plenty of remover and these on hand'. She pushed the box of cotton tips across the dressing table.

Sophie cleaned the mess she'd made, then kept trying and eventually got it.

'Nice work. Persistence is the key, much like with manual masturbation. Mascara next.'

'So... um... do I just poke my fingers around in there?'

Once she'd finished the mascara on both eyes, she replied, 'Best to start with rubbing the area, then go for penetration when you feel aroused.'

'Oh, okay.' Mascara done! She was getting the hang of it. The lip liner was a challenge too, but she got it with a few attempts and the lip gloss was easy enough.

'Oh, and don't forget to clean your hands before and after.' Candice added.

'Do you mean for makeup or masturbation?' Sophie asked.

'Both.'

෨෬

Sophie lay face down upon her bed with a framed photo on the pillow, dimly lit by her bedside lamp. She was wearing a new black satin negligee and trying to focus her thoughts on the picture of Derrick in front of her. It was difficult though. Her mind kept wandering.

Dinner was interesting that night. Sophie wore makeup and one of her new slip dresses. The moment she entered the dining room, everyone looked up and gasped.

'You look stunning, Sofia,' Mamma complimented her first.

Then Papà's attempt: 'Yes. You look quite respectable now.'

The oddest response of all came from Stefan. He didn't say anything. Just kept staring at her. Even with Candice sitting next to her, it was as though Sophie was the only person at the table. When they retired to the family room to watch a movie, Stefan put a hand on her shoulder and whispered, 'You look incredible, Soph.'

'Thanks Stefan,' she replied, then hugged him. It reminded her of the embrace from the previous night. There was something strange about it that she couldn't place.

This kept intruding upon her thoughts when she tried to focus on Derrick's image. She turned onto her back, closed her eyes and commenced rubbing herself. She visualised Derrick giving her that flirtatious smile. Still nothing. Then she remembered her reaction to the sight of Candice's naked body riding her brother. Dare she go there? Too late! The swelling had started. She relaxed and allowed her mind to return to that clandestine moment as she stroked her clitoris. Her opening instantly tightened and she could feel a tingling sensation throughout her lower region. Finally! She let her fingers explore the depths of her womanhood. The texture of the supple folds of internal skin were strange, but not unpleasant. Her mental images changed again, and she was being touched by her mysterious stranger. It was his rough fingers inside her. She began to moan as the tension built and her juices flowed. She was getting somewhere. Her anonymous lover thrust his hand harder, faster. Then her body convulsed as she rode the waves of her first orgasm.

Chapter Four

'Who's the new hottie?' Stuart, one of Derrick's soccer teammates, asked, calling him to attention.

Having just finished training, they were approaching the biology labs, and Derrick's mind had been busy working through the dissection method steps he'd read several times over the last week. When his eyes followed Stuart's—thankful he remembered his sunglasses—they were pleasantly surprised by the shapely backside barely concealed beneath a pink plaid skirt. And those legs! By God! He was instantly intrigued, especially since she was waiting outside the lab he was about to enter. *Surely it was too late in the semester for someone to start a new class.*

As the two guys moved in on her, the girl in pink turned to face them. 'Ah, ciao Derrick. Stuart.' Her smile was focused on Derrick. It was disarming.

Derrick blinked a few times to make sure his

eyes were not deceiving him. 'Sofia?'

'Yes? Are you okay, Derrick?' There was a playful twinkle in her eyes, and he noticed she was wearing makeup.

Stuart tittered. 'Hey Sophie. You look nice today.' Then he walked over to his prac partner.

A quick glance of her chest was rewarded by the delicious crevasse that her cardigan's open buttonhole revealed. He realised his mouth was agape. *Idiot! Don't lose your cool!* 'Yeah, sorry. I just didn't recognise you at first. You look… so different.'

'Oh, right. I decided it was time for a change. Shall we?' indicating with her manicured hand that she meant to enter the door that had just opened.

He followed her closely. Derrick had always valued his friendship with Sophie. They grew up together in neighbouring homes and their Italian community was tightknit. He had known about her crush for years and was flattered by it, but only friendship had ever been his intent with her. That was before. He had no idea she'd been hiding such a beautiful woman beneath those layers of baggy clothes.

When they reached their workbench, Derrick was a little disappointed that Sophie had to cover up with a lab coat. It was probably just as well: distractions were not ideal when working with scalpels. As she fastened her buttons, she inquired,

'How was your weekend, Derrick?'

He shrugged on his own coat as he replied, 'Good, thanks. Yours?'

Finished with her buttons, she looked up and grinned, 'Great actually.'

He became acutely aware of the way the hem of her white coat extended beyond that of her skirt. Cake (the band) weren't wrong about the appeal of this look.

'Planning to do these up?' She moved in close and fingered the buttons on his lab coat.

Forgive me Lord! Derrick couldn't control the lecherous desire that surged through his body in response to her slight touch. He felt ashamed. Willpower was usually one of his strong suits. 'Hmm? Oh right.' *Get it together, loser!*

'Here. Allow me.' She pressed her hands up against him.

Derrick couldn't object, even if he wanted to. He was enthralled. Her musky perfume overpowered the sterile smell of ethanol in the air.

'Right, well it's time we started. Greetings all,' announced Graham, their supervisor. 'You will each need to collect a specimen. Please ensure that you work with one of each gender in your pairs.'

Sophie removed her hands from Derrick's person and walked towards the front of the room. He felt compelled to stay close to the new Sophie. When they reached the specimen area, Sophie looked over her shoulder to ask, 'Did you want the male or female?'

'Female, please.' He was still uncomfortable with the thought of touching male genitals other than his own. He knew he'd have to get over these apprehensions if he was to be a doctor one day, but he'd worry about that later.

When they returned to their work area, his first instinct was to make some wisecrack about probing the introitus, but he suddenly realised that Sophie wasn't just one of the guys anymore. How should he act around her now? Could he see her as a girlfriend?

⁊

Candice watched as Derrick reluctantly walked away. 'He's got it bad now,' she observed aloud.

Sophie returned to her seat on the lawn. She looked perplexed. 'Got what bad?'

'Your plan to seduce him is obviously working. He couldn't keep his eyes off you all through lunch. Even the fact that he joined *us* for lunch speaks volumes.'

'I dunno. He seemed quiet and withdrawn in our prac this morning, despite my obvious attempts to flirt.' She was awkwardly trying to adjust her skirt and sitting position.

Poor, naïve girl. Candice was beginning to appreciate the downsides of Sophie's sheltered upbringing. But then much of what Candice learned about men was forced upon her much too early.

'That's *because* he wants you. He's being cautious because the stakes are higher.'

'You think so?' Sophie asked.

'I know so. Trust me.' Candice was fascinated by Sophie. She was humble and kind, unlike the other rich bitches from her end of town. But there was also a fragility to her that made Candice want to shield her from the harsh cruelty of the world. The problem was, she had no idea how to be a protector.

'God damn it! How can you stand sitting on the lawn with a short skirt?' Sophie exclaimed while scratching at her legs.

'Sorry, I didn't realise the grass would bother you. I've never had problems with it. Did you want to move?' At least that was something Candice could thank her father for. His strong genes meant she didn't have any allergies.

Sophie didn't need any more prompting. She was up in a flash. 'Yes please.'

Candice stood, then casually brushed the grass off her backside. 'Let's go to the library. I need to do some more physics research anyway.'

'Good plan,' Sophie agreed.

৪৩৫

Sophie spotted Dom sitting alone in one of the

group-study rooms in the library. She pointed out the room to Candice, who was sitting at one of the database computers.

'Go on. I'll catch up with you later,' Candice suggested.

As soon as the door was shut behind her, Sophie burst with her news. 'I did it!'

Dom looked confused. 'Did what?'

She sat down next to him and lowered her voice to a whisper. 'Masturbated.'

'Um… oh right. The pact,' he blushed. 'Sorry, I forgot.'

'That's okay. You still have till the end of the week.' She smiled encouragingly. 'You know what the weirdest part of it was?'

'I can't even begin to imagine,' he admitted.

Sophie looked around conspiratorially. 'It was thinking about Candice that got me aroused in the first place.'

Dom gasped. 'No way!'

She leaned in closer to him. 'Please don't tell her, or anyone else.'

'Scout's honour. But Candice? Seriously? You couldn't have a thing for a woman with some dress sense?' He looked bewildered.

Sophie looked out through the fishbowl windows at Candice, who was absorbed in her reading. 'I know it's weird… I don't feel anything when I'm with her, but when I visualise her naked…'

He shook his head. 'What about Derrick? Do you still want him?'

'Yes, of course. I still get butterflies around him.' She recalled her biology prac with Derrick. She had to admit his strange behaviour did include ogling. Perhaps Sophie had a chance with him after all.

'Maybe you're bi,' he suggested.

Sophie considered his words carefully. She'd never felt attracted to girls before, but then she had only recently felt any sexual urges outside of her dreams. 'Hmm… maybe. But how can I be sure?'

'I dunno. You could try some… lesbian porn.' Dom's face had never looked so red.

'I can't exactly walk into an adult store yet.' She paused for thought. 'But you could.'

He shook his head. 'Oh, no Sophie. I don't think I…'

Sophie grabbed Dom's arms and pleaded, 'Please… pretty please, Dom?'

He sighed. 'Fine, I will see what I can do. No promises, though.'

She hugged him. 'Thanks Dom. You're the best.'

☙❧

It's time to bite the bullet Sophie! This is the day. She stood in front of the mirror to apply her makeup. It had been five days since her first lesson with Candice and most of it was becoming second nature, except for the eye liner.

Derrick's strange behaviour had continued in their biology lectures. He even sought her out each day to spend lunch together. But why hadn't he made any moves?

Just as she was starting on her lips, there was a knock at the door. 'Come in.'

Stefan entered. 'Are you ready Sofia? Papà's—' he stopped dead in the doorway.

She turned to see what was wrong. Stefan's eyes were wide, and he was staring straight at her. 'What?'

'God damn, Soph. That outfit...' his gaze skimmed over the length of her body.

Sophie was wearing her black mesh number. She panicked a moment. 'What's wrong with it?'

'It's um... well it's very... um... nice.' Stefan had also been acting peculiar that week: when not avoiding her, he was awkward.

Her lip gloss was finished, so she made for the door. 'Thanks... um... I think.'

Her brother was still standing in the threshold, blocking her path. As she approached, his body stiffened. 'I've been meaning to ask... what's with the... um... new look?'

'I just got sick of being frumpy. I wanted to look... and feel sexy.... I guess it's an outward expression of my… inner changes.' Sophie moved in and embraced Stefan. 'You know, I've missed you this week.'

He cleared his throat, then his arms fell around her waist. 'Sorry. I've had a lot of study.'

Sophie felt his chin rest in the crook of her neck. The bristles of his goatee scratched her skin, but she didn't mind. It was comforting to be close to her twin. It made her feel whole. His lips brushed against her neck. She sensed he was about to speak, but he hesitated. The moment was electric, and she felt blood rush through her body. His lips closed instead, pressing a gentle kiss on her throbbing pulse. For split second, she thought she detected the faint smell of sandalwood cologne, but Stefan broke their hold and rushed downstairs, crying, 'We'd better hurry. Papà's waiting.'

ഗരു

Sophie's heart was pounding out the beat of her nerves as she approached the biology lecture. Her skin was prickly from the rush of blood and she felt hot, despite the cold, drizzly weather.

Derrick was leaning against the brick wall outside the hall, reading a textbook. Was he waiting for her? He looked gorgeous in his designer jumper and skinny jeans. When he looked up at the sound of her footsteps, his jaw dropped.

'Ciao Derrick.' Sophie had no doubt the

outfit was working.

'Ciao Sof—' his voice broke on her name.

Sophie was glad to catch him outside for her question. 'I've been uh… meaning to ask you…' She cast her eyes downward, too embarrassed to finish those dreaded words.

She heard his intake of breath. 'Ask me what?'

When she lifted her head, his eyes penetrated her. She forced the words out: 'Would you… uh… go to the debutante ball… with me?' There—it was out at last!

His eyes betrayed insecurity. 'Yes… I'd love to, but… are you sure there is no one else you'd rather ask?'

What? Did she hear right? Was that a yes? But why the uncertainty? She smiled. 'I'm sure.'

He put his arm across her shoulders as they entered the auditorium. 'Then I'd be honoured. Did you hear my parents have offered to host it this year? Apparently, the ballroom is undergoing renovations.'

Her skin tingled with excitement. 'Yes, Mamma mentioned something about it.'

ℬᏰ

Derrick couldn't believe his luck. As they took their seats in the lecture hall, he felt confident that Sophie's feelings were unchanged. It had occurred to him that her sudden change at the start of the week was the result of a new relationship or love interest and he couldn't put the idea out of his head. This assurance from her reaffirmed his conviction and the ball would be the perfect opportunity to show her how he felt. He wished he could do so sooner, but he was swamped with assignments and he would accept nothing less than a High Distinction for all of them.

He watched her with delighted fascination as she retrieved her notebook. Tucking her glossy, voluminous hair behind her right ear, she turned to him. Frowning slightly, she held up her notes on the nervous system and said, 'I found this week's reading confusing.'

'Perhaps I could tutor you during Swot Vac?' he suggested. Derrick had a natural gift for understanding biological systems, hence his ambitions in medicine.

'That'd be awesome. Thanks,' she beamed.

What a treasure! Derrick chided himself for not seeing her this way years ago. He felt ashamed for being so shallow. He settled in close to Sophie, returning his arm to her shoulders when the lecturer started talking.

ଚଡ଼ଃ

Stefan was sitting at the dinner table, already digging into his pasta, when Sophie burst through the front door squealing excitedly. *'He said yes! I'm going to the ball with Derrick!'*

His heart sank. He hadn't heard that name all week and the intimate moments shared with Sophie had allowed him to hope. How stupid he'd been. Of course she wasn't changing for him. 'That's great.' He spoke blandly, trying to hide his disappointment.

'That's wonderful news, Sofia!' Mamma responded, beaming with pride. 'He's sucha handsome *ragazzo*. And very rich too!'

'Mamma!' she cried reproachfully. 'But yes, it is wonderful. Only a matter of time now…' she winked at Stefan, then commenced eating.

Indeed. Stefan pictured his beloved Sofia with that brute. Holding hands… kissing… and more. He felt sick. He pushed the remainder of his meal aside, much to Mamma's horror. 'I'm not feeling well, sorry Mamma.'

'Oh, my dear boy! What-sa wrong?' She placed a hand on his forehead.

He forced an apologetic smile. 'Just a little queasy.'

Sophie looked up from her food, concern on her face. 'I hope you're not getting gastro.'

'I'm sure it's nothing.' He stood up and took his bowl to the kitchen.

'Well you betta stay home tonight and rest, just in case,' Mamma suggested.

He considered it briefly. His mood was not conducive to an evening of ballroom dancing. But he ought to make the most of the time he could get with Sophie. 'I'll be fine Mamma. Please don't worry.'

Mamma's frown eased. 'Well okay, but Sofia you keep close eye on him.'

Sophie nodded. 'Yes Mamma. I won't let him out of my sight... I better get changed.' She took her bowl to the kitchen, then dashed upstairs.

How did a jerk like Derrick deserve such a precious soul? Already dressed in his practice wear, Stefan moved into the family room to wait. He tried to push the depressing thoughts from his mind. It's not like he could have her anyway. It was safer this way.

When Sophie returned, Stefan was immediately aroused by her choice of attire. She wore a sleek, black, Latin dance dress with a hem that was angled from her upper left thigh down to her right knee. It was a big change from her usual track pants and left very little to the imagination. He couldn't fight off the devilish head-voice that told him she wasn't wearing this for Derrick, who didn't even attend the same lessons as them.

'Can I drive?' Sophie asked with her open hand out toward him.

He handed her the car keys. 'Probably best you do....' *You are far too much of a distraction*, he finished silently. They had both agreed to share the one car to save money.

Sophie started the engine of their silver Maserati. 'Did you want to pick a CD?'

Stefan smiled. He knew Sophie's taste in music was extensive, so he relished the opportunities to listen to something they both enjoyed. He flicked through the CD wallet and found *The Matrix* soundtrack.

As soon as Marilyn Manson screamed through the stereo, Sophie grinned. 'Good choice.' She pulled out of the garage and tore down their street.

Stefan grabbed the roof handle and braced himself. 'Jesus, Soph. I'd like to get there in one piece.' His voice was filled with humour.

'Sorry. I got a little caught up in the moment.' Stopping at a red light, she looked at him and grinned.

Sophie restrained her speeding for the rest of the drive, instead choosing to express her joy by singing along to the music. Stefan eased back into his leather seat and closed his eyes. The upholstery still smelt new, so the sensual fragrance combined with the patter of rain that blended with the music enhanced his fantasies. He was visualising Sophie, in that dress, climbing into his lap, stroking his face with her soft fingers, pressing her lips on his...

He was suddenly aware of the silence and

opened his eyes. The car was parked at the church hall and Sophie was grinning at him. 'Happy thoughts, I assume?' Her gaze briefly flicked to his crotch.

Stefan blushed, realising that she'd noticed his erection. At least she didn't know the cause. He gave her a cheeky smile, 'Perhaps.'

'Feeling better then?' she asked.

He'd completely forgotten his previous complaint. 'Yeah, the nausea passed.'

She placed her hand on his shoulder. 'That's good, but I did promise Mamma I'd keep an eye on you, so I'm gonna tell Cassie that you're all mine tonight.'

Choice words, my love! Stefan imagined that the passion coursing through his body was in fact the infernos of hell. Could Sophie see the fire in his eyes? It occurred to him in that moment that he was sick of hiding his desires from her. She wasn't repulsed or embarrassed by his visible lust. She wasn't even shying away from physical contact with him in his heightened state.

They both stepped out of the car, then Stefan took Sophie by the arm. 'Excellent… I'll be the envy of all the straight guys here tonight.'

She snorted, apparently trying to shrug off his compliment, but the twinkle in her eyes suggested that she enjoyed the flattery.

Chapter Five

The Pacini house was a bustle of activity. Mamma had insisted that Sophie have a professional hair stylist and makeup artist attend to her at home so that she looked her best for the ball that night. Sophie was surprised at how excited she was. She'd never been interested in formal nights in the past, but that was the old Sophie.

This night was also her opportunity to spend some quality time with Derrick and she was desperately hoping he would make his move. The last two weeks, since she asked him to be her date, had been arduous. They were both busy with assignment work and there were few chances to spend time together outside of class. Biology lectures had been her one solace. Derrick's arm had become a permanent fixture around her shoulders on these occasions. It assured her that he was just waiting for the right time.

Mamma was watching with excitement as

the hairstylist curled and pinned Sophie's hair in place. Sophie realised she hadn't seen her twin since breakfast, so she asked, 'Where's Stefano?'

Mamma shrugged, but then recollection dawned on her face. 'Oh, he has a date tonight. I think he left already.'

Strange. He didn't mention anything about a date to Sophie. A wave of disappointment washed over her. She was hoping Stefan would be there to see her all dressed up before she left. It was a shame that he was not attending the ball. He was one of the best ballroom dancers in their class.

With her updo of loops and curls complete, Sophie moved across to where the makeup artist was set up. Unable to talk, she sat still through the makeover, listening to Mamma boast about Sophie going to the ball with the son of Minister Vianello.

Once the makeup was done, Sophie looked at Mamma, who gasped. 'Stunning! It is a pity you cover your pretty face most of the night. Speaking of which, I gotta blue and white mask.' She put the mask on the table in front of Sophie. 'It's a butterfly.'

Sophie thought it looked more like a moth, but she didn't want to upset Mamma. 'It's lovely, thank you.' And it was, really. An authentic Venetian mask, hand painted with intricate glittering swirls. Given that the ball was being held in a Venetian style mansion, the masquerade was a fitting theme.

Getting dressed was not a simple matter. Sophie needed Mamma to help with the corset lacing. Then she stepped into her dress to avoid messing her hair or makeup. The garment was a white satin, embroidered ballgown with a deep, royal blue lining that showed at the back where the white layer tapered open.

Mamma fastened the dress, then offered her shoulders for support as Sophie stepped into her silver, strappy dance heels. It felt strange having Mamma buckle her shoes for the first time since childhood, but there was no hope of bending down to reach her feet. She assumed this was what it felt like for brides.

'There we go.' Mamma looked pleased when she stood up to inspect her debutante daughter.

Sophie looked in the mirror, amazed by her reflection. 'I just hope Derrick will be impressed enough to make a move.'

Mamma beamed. 'I don't-a think he will-a-be able to keep his hands away. Just-a be careful he don't try anything impropa.'

Sophie secretly hoped he would but smiled coyly. 'Of course, Mamma.'

Suddenly Mamma threw her hands up. 'Oh dear! I forgot-a the necklace!'

'What necklace?' Sophie inquired.

'I was gonna get pretty necklace to match.'

Mamma looked crestfallen.

'Don't worry Mamma. I want to wear this.'
She picked up the gold pendant that Stefan had
given her.

Mamma shook her head. 'Are you sure? I
don't think it matches.'

'I'm sure. It fits the theme.' And it meant
more to her than any other jewellery. She clasped
the chain around her neck, then pressed the
miniature gold mask gently against her chest. She
would still carry a token of her brother's love with
her, even if he couldn't be there.

The doorbell rang, then she heard Papà's
voice greeting their guest. Another man replied and
Sophie's heart jumped when she recognised
Derrick's voice.

She made her way downstairs with help
from Mamma and was met with a look of awe from
her date. He looked gorgeous in his black tuxedo
and he was holding a blue and white jester mask.
She remembered him asking what colours she
planned to wear because he wanted to match.

Derrick held his right hand out for hers. 'You
look stunning, my dear.'

Sophie gave him her hand and smiled.
'Thank you, Derrick.'

ഇരു

Sophie was entranced by the splendour from the

moment she stepped through the front gate. She had been fortunate to spend much of her childhood playing in and around this grand mansion, but she had never seen it decked out for a ball. Fairy lights twinkled from the palm trees lining the long white granite driveway. White chiffon draped between the marble statues which topped the railing of the front steps. Sophie was thankful for Derrick's strong grip when they ascended the steps. She had spent the last few ballroom lessons wearing in her new shoes, but she still wasn't used to climbing stairs in them.

More fairy lights and white chiffon were draped about inside the entranceway and a string quartet was playing classical music from the first landing of the spiral staircase. It sounded pretty and Sophie decided she would have to learn who the composer was.

Derrick presented her to his parents, the only people not wearing masks. 'Mamma and Papà, this beautiful lady is Sofia.'

Paolo, Derrick's Papà, looked every part the distinguished gentleman in his tailored tuxedo and Italian leather shoes. His salt-and-pepper hair was slicked back, and his face was sporting the grin that he always wore in public. 'Ciao, Bella. You look absolutely stunning.' He took her hand and pressed it to his lips, which lingered longer than she found comfortable or appropriate. His mamma did not seem to notice; or if she did, it didn't bother her. She simply smiled at Sophie.

'Um, thanks, Mr. Vianello.'

'Please, call me Paolo. With all the time you have spent in this house, you are practically family, sì?'

'Yes, thank you, sir—I mean Paolo.' She had always felt awkward around Derrick's parents. Her own parents were wealthy, sure; but the Vianello family were like royalty.

His smile widened. 'You are most welcome. I trust that my son will take good care to ensure you enjoy your evening.'

With that, Derrick led Sophie into the ballroom. She took a moment to admire all the guests in their finery. She recognised a few people from her church congregation, but most people's identities were concealed behind their masks. It was exciting to think that she could be mixing with celebrities without realising it. She wished she knew what Dom and his date, Tegan, would be wearing. Would she get a chance to identify them before the unmasking?

'Good evening ladies and gentlemen.' The din of voices hushed as Paolo commenced the formalities. 'On behalf of the parish committee, I would like to welcome you all to the annual Toorak Debutante Ball. It is with great pleasure that I invite you all into my home this year. I am delighted to see that most of you have embraced our theme. In keeping with the spirit of masquerade, I hope that you will refrain from revealing your identities until the appointed time. Let the festivities begin!' A loud cheer was heard through the crowd as everyone applauded.

৪০৫৪

'You've got some impressive moves, my dear,' Derrick commented as he twirled Sophie about, jiving to 'Footloose.'

Sophie was overjoyed by his flattery. It was a few hours into the ball, and she was on top of the world. She'd danced with several other young men but kept returning to Derrick. 'Thanks. You're not bad yourself.' Derrick used to attend lessons at the church, but he moved on to a professional studio a few years ago and it showed in his skill level.

When the music changed to the deep, husky voice of Nina Simone singing 'I Put a Spell on You,' Derrick pulled Sophie in close. 'Let's tango to this one.'

'Certainly.' Sophie was ecstatic. The ultimate dance of passion and Derrick wanted to do it with her! The feel of his hands gliding across Sophie's back was thrilling; the intensity of his eyes looking into hers, electrifying. For those precious minutes, it could have been just the two of them in the room. Sophie imagined them dancing like this in Derrick's bedroom, but with much less clothing. She grinned.

'I'd love to know what's on your mind right now,' Derrick drew her back to the present.

She replied in the sexiest voice she could muster, 'I'm sure you would.'

'Do I get any details?' he prompted her with his own seductive tone, then swung her out and back into his arms.

'Maybe… later.' She was enjoying the teasing nature of their conversation. It suited the dance.

He pulled her closer so that his mouth was touching her ear, then whispered, 'Well, I look forward to… later.' Then he spun her out again.

Sophie could barely contain her excitement. He clearly wanted her! She briefly considered escaping the ballroom with him early. But she didn't want to appear too eager or easy.

The song ended and they were interrupted by another couple. A girl with long blonde curls in a sleek white and gold dress addressed Sophie, 'Do you mind if I have the next dance with your partner?' Her voice sounded familiar, but she couldn't put a name to it.

She looked doubtfully at Derrick. She didn't want to let go of him, but then she remembered that the point of the evening was to mingle. 'I guess I can spare him briefly.'

As she released Derrick's hand, he whispered, 'Later,' then walked across the dance floor with the blonde.

৪১ন্ড

Sophie turned and looked at the man standing beside her. He'd been the blonde girl's partner for most of the night and he was holding out a hand to her, offering to dance. He wore a full-face mask of gold, black, and white with decorative patterns of musical score. She accepted his hand and a spark instantly ignited as their skin made contact. His fingers felt rough in contrast to the soft, velvety texture of Derrick's. When their eyes locked, the chemistry was undeniable, and she detected the hint of a grin beneath his mask.

Norah Jones was halfway through singing 'Come Away with Me,' so he led her into a short waltz. She considered talking to him, but somehow the silence between them added to the mystique. She admired his graceful movements. He had already abandoned his suit jacket, and, thanks to the tight-fitting shirt, Sophie could tell that his figure was slim yet well-toned.

When the music changed, she found herself dancing a samba to 'Ain't It Funny' by J. Lo. The moves came naturally to them both and she wiggled her hips to the Latin rhythm. Then she gasped as it dawned on her: the reason she recognised him. It was the cologne: sandalwood. It was the way he touched her skin: calloused fingers.

It was the facial hair escaping the edges of his mask: scratchy stubble. Could this really be him? Her mysterious stranger? In a matter of minutes, she'd forgotten Derrick entirely. Fire coursed through her veins. Electricity surged through her nerves. She had to know this man... intimately.

She found her hands on his chest. He inhaled sharply, then spun her out. When he pulled her back in, he pressed up against her body, their masks touching. His right hand brushed along her side. They moved together in a close embrace. Then they were suddenly twirling. Sophie's feet lost contact with the floor and she realised that one of his arms was tucked under her legs. She giggled with delight. When she returned to earth, the song reached its interlude and they circled each other slowly.

⁃р

After waltzing to Norah Jones, Tegan pulled Dominic outside for some fresh air. Once outside, he took a moment to enjoy the view. He had to admit that Derrick's house was impressive. It was incredible how closely the architect had imitated the Venetian Gothic style. It even had ogee arches and quatrefoil openings.

'Stunning, isn't it?' Tegan stood close behind him and he felt her breath tickle his neck. It was just as well his date was someone with a similar appreciation for architectural beauty.

He turned and smiled, removing his Phantom of the Opera mask. 'Yes, it's incredible.' Something in the garden caught his attention then. 'Oh look, a hedge maze!'

Tegan tossed her Harlequin mask aside. 'Awesome! Come on, let's get lost!' She ran off towards the topiary.

Dominic had a hard time keeping up, but at least she waited for him at the entrance. Wow! They'd even put lights and decorations up around the maze. For a second, he imagined that they stepped into a fairy realm. He wished he could show his World of Darkness role-playing group this place!

Tegan grabbed his hand, then led him into the depths of the labyrinth. When they found an alcove with a stone bench, she sat down. Dominic followed suit and Tegan slid closer, their legs touching. Did she mean to seduce him here? He wondered what it would feel like to kiss her. Would he enjoy it? Sure, he liked her, and she was pretty, but...

His train of thought was cut off when Tegan's soft lips pressed against his. It was a pleasant feeling. She pulled back and asked, 'Is this okay? Can I kiss you more?'

'I guess so.' He leaned in for it this time. But Tegan moved. Then he was a little startled when she mounted his lap. Her hands reached behind his neck and their lips locked again. This time her tongue licked his lips, then pushed them apart so that she could explore his mouth. He wasn't sure what do, having never kissed anyone before, but it didn't matter. Tegan was happy to guide him through the process. He welcomed the heat she was radiating. The night air was chilly, but dry at least. The kiss continued for what felt like an hour or more and Dominic was enjoying it. It didn't possess the fire and passion he'd always imagined, but it was warm and comforting. He was happy.

ℰℭ

Stefan recognised his new dance partner as soon as they joined hands. He'd know those soft, delicate fingers anywhere. A glimpse of the gold pendant she wore merely confirmed his guess. By God, she looked exquisite! The white dress with a splash of blue was a good fit on her perfectly sculpted body. He considered complimenting her during their waltz, but he knew his voice would give him away and he wanted to honour the spirit of masquerade. She would have to guess his identity from his dancing, which they'd done together countless times over the last seven years. Of course, his cover would be blown if she did. He was here to chaperone from the shadows because he didn't trust Derrick. That was the excuse he'd given Mamma anyway.

Soon after J. Lo started her first chorus, Sophie gasped, and her eyes lit up with recognition. Stefan nearly spoke, but then she did something that rendered him speechless. She drew in closer and placed her hands on his chest, sending shockwaves through his body. There was no mistaking the passion in her eyes. She wanted him. She knew him and wanted him. From this point, they were dancing a delicious samba of seduction.

When the song reached its interlude, they circled each other slowly. Then Stefan pulled her back in. Her hands encircled his body, sliding up and down his back then across his waist. The cotton shirt did little to muffle the sensation. The heat between them was intense. It took all his concentration to maintain his footwork. He sent her into a double spiral turn. When she returned to embrace him, he felt her breath against his neck. Her lips brushed his skin. Desperately wanting to meet her mouth with his own, he silently cursed his choice of mask. But a quick glimpse of their surroundings suggested this was for the best. There were several sets of eyes on them, including what he presumed to be Derrick's. This state of anonymity wouldn't last all night. What would they all think when the masks came off to reveal that this couple of dirty dancers were siblings? He was such an idiot!

As the song faded out, Stefan broke their grip and whispered, 'I need some air,' then made his escape. He sensed her attempt to follow him, but Derrick moved in to block her egress. Damn that bastard! He was hoping Sophie would join him outside, somewhere private. He sought his solitude in the back garden. It was an icy cold night, and he forgot his jacket, but he didn't mind. He needed to cool off. If Stefan's feelings for Sophie were mutual, the twins would have to proceed with caution. They could not afford such public displays.

⁝⁞

The first words spoken between them were a whisper. He needed air. It sounded like an invitation to join him. She walked after him, but Derrick stepped in front of her. Oh Shit! What must Derrick think? Did he see how sensual her dancing had been?

His suspicious eyes pierced her. 'Who was that?'

'I... I don't know.' Her gaze tracked the exit route of her mysterious stranger.

Derrick's hand gripped her left arm tight. 'Oh? So, you'll dance like that with anyone?' He was trying to sound light-hearted, but Sophie could detect a darker tone underlying his question.

'Well no, but...' What the hell could she tell him? That she'd just met the literal man of her dreams? She shook her head, feeling torn between her love for Derrick and her strong desires for a man she'd just met yet somehow knew intimately. She felt him embrace her and resigned herself to the familiar comfort and safety of Derrick's arms. Her mysterious stranger would have to wait.

଼ଓଔ

It was good to have Sophie back in his arms, but Derrick couldn't help feeling he'd lost her. The passion of their tango was gone, stolen by another man, and a stranger no less. He'd watched them dancing their samba as though they were hidden within the confines of a boudoir, not in a crowded ballroom.

He led her back to the dancefloor and tried to make small talk as they swayed together. It was useless. She was too distracted, her eyes constantly scanning the room. He considered taking her upstairs, but what was the point? If she didn't want him, he couldn't force it. He needed to find another way to win her back. She'd responded well to flattery before, so he'd start there. 'You ought to know, my dear, that you are the most attractive lady here tonight.'

'Thank you Derrick, although I know you're lying.'

He placed a hand on his heart and gasped to feign disbelief. 'I would never tell such falsehoods.

But I will admit that beauty is a matter of subjectivity and that to my eye, there is no competition for you. Not here… not anywhere.'

That must have caught her off-guard because she stumbled. Luckily, Derrick caught her. She looked straight into his eyes to ask, 'Do you really mean that?'

Before he was able to answer, Papà's loud booming voice filled the room. 'May I have your attention ladies and gentlemen?' The room went quiet. 'We are approaching the end of this evening's festivities, with but one dance left. This means it is time for the unmasking, followed by the presentation of the debutantes.' An excited murmur was heard through the crowd.

Derrick noticed Sophie searching the room again, then her eyes settled on someone. He followed her gaze and found the stranger in the musical mask, who was watching them both intently. Damn it! He was going to have to try harder. He placed a protective arm around Sophie's waist.

His Papà continued, 'On the count of three. One…'

Sophie's delicate frame stiffened in his grip as she moved her left hand to her mask, mirroring the mystery man.

'Two…'

Derrick moved his right hand up, keeping

his left firmly gripping Sophie's hip.

'Three!'

What the? He couldn't believe his eyes, or his luck. He quickly hid his amusement as he realised the impact that this the revelation had on Sophie.

She let out a small whimper. 'No!' Then a single tear slid down her cheek and her visage went deathly pale.

He looked back at Stefan and saw a face of worry and confusion that was pushing forward through the crowd. How could they have not recognised each other? They were twins for Christ's sake.

As if she couldn't bear to face her brother any longer, Sophie rushed into an embrace with Derrick, pressing her face into his chest. He was suddenly in two minds about how to proceed. Given the state she was in and their history, Derrick was confident that he could get what he wanted that night. But would it be right? He didn't think so. If he had any hope of future happiness with Sophie, he would have to make the moral choice.

❧❧

'No!' Sophie was flabbergasted, horrified. *How could he be Stefan? My brother! Born of the same womb.* She felt ill. He was moving toward her, but she couldn't face him, not yet. She hid herself in Derrick's arms. She was safe and warm there.

'Come on Soph. It's time for the presentation.' Derrick's voice was soft and smooth, like velvet. He was guiding her towards the stage.

How on earth was she going to manage to stand up in front of everyone? And pose for photographs! 'I can't do it,' she whispered.

'It's okay Soph, you don't have to if you don't want to. But are you sure?' Derrick's eyes were concerned.

'I'm sure. I feel sick. I just wanna get out of here.' Sophie looked up at him hopefully. 'Will you take me upstairs? I'm not ready to… go home.'

'Yes, of course.' Derrick's arm was around her again. She was vaguely aware of him excusing her. '… not feeling well… take her to rest…'

Next thing she knew, she was being led upstairs. She tripped after a few steps, so she kicked off her shoes.

This was when Stefan caught up with them. 'Derrick! What are you doing with Sophie?'

'Putting her to bed. She's not feeling well.' Derrick's voice betrayed anger, despite his efforts to stay calm. Sophie kept her face hidden against his chest. She was still too afraid to look at Stefan.

'I can take her home. She'd be better off resting there,' pleaded Stefan.

'She doesn't want to go home. Not yet.' He was being protective, which made her heart swoon.

'But…'

'Give it a rest Stefan. She needs time.' With that, Derrick picked her up and carried her up the stairs.

Before long Sophie was sitting on a bed, Derrick beside her. She looked around and recognised the room from sleepovers of the past. It was a spacious guestroom with a comfortable king-size bed. The elaborate walls and furnishings colour-coordinated in white and silver, much like the rest of the house.

She turned to Derrick, who was watching her intently. 'Are you feeling any better?'

'A little, thanks.' She studied his dark brown eyes. They were almost black. The sudden desire to kiss him surged through her body, but she remained frozen by his gaze. She couldn't make the first move. She'd never French-kissed anyone. Instead, she channelled all her longing into her own gaze, hoping he would read the signs.

They remained this way for several excruciating minutes, then Derrick stood up. 'I'll get you something more comfortable to sleep in. Be right back.'

He closed the door, leaving her alone to think. She'd been fearing the moment when she would have to confront her thoughts and feelings. Unconsciously she fiddled with her pendant. That's when it struck her. Oh God! Surely Stefan saw her necklace? He must have known he was dancing with her. Did that mean he…? she couldn't bear to think it. No, she refused to believe her dear brother would deceive her so. The whole business had been a huge misunderstanding. She took the necklace off, placing it carefully on the bedside table.

Derrick returned with a pair of flannelette pyjamas. 'Here, I hope they fit okay. I'll give you a few minutes to change.' He handed her the sleepwear, then turned toward the door.

'Wait… I um… need help with my dress.' Blushing, she stood up, gesturing to the zip and bow at the back of her dress.

Derrick sucked in a deep breath, then moved behind her. Sophie's skin ignited at the unavoidable touch when he unfastened the garment. The white and blue satin fell to the floor, revealing her corset and hosiery. She heard a sharp exhale from Derrick, then turned to face him. She could see lust in his eyes, in the slight curl of his lip. She grabbed onto his shoulders so that she could step out of her dress. When she let go, Derrick was still staring at her, all of her. *Why won't he kiss me?* Did he need more persuasion? She commenced unclipping the front of her corset. Derrick remained transfixed. Once the last catch was freed, she let the corset fall behind her, exposing her naked C cup breasts. She advanced on him.

Her motion broke the spell he was under, enabling him to speak. 'I'll let you rest. Good night

Sophie,' and he walked out.

What? Why? She threw herself on the bed, frustrated and ashamed. She pondered how awful her night had turned out. Stefan wanting her too much and Derrick not wanting her enough. There was nothing for it but to let the tears flow.

ℬℭ

How could I have been so stupid! Stefan slumped down on his bed after another failed attempt at conversation with Sophie. Three days later and she still wouldn't talk to him; she wouldn't even look at him. He never should have indulged his desires so openly without being more certain of her feelings. A twinkling light in the corner of his vision caught his attention and he looked across to his bedside table. It was the glittery mask that Sophie had worn, catching the lamp light.

When he found it discarded at the ball, he rescued the costume piece and brought it home. Intending to return it at first, the accessory became a fixture in his room. Picking up the mask, he caressed it with his fingers. He assumed she had gone for a butterfly, but the shape reminded him more of a moth. Sophie had been fascinated by butterflies as a young child. He remembered going to butterfly houses with her on numerous occasions. It was a joy to see her frolic and squeal with delight as she danced amongst her winged friends.

There was a knock at the door, so he quickly stuffed the mask under the bed. 'Come in.'

Sophie stood before him. She was wearing a short, loose-fitting white cotton night shirt. He couldn't help but notice the slight transparency of the fabric, or her bare legs. His cheeks burned as she moved closer. For a moment, he thought he was dreaming. It was one of his fantasies about Sophie coming to his bed, desperate for his touch. His groin began to stir.

But she didn't climb into his lap. She sat alongside him, then spoke softly. 'I'm sorry, Stefano. I needed time... to process. I... I didn't realise it was you... You resembled... someone else... Can we put this whole awkward misunderstanding behind us?'

Was that all it was to her? He felt a proverbial knife in the gut. He stuttered, 'Y—yes of course. That's... what... I want too.'

She forced a smile. 'I've missed my brother.' She threw her arms around him.

He tried to relax as he returned the embrace. He still loved his sister, even if he couldn't have her completely. 'I've missed you too.'

Chapter Six

Dominic hadn't forgotten Sophie's request; it just took a few weeks to pull together the courage to step into the adult emporium. She would be eighteen the next day anyway, but he figured this would be a nice addition to her gift that would at least save her the embarrassment he was subjecting himself to.

As he browsed the shelves, he thought about Tegan, wondering what she would think of him shopping for porn. On Monday he had worried that things would be weird between them at uni, but she made of point of defining their relationship first thing. So, it was settled: Tegan was officially his girlfriend. He smiled as he thought about her hand in his wherever they went together.

This must be the lesbian section. He blushed at some of the titles. And the covers. Oh God, the cover pictures! He settled for something that looked relatively tame. Sophie might freak out over the kinkier stuff. Should he get something for himself?

He wasn't even sure what would appeal. The girl-on-girl pictures didn't do much for him. No, what he needed was something to help him learn how to use his own equipment. The 'Educational' section looked like the ticket. He grabbed a couple of instructional DVDs, then something else caught his attention. It was the way the bodies were so artfully posed that intrigued him. Should he purchase it? He couldn't imagine watching something like that, or could he? No, he pushed the idea out of his mind, then made his way to the counter.

'You're new here,' the guy at the counter observed with a friendly smile.

'Um, yeah. I'm kinda new to this sort of shopping.'

'Well let me know if you ever need any help or advice with the products.'

Something about the man's demeanour eased Dominic's tension and he smiled. 'Thanks.'

'My name's Patrick, by the way.'

'Nice to meet you. I'm Dominic.' After paying for the products, he began to turn, but paused. 'There is something I was curious about.'

ՏᎦᏟᏒ

Plans for Sophie and Stefan's eighteenth birthday had progressed perfectly, and the 21st of May was suddenly upon them. Sophie had suggested a house party because neither of them had a huge guest list and their home offered more freedom. The family room and outdoor entertaining area had been decorated with balloons, streamers, and table scatters of black, silver, and gold. Papà had even cleaned out the pool and spa for the guests willing to brave the cold of late May. Mamma had set up a fully stocked bar and hired some bar tenders to serve cocktails. She had also instructed all family members to bring a dish, as was the tradition. The result was several trestle tables loaded up with casserole dishes, cheese platters and dessert plates. No one could complain of hunger at a Pacini party.

Sophie chose to wear a black and gold cocktail dress with black stockings to keep her legs warm. When Stefan first emerged from his room in jeans and a Karnivool t-shirt, she chided him. 'You can't dress like that!'

He grinned. 'Why not? I thought the point of a house party was to feel comfortable.'

'But tonight's special!' she cried.

Candice, who had been there to help her get ready, laughed. 'If I can do it, you ought to try a little harder.' She was referring to the dress that Sophie had picked out for her. If not exactly gothic, at least it was black.

'Fine,' he sighed, then returned to his room to change.

'Oh yeh, before I forget. You should open this before everyone gets here.' Candice shoved a large giftbag into Sophie's hands. Looking inside, she found it was filled with a range of sex toys. 'Just a few essentials. I'll take you shopping for more later.'

'Oh wow! Um... thank you. I better put these away.' Sophie ducked back to her room and stuffed them under her bed.

The first hour had been spent greeting their guests, the majority being extended family. Dominic arrived in a group of three: Tegan, his new girlfriend, had brought a friend. 'This is Owen. I hope you don't mind. Dom suggested that it'd be okay to bring him.'

Sophie looked Owen up and down. He was dressed on the casual end of the semi-formal spectrum, but he looked respectable and friendly. 'Of course not. You are most welcome Owen.'

He beamed, 'Cheers Sophie. And happy birthday! Here's a little something.' He handed her a bottle of red wine. She didn't recognise the label, but she didn't know much about wine.

She thanked him, then Dom moved up to hug her. He gave her a beautifully wrapped gift. 'This is from Tegan and me.'

She unwrapped the parcel and was delighted to find the *Buffy* DVD boxset. 'Awesome! Thanks guys.'

Dom grinned, then leaned in to whisper, 'I added something extra beneath the first disc. Don't open it until you're alone.'

Blushing, she whispered, 'Understood.'

When Derrick arrived, Sophie's nerves kicked into gear. Damn it! She forgot he was coming. She'd made a point of avoiding him all week, attending alternative classes where possible. The humiliation of exposing herself when he didn't want her was too much. This was the first time she'd seen him since.

As if sensing her trepidation, he inquired, 'I hope that my presence is not an intrusion tonight.'

She forced a smile. 'Of course not. Welcome, Derrick.'

He appeared to relax. 'That's a relief. I was worried when I didn't see you all week. Have you recovered from… the ball okay?'

Assuming he referred to the Stefan incident, she replied confidently, 'Yes. I'm fine now.'

'Good. Here, I got you a gift.' He handed her a small box, elegantly wrapped in gold foil with a white bow. 'I know you don't wear much jewellery, but I thought this would suit you.'

Upon opening the box, she gasped. 'It's exquisite.' Picking up the gold bracelet covered with dazzling diamonds renewed her with hope. She knew men didn't give diamonds to just anyone. She began to put it on.

'Here, allow me.' Derrick took the bracelet and clasped it around her left wrist.

He paused with his hands wrapped around hers and looked into her eyes. The skin contact was electrifying, the gaze exhilarating. Sophie's heart cried out for him to kiss her.

'Ahem.' Luke's voice broke their trance.

'Oh, hey Luke.' She tried to hide her displeasure.

'Hey, Soph. Happy birthday.' He looked at Derrick, then added, 'Sorry for the interruption.' Turning back to Sophie, he handed her a black gift bag. 'This is for you.'

'Thanks Luke.' She peeked inside the bag. It was a bunch of Xbox games. She smiled. 'We'll have to try these out next gaming night.'

'Yeah, should be good. I'm gonna find Stefan now. See ya round.' He patted her on the arm, then walked out the back.

Smiling apologetically at Derrick, she dropped the bag with the rest of her stash. 'Let's grab a drink,' she suggested, then led him to the bar.

'Sounds good.' He followed her closely.

ℰↃℂℛ

After a few hours and several drinks, Sophie was feeling cheerful. The playlist was the perfect mix of alt rock and metal, with the occasional pop song thrown in to appeal to some of the other guests. The party had split such that the older generation were sitting inside, while Sophie sat outside with her friends and a few cousins.

'Right, let's play some party games,' Sophie declared. 'Who's in and what do we feel like playing?'

'What are the options?' asked Cousin Isabella.

'Hmm, well we have *Apples to Apples*, *Things*, *Pictionary*, *Scattergories*, and *Balderdash*.'

'Ooh, I love *Things*—let's play that,' suggested Dom. A few of the guests were giving him blank looks. 'It's a fun and simple game, trust me.'

'I'm down. Stefan?' Sophie looked to her twin for consensus.

'Sure. I'll go get it.' He disappeared into the house, returning a few minutes later holding a wooden game box.

Sophie let Dom explain the rules. When everyone had their pencils and paper, she started the first round. 'Tell me things you would ask a psychic.'

The group went quiet briefly as they wrote their answers. Sophie finished writing her answer, then looked at Derrick who was sitting to her right. It occurred to her that he had chosen to sit next to her, in fact he'd barely left her side all night. When she had all the answer slips, she read them aloud: 'So things you would ask a psychic include...

"What is Love?" (Sophie giggled), "Will I graduate from uni?", "The winning Lotto numbers," "When will I be kissed?" … (several responses later), and um, well this one says, "Who Sophie really wants." She thought it was an odd response and became very curious to know who wrote it.

Stefan, who was on Sophie's left, started the guessing. 'Luke, did you write "What is Love?"'

He was met with a 'No.'

Curious, Sophie thought. She guessed Stefan had submitted that one and couldn't think which other response he would have given.

When the guessing got around to Derrick, there were only a few options left. With accusing eyes, he asked, 'Stefan, did you want to know who Sophie really wants?'

Sophie wanted to sink into the floor. Why did he have to challenge Stefan directly in front of everyone? She hadn't told any of her friends about what happened at the ball.

'No Derrick, that wasn't me. I already know who she wants,' Stefan replied in an ice-cold tone.

Was that jealousy she detected? Sophie quickly dismissed the thought. It was her turn to guess. The Haddaway reference had already been attributed to Dom, so she decided to try her luck with 'Who Sophie Wants.' 'Was it you, Luke?' He was the most likely candidate left in the pool. 'Did you write the one about who I want?'

'Yeah, ya got me. Pity there aren't any psychics around huh?' Luke winked at her.

What the hell? Did he know about that incident at the ball? Or did he have a thing for her? She decided to have a word with him later.

'Well Soph, I guess that means the kissing one is yours,' Stefan was glaring at Derrick as he spoke.

'Yeah that's me.' Things were getting weird. 'I'm getting another drink.' Sophie stood up and went to the bar. She found Luke there. 'Hey, what was with that response in Things?'

'Ah, that would be telling. But I'm guessing you don't even know who you really want.'

'I'm pretty sure I want Derrick. Always have.' Sophie was confused by his cryptic words.

'Well if you're sure…' With that, he walked off.

She grabbed another cider, then returned to the group. The game had continued without her, although Candice, the cousins and Stefan's other band mates had dropped out, preferring to converse in the smoking area. Candice wasn't a smoker, but Sophie suspected she was trying to hook up with Chris, the bass player.

As the game progressed, Sophie found herself giggling as she wrote 'Masturbation' in response to 'Things that are harder than they look.' It was the winning answer too, since no one guessed it was hers.

When the game was over, most of the group went for drinks, leaving her alone with Stefan. He leaned in to ask her, 'So, when did you start masturbating? I thought you found the idea repulsive.'

Sophie blushed. 'I used to, but that was before... my awakening.'

He gave her a lewd grin. 'Surely it can't be that difficult for girls? Perhaps you just need to be shown how.'

'I figured it out eventually. I just needed the right... stimuli.'

'Stimuli you say. I suppose that involved Derrick somehow. A picture perhaps?' Stefan's interest in the matter was disturbing, considering recent events, but Sophie tried to shrug it off. She had always enjoyed talking to him about her deepest, darkest secrets.

'No, actually. That's how I started, but it wasn't his image that got me there.'

'Oh? Colour me intrigued.' He looked around conspiratorially, then continued his questioning. 'Pray tell, whose was it?'

She hesitated. Should she tell him about her dark fantasy? 'The mysterious stranger of my dreams.' *There, it was out.* It sounded so lame when she said it aloud.

'Curious. What does this stranger look like?'

Stefan didn't scoff or tease her. He was genuinely interested.

'I don't know. I'm always blindfolded, but…'

'Here Soph, I got you another drink.' Derrick had returned, holding a cider out for her. 'We're gonna play a drinking game now.'

෨෬

Stefan speculated over Sophie's revelation. Was it the mysterious stranger who she mistook him for at the ball? If so, why? Was it possible she thought the stranger was real? That she'd seen him before or knew him? Or that…

'Five's guys! Come on Stefan, take a drink!' Sophie was prodding him.

Oh right. The game of King's Cup had started. He sipped his drink, then drew the next card. 'Nine is rhyme.' He grinned at Sophie. 'Okay then, my word is "stranger."'

She responded without shifting her gaze from him, 'Danger.'

He was vaguely aware of the rhyme continuing around the circle, but his attention was locked in with Sophie. Could it be?

෨෬

It was that time of night when the party divided into smaller groups. Sophie was with Derrick and a few of her cousins; Stefan was jamming with the musos in the rumpus room; the oldies were gasbagging in the living room; and Dominic was left sitting with Tegan's scruffy friend, Owen, at the patio table. Tegan excused herself shortly after the drinking game. Feeling ill from too much alcohol, she claimed a spare room. Dominic had offered to stay with her, but she wanted to be left alone.

Feeling a little awkward, Dominic emptied his wine glass, then tried to start a conversation. 'So, you study visual art at Melbourne U, huh? What's your speciality?'

Owen smiled so warmly that Dominic imagined beams of sunlight radiating from him. 'Sculpture is my greatest passion. I love painting, too. How about you Dom? What's your design major gonna be?'

Dominic felt compelled to return Owen's grin. 'Architecture. I love all forms of creative expression, but structural design is where my strengths lie.'

'Sweet. What's ya fave style?' Owen was leaning forward, listening intently while sipping his wine.

Dominic was a little unnerved by the attention. He wasn't used to people other than Tegan or Sophie showing genuine interest in him. 'While I can appreciate the beauty of older ornamental styles, I would have to say postmodern excites me the most. I love the idea that a building can be also be a sculpture. Speaking of which, I'd love to see your work.'

Owen refilled his glass from the bottle of shiraz on the table. 'Yeah? You should come over sometime. I got my own flat in Fitzroy. Although you might find my latest work hard to digest. A lot of people do. Wine?'

Holding out his glass, Dominic thanked him then inquired, 'What's your latest work?'

'It's a sculpture about gay love,' he said frankly.

'Oh? Are you…' Dominic felt himself blush.

'Gay? Not quite. I'm bi. Does that unsettle you?' Owen eyed him apprehensively.

Dominic considered for a moment. He thought about his conservative parents and his church upbringing. He thought about the contemptuous way his father would use words like 'queer' and 'poof' and the way the bible judges 'a man who lies with another man'. A sudden incongruity struck him, between all of this and something his priest said in a sermon years ago that inexplicably had lodged in his memory ever since:

'When we fallible men and women appear to attack one another, that is really an attack against oneself, projected outwards. We see things in others, and we hate them, because we recognise in them aspects of ourselves that we have neither confronted nor resolved.'

Abruptly Dominic came to himself, unsure of

how much of his reverie he may have spoken aloud. He met Owen's eyes again.

'No,' he said.

Owen nodded his understanding. 'I can see why Tegan loves you.'

⁊⦶

A small group had moved the party to the spa. Derrick was among those who sought the comfort of the hot, bubbling water. Sophie's cousins were good company, especially Angelo, who loved soccer as much as Derrick. When he observed Sophie approaching, having just changed, he was impressed by the sight of her in a tiny black bikini. It returned his thoughts to the night of the ball when she'd undressed in front of him. His urge to take her then was just as strong, but he knew he needed to exercise restraint that night.

She was staggering by this point, obviously drunk, and lost her balance on the edge of the spa, making quite a splash as she fell in. Derrick helped bring her back to the water's surface. 'Oops,' she giggled.

Derrick gripped her arms tight. 'I think I'd better hang on to you, so you don't drown.'

With a lustful grin, she pressed up against his chest. 'No complaints here.' She was even slurring her words.

Damn it! Once again, he was at risk of taking

advantage of Sophie. It didn't help that his own inhibitions were lowered. 'Are you okay? No injuries from that fall?'

'Yup! All good. Especially now.' Her hands were strategically placed, one on the waistband of his board shorts, the other on the bare skin of his back. 'Are you having a good time?' she asked in a low, suggestive voice as her fingers began to trace the definition of his abdominals.

'I am, now that you're here.' He couldn't help but feast his eyes upon her cleavage with so much of it on display.

She gave him a knowing look, then her pupils dilated as that gaze of hers took over: the one that screamed 'Fuck me now.'

Derrick wished he could, but there was something other than her level of intoxication holding him back.

As if sensing their need to be alone, the cousins made a quick exit from the spa.

'Good. Now that I have you to myself, there's something I'm dying to know.'

She briefly sucked on her lower lip before responding. 'And what could that be?'

He tucked some wet strands of hair behind her ears to stop them covering her luscious blue eyes. 'Why would Luke question who you really want?'

In a split second, her countenance changed.

She became anxious and withdrew her hands. 'I... I don't know.'

Shit! He knew it. She was conflicted. Luke must have seen it too. It was a sickening thought. Well that's one way to temper his lust. 'I see... excuse me a moment. I need some... air.' He released her arms, then made a dash for the bar.

෫෭ඏ

Sophie watched as Derrick walked away from her, shattering her heart. She couldn't have been more obvious about what she wanted, yet he left her high and dry again. Well maybe not so dry this time. She dragged herself out of the spa and grabbed her towel. She could feel the tears welling up as she traversed the wet pavers with great care. Once she was past the pool gate, she decided to make a run for the privacy of her room.

Halfway up the stairs, she tripped and fell. Damn it! Her ankle was twisted, adding physical pain to her list of woes. She couldn't hold it any longer. The flood gates opened.

'Sofia? Shit! What happened?' The familiar comfort of her brother's voice coming to her aid. When she looked up, he was rushing down the stairs toward her. She also spotted Luke on the top landing. Then Stefan's arms were around her, lifting her up.

She winced, then looked down. 'My left

ankle.'

'Okay, hang on to me and the railing. Let's get you downstairs, then we'll find somewhere to elevate it.' He started to turn her around.

'No! Take me up. Please!' She couldn't bear to face the party guests in this state.

Her towel came untied in that moment. Stefan was quick to react, tucking the loose corner into her shoulder strap. 'Are you sure? Going up will be much harder than down.'

'I'm sure.' With her brother's help, she limped up the stairs. Slumping onto the couch in the gaming room, she noticed the Xbox was on. The guys must have been playing.

'Luke, can you grab an icepack?' Stefan was shifting her into a reclined position, then gently stuffed cushions under her injured foot. It was incredible to see how expertly he responded to the incident.

Once Luke was off on his quest, Sophie summoned the strength to explain, 'This ankle pain is the least of my concerns right now.'

'Why? What else have you injured?' He was trying to stay calm, but his eyes betrayed worry.

When Luke appeared with the icepack, Stefan carefully placed it on her injury, then returned to her side.

Sophie teared up again. 'It was Derrick.'

All of Stefan's composure was lost, replaced

with a fierce rage. 'What has that bastard done to you?'

'Nothing. That's the problem,' she sobbed. 'I really thought he wanted me this time.'

'*Right!*' In a flash, Stefan bolted down the stairs.

'*No! Stefan—don't*' she cried out to him, but in vain. He was gone, leaving her with Luke. She looked at him and pleaded, 'Please stop him, Luke.'

ഇൻഈ

Stefan was furious. How dare that prick toy with Sophie! When he burst through the living room, he heard several alarmed cries from his aunties. He continued to the patio. Quickly scanning the area, he spotted Derrick talking with Angelo near the brick fence toward the back of the yard. He marched on, each step feeding his rage, thinking of Sophie's fragile state. Reaching his target, he used momentum to slam into Derrick, pinning him to the fence with all his weight. His left hand was gripping Derrick's shirt, the right gripped the man's shoulder like a vice. '*Listen arsehole!* Stop leading her on. If you want Sofia, then show her! Otherwise, just leave her the hell alone.'

Derrick didn't attempt to free himself, he just sneered. 'Oh, but I do want her. I just don't take advantage of trashed or vulnerable girls. But hey, you might get lucky with her tonight!'

Stefan felt all his fury funnel into his right fist, landing a blow on Derrick's jaw as he exclaimed, '*She's my sister, you dick!*'

Turning his head to the side, Derrick spat a little blood. When his gaze returned to Stefan, his visage was less amused, but remained cool. Breaking free of Stefan's hold with ease, Derrick pushed him back with enough force to knock him to the ground. 'Get out of my face, loser.' Then he walked off.

Sitting there with his wounded pride and bruised knuckles, Stefan scolded himself for giving in to wrath.

'Hey man, you okay?' Looking up, he saw Angelo offering a hand to help him up.

He graciously accepted. 'Yeah. Derrick just gives me the shits.' Then he remembered what Derrick had said about wanting Sophie. Should he tell her?

Chapter Seven

'Oh God, Derrick! I'm so sorry.' Sophie rushed through his front door to embrace him. 'I didn't think he would lose his shit like that.' Taking care to avoid touching the split lip and swollen lump on the left side of his jaw, she cradled Derrick's face in her soft hands. She inspected his injury, gently turning his head from side to side to get a close look. 'Is it bad?'

'It's okay. Nothing's broken.' He'd had worse, but the previous night's encounter with Stefan's fist still hurt like hell. The blow came as quite a surprise. Sure, he'd touched a nerve, but Derrick didn't think Stefan had it in him.

When Sophie stepped back, he took a moment to look her over. She looked hot in her low-rise denim jeans and purple cardigan.

Her words brought his attention back to her eyes. 'Can we go upstairs… to talk?'

'I dunno Soph…' he winced, 'talking is still painful.'

A lone tear slid down her perfectly sculpted cheek as she whispered his name. 'Oh, Derrick.' Then her arms were around him again. Her hot breath tickled his ear when she continued, 'I just need to tell you something… important.'

Drawing back just enough to look into her eyes, Derrick's inquiring eyes prompted her to go on. He wasn't in the greatest mood for conversation, but he was eager to know Sophie's mind.

'In private,' she added, casting her gaze towards the stairs.

Taking her hand in his, he silently led her up. He noticed that she had a slight limp and once they were in his room, he looked at her foot inquisitively.

'Oh, that. I tripped on the stairs last night, just before…' she blushed. 'I'm sorry for doubting you Derrick. I… I understand why you didn't…'

Sensing her anxiety, Derrick's interest was piqued. What was she trying to say? He was already standing near her, but he advanced forward a couple of steps to encourage her.

Biting her lip, Sophie shoved her hands in her pockets and slouched against the wall adjacent to his door. She lowered her gaze to gather her thoughts. When she looked up again, there was passion in her eyes. 'I want *you* Derrick, now more than ever.'

Those words of confession penetrated his life

force, pushing all fears from his mind and sending much stronger signals firing through his nervous system. He crashed into her body, pressing her firmly against the wall. Forgetting his wounds for a second, he pressed his lips against hers, then cursed, 'Ow, shit.'

Sophie brought her hands up to hold the back of his neck. 'It's okay. I can wait till you've healed.' Her voice was gentle and soothing, but her eyes betrayed an intense hunger.

Derrick lightly brushed Sophie's moist lower lip with his thumb. The pain of his jaw had little impact on the extent of his desire. He groaned deeply before replying 'I can't wait.' He gripped her magnificently toned buttocks, then hoisted her up.

Clearly startled by her sudden elevation, Sophie gasped, but then grinned as she looked down upon Derrick.

He carried her across his room, eased her down on his bed, then he was on her. His hands explored as much of her clothed body as possible, nuzzling against her soft skin with his nose rather than kissing her where possible. He breathed in her perfume as though it was more important to him than air. The urge to strip her bare was overwhelming, but his throbbing erection warned him that he wouldn't be able to resist her if he did. He didn't, however, want his busted mouth to spoil the experience, so he exercised some self-control.

He growled in her ear, 'Once this heals, I promise to kiss every square inch of your body.'

She moaned. 'Mmm, I look forward to it.'

සාලි03

She could hear his fast, heavy breathing; smelt his sandalwood cologne; tasted his salty lips as they pressed against hers; felt the stubble on his cheeks scratch her skin. She welcomed the touch of his calloused fingers as they explored her body, starting from her face and gradually working their way down. As they reached their destination, her senses blurred, then...

Sophie awoke, hot and sticky, pulse racing. Why was her mysterious stranger still haunting her dreams like that? She'd just spent an afternoon in Derrick's wonderful arms; she should be dreaming of him. It should be his tangy cologne, his smooth cheeks and velvety fingers touching her.

Feeling extremely aroused, Sophie decided to try out one of her new toys. She grabbed the black bag from under her bed and read the note from Candice that explained what each implement was and how to use it. She couldn't help but giggle. After briefly testing the two powered items, she settled on using the dildo. The noise from the vibrators might travel and she didn't want to wake anyone.

After sanitising the large plastic phallus, she

relaxed and thought about her make-out session with Derrick. The problem was that aspects of her mysterious stranger kept superimposing themselves upon her visualisation. She sighed, then let him take over her fantasy completely.

∽∾

The increasing volume of the rumbles and apparent wind direction suggested that the storm on the horizon was approaching. Sophie watched anxiously through her window. It was Saturday night and she was about to embark on her first official date with a boyfriend. Wow. She took a moment to let that thought sink in. Derrick was her boyfriend!

The days following her first sort-of kiss with Derrick had been wonderful. It was their final week of classes for the semester and she spent every spare minute with him either cuddling or holding hands. She felt sorry for Candice, who'd almost become a fifth wheel, spending every lunch with them as well as Dominic and Tegan. But her goth friend didn't seem to care.

There he is! Sophie recognised the black, convertible Lexus that pulled into her driveway. It had been Derrick's eighteenth birthday present from his folks. Her heart rate increased at the sight of him stepping out his car. She rushed to her bedroom door, stopping briefly to inspect herself in the mirror. Her makeup was good. She straightened the hem of her short, black dress. Given the weather, she was thankful that their plans were all indoors.

When she reached the front hall, the doorbell rang. *Perfect timing!* It was left to her to answer. Her parents were out, and once Stefan knew Derrick was coming over, he'd made himself scarce.

Derrick let out a whistle when he entered the house. 'You look gorgeous, my dear.'

She beamed. 'Thanks, so do you.' In those skinny jeans, striped dress shirt and leather jacket. His face had healed up nicely, too.

After pulling Sophie into his arms, Derrick pressed his lips to hers and kissed her properly. The tangy scent of his cologne encompassed her. His lips were soft, and the kiss was slow and gentle. She felt dazed when he eventually pulled away.

Derrick squeezed her hand and smiled. 'We'd better get going.'

Sophie loved riding in Derrick's car. It was even more luxurious than her own and there was always good music playing through the stereo. On this occasion they were both rocking out to Muse along their short journey.

Their entertainment for the evening was in South Yarra at the Jam Factory. A shopping complex had been developed within the walls of the original mid-nineteenth century structure. Sophie loved the building's blend of old and new. It was a feature she admired about Melbourne in general. When they arrived, the storm had caught up and it was raining heavily. At least their parking was undercover.

After a delicious dinner that Derrick insisted on paying for, they made their way to the cinema. Lining up at the ticket sales counter, he asked, 'Have you seen *Star Wars Episode III* yet?'

'Um, no, b...' Before she could finish, they reached the front.

Derrick turned to the cashier. 'Okay, two tertiary students for *Stars Wars*, please.'

Dammit! Stefan was going to be pissed with her. They had planned to go together once exams were finished. Well, too late now. She would have to make the most of it.

With tickets in hand, Derrick led her to the candy bar. 'I know you're a *Star Wars* fan, so I couldn't miss this opportunity.' His smile was infectious. 'What snacks did you want?'

She couldn't really think of her stomach. 'Anything chocolate will do. Oh, and some sugar-free cola. Thanks.'

To begin with, they snuggled together as though they were sitting in a lecture, but when the lights dimmed, Sophie felt Derrick's hand move to her thigh. Fire surged upward from the point of contact.

෨ඥ

When the credits started rolling, Derrick whispered into Sophie's ear, 'Your place or mine?' His hand was still gripping her thigh firmly.

Sophie grinned then replied, 'Yours.' She was keen for more intimacy with Derrick and didn't think her home was the best place for it.

The full implication of the response to his question occurred to her as they approached his car. She was about to spend the night at her boyfriend's house. *Would he want sex? Am I ready?* Her mind raced and her heart pounded.

Settling into the leather passenger seat, Sophie tried to calm her nerves as Matt Bellamy's beautiful voice permeated through the speakers.

Once the Lexus was cruising along Toorak Road, Derrick asked, 'So, what did you think of the movie?'

Thankful for the distraction, Sophie considered her answer. 'It was better than the previous prequel movies. There was still too much Jar Jar, but I enjoyed it otherwise. What did you think?'

'I liked it. Good action scenes.' He turned a corner, then continued, 'But then it doesn't take much for a movie to impress me.'

'So long as there are enough fight scenes, car chases or explosions, you mean?'

'Hey, I like mystery and suspense too.' Derrick's tone mocked injury.

'You don't enjoy mysteries. You over-analyse them and spoil the ending for everyone there.' Sophie's tension had gone. It felt good to talk freely with him again.

'Hey, I can't help it if scriptwriters make it too easy for me.' Derrick pulled to a stop in his garage, then looked across to Sophie and grinned. 'We have the place to ourselves tonight.'

Just like that, her anxiety came flooding back. She looked at him and tried to sound suggestive. 'Good to know.'

They both stepped out of the car. Derrick unlocked the inside door and gestured for Sophie to go first. Such a gentleman! But then as soon as they were both inside, he grabbed her, and the genteel behaviour ceased. They kissed with a lustful vigour that was in direct contrast to her first kiss that evening. Derrick's strong tongue manoeuvred across her lips and into her mouth with expert finesse, his hands all over her.

Within a few minutes, Sophie found herself falling into a suede leather couch. She hadn't even noticed them moving across the room! Derrick stood above her, removing his jacket, which he then threw on the adjacent armchair. His eyes bore deep into her soul. Kneeling, he unlaced his shoes then put them aside, all without shifting his gaze from her. 'I'm sure you want out of yours too. Here, allow me.' He slipped Sophie's heels off, then ran his hands and eyes up along her black stockings until he found their suspender straps. Returning his gaze to Sophie's face, his lip curled. 'Are you wearing another corset?'

Sophie smiled coyly. 'Maybe. You'll just have to find out for yourself.'

He stood up. 'Right then. Come here.' He offered her a hand and pulled her up. Wrapping his arms around her, he found her zip. Before she knew it, Sophie's dress was falling to the floor. Derrick stepped back a moment to admire the view. 'Very nice.'

She was wearing a black and red lace corset that Candice had picked out for her when they'd been shopping on Thursday night. Sophie stepped out of her dress and moved in close to Derrick. 'My turn now.' Her nervous hands got to work on his shirt buttons, fumbling a few times along the way. When the fabric fell free, she took a moment to run her hands along his smooth six-pack. Wow, he felt even better than he looked! Then she moved to his belt and the waistband of his jeans. He helped her peel away his pants, then stood before her in nothing but designer boxer briefs. The impressive size of his bulge aroused and intimidated her.

The heat in the room was intense. Sophie wondered how much of it was climate control.

Derrick sat on the couch, then pulled her into his lap. Their lips locked. As passion stirred between her legs, Sophie noticed Derrick's desire growing. Their hips began to grind together. She groaned with pleasure, letting her mind float in an altered state of consciousness.

Derrick's smooth voice brought her back to reality. 'We better take this upstairs, before we wreck the couch.' He was grinning in the direction of their underpants.

'Huh?' Then she noticed the moisture she'd be secreting. 'Oh.' She jumped up and blushed.

'Relax, my dear. It's perfectly natural.' He stood and embraced her. She felt his erection pushing into her belly. 'You're still a virgin, aren't you?'

Was it that obvious? She nodded and gulped before giving her verbal reply, 'Yes, but... I think I'm ready.'

Derrick eyed her cautiously. 'We'll take it slow.' After gathering up their pile of clothes into one arm, he took her hand in his and led her upstairs.

Sitting on his bed, he pulled Sophie between his legs, then unclasped her suspenders. Pulling one foot on to his knees at a time, he carefully rolled each stocking down, kissing her exposed skin as he went. The feel of his lips against her was divine.

'You have the most incredible legs.' Derrick

was pulling her into his lap. He deftly unclasped each hook of her corset, working up from the bottom. He sucked in a breath as the last one came away. 'And these are perfect.' Cupping her breasts, his mouth became acquainted with each of her hard nipples.

The contact sent a signal straight between her thighs and she spasmed. 'Oh God that feels good.'

His mouth was upon her lips again and they kissed fervently. Derrick lay back, letting Sophie fall upon his firm body. Then he turned them over, so he was on top. He gave her a lascivious grin. 'Now to make good on my promise.'

Sophie moaned as he explored her body with his mouth, her skin prickling with goose bumps.

He removed her G-string then gently kissed the exposed flesh. The moment his tongue entered her, she exploded.

ॐ

Sophie's conscious thoughts returned. Derrick was spooning her. She had no idea how much time had passed, but she was confident that Derrick had spent considerable time down there. Enough for her to black out. 'Wow! That was intense.' she whispered. When Derrick didn't respond, she turned to face him. He was asleep. Glancing at the clock beyond his shoulder gave her a shock. It was past three in the morning. She panicked, worried that she had left him unsatisfied. Would he be angry or upset with her? Embracing him, she ran her hands down his back and found that his underpants were still on.

He stirred at her touch, then opened his eyes. Relief washed over her when he smiled warmly. 'Welcome back, sexy.'

Sophie blushed. 'I'm sorry for passing out before… reciprocating.'

'It's okay. I intended it that way. I don't want to rush things with you.' He kissed her gently. 'We'll do it all when the time is right. Let's sleep for now.' Another kiss, then he drifted off.

Sophie followed soon after.

Chapter Eight

Having made it all the way to her bedroom door without detection, Sophie let out a sigh of relief. She'd managed to sneak back shortly after dawn. With any luck her parents would be none the wiser. Even though she was an adult, Mamma would still freak if she knew Sophie spent the night in her boyfriend's bed. Virtuous unmarried ladies didn't do that sort of thing.

'Busted!' When Sophie opened her door, Stefan startled her. He was lying in her bed, wearing pyjamas.

She backed up against the closed door. *Has he spent the night there, waiting for me?* 'Stefano! What the…?'

He pierced her with his inquisitorial stare. 'You spent the night at Derrick's, didn't you?'

What could she say? She stood there, staring blankly, pulse racing.

He threw a pillow at her. 'Don't worry, your secret's safe with me. You ought to know I'd never

110

sell you out to our folks.'

After catching the pillow, her tension eased. She sat on the edge of her bed. 'Yes, I spent the night with Derrick.'

'And?' Stefan was lying on his side.

'And what?' Sophie lay down to face him.

'Did you sleep with him?' His gaze was fixed on her intently.

'Technically yes, but we didn't have sex, if that's what you're really asking.' She hated how awkward it was to talk to Stefan about this stuff. There was a time when they would share everything they did or felt with ease and talking about sex never used to be a problem.

'Interesting. That man's got incredible self-control. I'd call him honourable if he wasn't such a jerk to me.' He began stroking Sophie's hair in way that was completely normal for them. But Sophie sensed something else in his touch. Was it because of their dance at the ball? Their eyes remained locked for a couple of minutes.

For a second, she almost forgot that this man was her brother. She quickly snapped herself out of it. 'I'm gonna get ready for church.' She jumped up and made a dash for the bathroom.

What the hell was that? She paused with her back against the locked door that separated her from her twin. Her attempt to shrug it off as she undressed amounted to naught. As the warm water cascaded across her naked body, her thoughts kept returning to that moment. Was she attracted to Stefan? Surely not! It must be the combination of her mistaking him for her mysterious stranger and the residual hunger from her night with Derrick. She pushed it all from her mind and focused on getting ready.

⁎⁏

Mamma entered the church and genuflected. When she stood up, she waited for Sophie to follow suit, then asked, 'Shall we sit with the Vianellos?' She had been overjoyed by the fact that Sophie was dating such a distinguished young gentleman, as she put it.

'Sure.' Sophie looked around, then spotted Derrick sitting with his parents. She walked over to join them; her family close behind her.

Derrick looked up when Sophie approached and smiled, gesturing for her to join him. 'Ciao Sofia.' Then his gaze moved past her, and he scowled slightly. 'Stefan.'

'Derrick.' Her brother's response was abrupt.

The fact that they greeted each other at all showed they were trying for Sophie's sake. She slid along the pew to sit next to Derrick, who grabbed her hand and kissed it chastely. Sophie noticed Stefan rolling his eyes as he sat next to her. Her parents circled around to the other side of the seat to join Derick's parents. She knew they got along well; Derrick's father was in fact Papà's biggest accounting client.

As mass started, Sophie became acutely aware of her proximity to Derrick and Stefan. Both men were pressed close enough for their legs to touch hers. In Stefan's case, it was likely due to the number of other parishioners who squeezed into their row; but she couldn't help wondering if that was the only reason.

During the Penitential Act, Sophie chanced a glance at Stefan. His face was downcast, but he must have sensed her eyes upon him because he looked up and returned her inquisitive gaze. A strange and confusing desire surged through her body. 'Lord have mercy.' She remembered how good it felt to dance with Stefan at the ball. 'Christ have mercy.' Looking away, she tried to focus on reciting the hymn.

Feeling guilty for letting her mind drift during a time of worship, she closed her eyes when the priest said, 'Let us pray.' *Forgive me Lord, for such sinful thoughts.* Trying in vain to concentrate on the Liturgy of the Word, she looked at Stefan again. This time he was already watching her from the corners of his eyes.

Looking away quickly, she turned her attention to Derrick. He had been engrossed in the ceremony. She studied him, in awe of his piety. It was amusing to think that this was the same man that pleasured her into oblivion the night before. Resigned to the fact that she was unable to focus on the service, she let her mind return to her night with Derrick. At least this was a safer train of thought than the alternative.

కోం

Soon after the congregation dissipated, Stefan caught Sophie looking at him again. It was brief, but like the others that day, he was convinced there was something to it. What was on her mind? He decided he would question her later, but he had to survive lunch first. His parents had accepted an invitation to dine with the Vianello family at a local café before heading home.

When they took their seats, Sophie chose the place directly opposite Stefan. He had mixed feelings on the matter. On the one hand, he would have more opportunities to look upon her, but on the other hand, he would have to see her being affectionate with Derrick. It was sickening to see them together.

While Derrick was busy ordering, Sophie glanced across the table and locked eyes with Stefan. Was it a coincidence that she only seemed to look at him when she knew Derrick wasn't watching? Or was he jumping to conclusions again? It was time to test his theory. He intensified his stare, undressing her in his imagination. She held his gaze until she saw Derrick returning. *First piece of evidence.*

Stefan's investigation made for a good distraction from his dislike for Derrick. During the meal, when Derrick got caught up in a conversation about politics, Sophie's attention was diverted by Stefan again. This time he gave her the full smouldering look. She blushed but didn't avert her eyes until the conversation shifted and Derrick was talking to her again. *Second piece.*

The *third* time, Derrick was distracted, taking a bathroom break; they sought each other's eyes, but Papà pulled him into a discussion about business finance. It was still evidence though.

೮೦೧೪

Stefan couldn't help himself. It was too tempting to eavesdrop on Sophie's phone conversations with Dom and Candice. He pretended to play on the Xbox while listening through her bedroom door. He was still waiting for an opportunity to talk to her about the way they had been fucking each other with their eyes several times that day. The first call to Dom including a recap of her night with Derrick, but she kept the details to a minimum. The graphic retelling, instead, came when she spoke to Candice. While knowing that Derrick had done that to her angered him, he also felt aroused by the thought of her being pleasured that much. *By God, Stefan! You are one sick bastard!*

When she signed off, he put his headphones back on to maintain his cover. She came out of her room and sat next to him on the couch. He took the headphones back off and looked at her. 'Wanna play?' He gestured to the game of *Halo 2* on the screen.

She smiled. 'Would love to.'

He handed her a controller. 'PVP or Co-op?'

'Co-op, thanks.' She took the controller.

They played through a mission before Stefan broached the topic. 'So… was there anything you… wanted to discuss with me?'

She faltered in the game, flipping the warthog, a clear sign of distraction for her. 'Why would there be?'

'Oh, I dunno. Those looks you kept giving me this morning suggested… something's on your mind.'

Sophie froze, leaving her character wide open, so he paused the game for her. 'I… I don't want to talk about it.'

Nailed it! She never shied away from divulging her thoughts to him. The only reason he could think she was hiding them from him was because they were about him. Was she struggling with her feelings? It was understandable. It took him years to come to terms with his and he still reproached himself for being sick and perverted because of them. 'It's okay Sofia. I can wait till you're ready.' He left it at that and resumed the game.

ഔരു

The door lock clicked, and the heat of the room intensified within seconds. He was upon her in a flash. Sophie couldn't see him, but she heard his fast, heavy breathing; smelt his sandalwood cologne; tasted his salty lips as they kissed her before exploring her body. When his tongue reached its destination…

She awoke panting. That was the first time her mysterious stranger had tried that approach. It was probably because of her recent experience with Derrick. But why wasn't it Derrick in her dream? An uncomfortable thought was nagging at her, but she resisted entertaining it.

Her mouth was parched, so she fetched a glass of water from her ensuite. When she returned to her room, she caught a glimpse of the DVD boxset that Dom had gifted her. Remembering what he'd told her, she opened it and looked behind the first disc. Hidden beneath was a film entitled *Beautiful/Nasty*. Too stimulated for sleep, she snuck out to the gaming room and set up to watch the porn with headphones.

The lesbian sex scenes were intriguing, even

educational, but she didn't find them arousing. Putting her hands between her legs, she closed her eyes and tried some visualisations. When she thought about that time Candice was with Stefan, she isolated the image of Candice's naked body. Nothing. She imagined doing some of the stuff from the porn flick with Candice. Still no result. So why had she been so turned on that night? She'd heard about voyeurism being a thing. Was that it? She resolved to discuss the issue with Dom as soon as possible.

❧❧

Dominic waited anxiously for Sophie's arrival. Her text message didn't indicate urgency, but she'd said she wanted to discuss something important and needed complete privacy. He couldn't help but worry. His family were out all day, so he invited her over to his house.

When the doorbell rang, he ran to answer it. 'Oh my God, Soph. Are you okay?' He hugged her tight.

'Um, hi Dom. I'm okay.' As soon as she was able to pull out of his embrace, she asked, 'Are you okay? You seem worried?'

He inspected her eyes for signs of tears. No redness or swelling. 'Your text message spooked me. Are you sure you're okay?'

She smiled. 'Yes, I'm sure. Just confused. Can

we sit and talk?'

'Yes of course, come in. Did you want a coffee?' He led her into the living area.

'Mm, yes please.' Sophie made herself at home on the sofa.

Once the cappuccinos were ready, he took their cups across the room and placed them on the coffee table. 'So, what's up?'

She sighed. 'I watched that porn vid you gave me.'

'Oh. And?' If she was about to come out, the timing was interesting.

'Nothing. I'm not a lesbian. I'm wondering if the reason I got turned on by the sight of Candice with Stefan has more to do with some innate desire for voyeurism. What do you think?'

'Hmm... could be. I don't know how you could test that one, though. Maybe ask Candice to let you watch the next time she hooks up with someone?' It was a strange thought.

Sophie continued, 'There's something else. But first, I need to tell you about these dreams I've been having.'

He listened intently to her description of her mysterious stranger. It was a pretty hot dream, but he was unsure what it had to do with her questioning her sexuality.

'So, this other thing I mentioned...' she paused to sip her drink.

'Yes?' he prompted her.

'It happened at the deb ball. We never really had a chance to debrief on that night properly. I know it went well for you,' she grinned.

'Yes, well…. But do go on.' The suspense was killing him.

'I thought I met my mysterious stranger that night. When some blonde girl stole Derrick away from me briefly, I ended up dancing with a man in a full mask. When we started our samba, the similarities struck me. His calloused fingers, the same cologne… and I could even see stubble escaping the edge of his mask. The thought was a serious turn-on, and we ended up dancing the hottest samba of all time.' Pausing again to drink more coffee, she stared into her cup.

Curious. Dominic wondered why she still ended up with Derrick if she'd met the man of her dreams.

She looked up again. 'Did you see me leaving before the presentation that night?'

Dominic felt a little guilty for not being more attentive to her that night. 'Yeah kind of. I noticed you weren't presented. Why, what happened?'

'The unmasking happened. The man I thought was my mysterious stranger revealed his identity.' She shuddered.

'And? Who was he?' How could the unmasking have been so bad?

A few tears streamed down her cheeks. It must have been a painful memory to recollect. She looked into his eye as she replied, 'He was Stefan.'

'Oh shit, Sophie! I... I'm sorry.' Dominic pulled her into his arms. Well no wonder!

She wiped her tears and tried some deep breathing. 'There's more. Things have been awkward between me and Stefan since then, as you might imagine. But I've also noticed him looking at me a lot more lately. And the way he looks at me... I think he might have the hots for me.'

Dominic considered her situation for a minute. 'There's more to it, Soph. I can tell you're holding something back.'

She was flicking her fingers against her cup, a sign of nerves. 'Why do you say that?

'I think you're afraid to admit it to yourself. The real reason for your attraction to Stefan when you thought he was your mysterious stranger. It's the same reason you were turned on when you saw Candice with Stefan.' He gave her a moment to process what he was suggesting.

She shook her head. 'No.'

'Soph. Listen to me. Stefan *is* your mysterious stranger. It makes perfect sense. I've often thought the two of you were closer than any other siblings I know. I used to put it down to you being twins, but I can see more to it now.' Her crying intensified, so he hugged her again.

'It… it's too wrong,' she sobbed.

'I don't think so. You guys have a beautiful connection. I don't see anything wrong with your desire to express your love for each other.' He thought about his own recent desires. 'Besides, I'm not in any position to judge.'

She looked up at him then. 'Why? Do you have the hots for Amelia?'

Amelia was his younger sister. 'Hell no! I can't imagine what anyone would see in that skank. But I do have a crush on my girlfriend's best friend.' When he got a blank look from her, he went on. 'Her best friend, Owen; the guy you met at your eighteenth.' Realisation dawned on her face. 'I think I might be gay, Soph. Or bi… I dunno.'

'Wow, Dom. That's huge! When? How?' Her mouth was agape.

He told her about the gay porn that had caught his attention, then about his fascination with Owen when they were left alone at her party. Ever since then, whenever he met Owen for coffee with Tegan, he found himself admiring the man's features.

'Have you told either of them?' she asked.

'Not yet. I don't know how to approach the topic.' He really liked Tegan and didn't want to upset her.

'Yeah, that's a toughie. But the longer you put it off, the more it has the potential to hurt someone.' She finished her coffee and put the cup down.

'Yeah I know. I was planning to wait till after exams, but maybe I should do it sooner.' He sighed, then took Sophie's empty cup, along with his own, to the dishwasher. He poured them both a glass of water. When Sophie joined him at the breakfast bar, he asked her, 'So what are you going to do about your predicament?'

Frowning, she took the water glass he offered her. 'I don't know. It's not like I can openly date Stefan. Besides, I still love Derrick, and he's been a wonderful boyfriend. It's probably best if I keep my feelings for Stefan to myself.'

ॐ

Having squandered her first day of Swot Vac chatting with Dom, Sophie settled in for an early night with the intention of getting up refreshed for some effective study the next day. She pondered what Dom had said regarding her dreams and feelings for Stefan. While she suspected he was right, it was a very weird and disturbing revelation, so she decided to test the hypothesis.

She was wearing a black satin slip, much like the one in her dreams. To eliminate other variables, her experiment would have to use the manual method, so she didn't employ any of her new toys. She brought the images of her dream to mind;

except this time, she wasn't blindfolded. When her lover came to her, she could see that he was Stefan. Letting her hands explore her own body, she imagined them to be Stefan's. When they reached between her legs, the reaction was instant. She convulsed and moaned as the fantasy took hold.

After climaxing several times, she collapsed and whispered to herself, 'Well fuck! I guess I'm going to hell.'

Chapter Nine

Refreshed was exactly the opposite of what Sophie felt when she awoke the next day. The little sleep she'd had was riddled with nightmares of being tied to a rotisserie that was positioned over hellfire while demons prodded her with pitchforks. She rolled over and turned off her alarm clock, then attempted to get back to sleep. It was useless. She tossed and turned to no avail for about an hour, then got up. She still wore her black satin slip, so she just threw her plush dressing gown over the top and headed downstairs.

The kitchen was empty, her parents already gone, so she brewed a new pot of coffee. She was buttering her toast when footsteps came pelting down the stairs. Oh crap! Her heart started thumping.

'Ah, ciao Sofia. Is that a fresh brew?' Pulling her into a sideways hug, Stefan kissed her on the cheek, then released her to grab the coffee. He was dressed in black track pants and a band shirt. The familiar, spicy smell of his shower gel wafted through the room.

'Um, ciao Stefano.' Heat radiated from where his lips had touched her skin. *Dear God, help me control these urges.* She poured herself a short black, then sat down to her breakfast.

Stefan joined her on the opposite side of the table. 'How's the exam prep going?'

'Fine,' she lied. Being blatantly dishonest with her twin made her cringe. It felt like a betrayal to herself. But she couldn't tell him why she'd been distracted. 'Yours?'

He swallowed a mouthful of toast before replying, 'Yeah, okay, I guess. Accounting and quants are easy enough. I'm a bit worried about the economics exam, though.' Looking up from his meal, he gazed upon her properly for the first time that morning. 'Are you okay, Soph? You look a bit… flustered.'

'I uh… didn't sleep well.' *Please don't ask why!* She wanted to avert her eyes but couldn't. How had she not seen it earlier? Stefan was steaming hot. There was no doubt that he was her mysterious stranger. *It was so fucking wrong!*

'Oh really? Something plaguing your mind?' He gave her that sexy look again as he bit into his toast. Had he guessed at her feelings?

She looked down and sipped her coffee. 'It's probably just exam stress.' If she could just resist the temptation to commit the act, perhaps her soul could still be saved.

'Hmm, well don't overwork yourself. Perhaps you should take a break and ease some tension.' He leant back in his chair and smiled. 'I'd be happy to help you relax.'

Sophie gasped, which caused her mouthful of coffee to go down the wrong way. Her bout of coughing was eased when she sipped the water that Stefan had brought her.

Sitting next to her, he placed a hand on her shoulder. 'Are you okay?' He looked worried.

'Yes. (cough) thanks (cough) for the water.' She took a few deep breaths and sipped more water. 'I must've drunk too much coffee at once.' Sophie was acutely aware of Stefan's hand on her body.

Stefan's look of concern was suddenly replaced by a devilish grin. 'So, as I was saying, I'd be happy to help you relax. If you feel like a round of *Halo 2*, for example.'

'Thanks, but I was thinking of going for a drive. That's if you don't need the car?' She decided it would be safer if she got out of the house.

He stood up, pulling his hand away from her. 'No, it's all yours. I'm not going anywhere today.'

It was a relief to be free of his grip; but at the same time, she ached for more of his touch. *Damn it!*

She finished her breakfast, then cleared her dishes. As she turned to say goodbye, her dressing gown fell open, revealing her satin negligee. His eyes were drawn straight to the sight of her scantily clad body. She blushed. *Try to act normal you idiot!* He'd seen her like this plenty of times before. If she reacted, he would surely suspect something… if he didn't already. 'I'm gonna head out soon. See ya later.'

His eyes remained fixed on her. 'Yeah, see ya, Soph.'

She turned and made her way back upstairs.

⁕⁖

Sophie parked outside the West Melbourne church, waiting for a break in the weather. It had been bucketing down all morning and she forgot her raincoat. The Gothic style cathedral was a sight to behold, even in its state of restoration. She had decided it would be better to speak to a priest outside of her own parish, given the delicate nature of her concerns. Having attended midnight mass in this church before, she'd never forgotten its splendour.

After locking the car, she dashed inside when the rain eased slightly. She was met by a smiling priest. 'Welcome. How may I be of service?'

'Morning Father. I wish to take confession and seek your guidance. I know I'm a little early, but this is somewhat urgent.' She shivered a little, partially from cold.

'I suppose I can spare a few minutes. You're not a regular here, are you? I don't recognise your face. What's your name, young lady?' He led her towards a confessional.

Sophie followed, admiring the decorative columns and stained glass. Dom would love this place. 'Sophie. And no, this is not my usual parish, but I would feel awkward talking to my regular priest.'

'Hmm, I see. Please have a seat, Sophie.' He sat down and gestured for her to take her place on the other side of the booth. 'What troubles you?'

'I come seeking forgiveness for lustful thoughts. I can't stop thinking about sex; in fact, I have been guilty of masturbation and using pornography.' She paused, bracing herself for the more difficult part of her confession.

He must have taken her silence to mean she was finished. 'Yes, these are grave sins indeed, but...'

'Wait, there's more. Many of these lustful thoughts have been... directed towards my twin brother.' There—it was out.

The priest gasped. 'Have you acted upon these desires?'

'No Father. I haven't even spoken to my brother about these feelings because I fear they're mutual. It is very difficult to be alone with him now because the temptation is strong.' Even as she spoke, the thought of Stefan touching her was making her moist.

'Indeed. It is good that you haven't told him. You must be very careful. Incest is not only a sin, but it's illegal. Any form of sexual interaction with your brother could land you both in gaol.'

Prison? Really? The severity of it shocked her. 'Oh wow, that never even occurred to me. Thank you for your counsel Father.'

'Does that conclude your confession, Sophie?' he asked.

'Yes Father.' Sophie recited the Prayer of Contrition.

After issuing her with some prayers as penance, he absolved her of her sins, then bid her farewell.

With the gravity of situation at the forefront of her mind, she decided to go to a library to study for the rest of the day.

৪০C₃

'Okay so what are the small molecule neurotransmitters?' Derrick was lying on his bed, with his hands laced behind his neck. The sight of him in nothing but track pants was extremely distracting.

It was the last day of Swot Vac and Sophie

sat at the desk next to his bed with her notepad closed. 'Acetylcholine, ATP, adenosine, glycine, GABA, and glutamic acid.'

He sat up and looked at her. 'Right, but you forgot the biogenic amines. Do you remember those?' His capacity to switch so easily from playtime to work was astounding.

'Oh right. So, they include dopamine and serotonin, right?' She started sifting through her notes.

Walking over to her, he put his hands on her shoulders. 'Among others, yes. Come on Soph, you had this before.'

'Yes, but you're not helping.' The physical contact was giving her more practical experience with neurotransmitters.

'I'm trying to help, Soph, but....' He sounded exasperated.

'I mean your proximity and the fact that you're half naked isn't helping. I can't focus when all I can think about is getting completely naked and putting all this theory to practice.' Standing up, she tried to kiss him.

He backed away. 'You're not even trying to focus. We've already spent half the morning making out. If you want to do well at your exam you need to apply yourself more.'

'Geez, Derrick. You're not my Papà. You know what, you don't *have* to help with my revision.' She snatched her notebook up and started towards the door.

Grabbing her arm, he pulled her back into an embrace. 'Wait, Soph. I'm sorry. I was just trying to help.'

'I know, but I'll do okay. I don't need perfect grades. But I do need you. And right now, what I need more than anything is sex.' She'd been very frustrated since learning just how out-of-bounds Stefan was. She had avoided being alone with him, but family meals had become excruciating with their exchanged glances. And Derrick had been busy studying for most of Swot Vac, so this was their first chance at alone time all week.

Holding her tight, he whispered, 'I can go down on you again if you like.'

The thought was enough to make her womanhood quiver. 'Mmm, that would make a nice start, but I'm ready for more, Derrick.'

He sighed and released his hold of her. 'I don't know, Soph. I don't think it's a good idea.'

'What? Why not?' She couldn't understand his reluctance.

'Well, you're still a virgin and I respect that.'

Was he for real? 'But I'm ready. More than ready.' She sat on the edge of his bed.

He sat beside her. 'The thing is, I regret giving away my virginity to someone who meant nothing to me. I don't want that for you.'

Sophie ran her hand up his thigh. 'But you do mean a lot to me, Derrick.'

He brushed her hand aside before it reached between his legs. 'I just think we should wait until we are sure.'

Sophie could feel tears building. 'Jesus, Derrick. I love you. I've been in love with you for years. What more reassurance of my certainty do you want?'

He was suddenly upon her, pinning her to the bed. 'Do you mean that?'

'That I love you? Yes, of—' Sophie couldn't speak anymore. Derrick's lips crashed into hers with a force that would've hurt if it wasn't exactly what she needed.

After a few minutes, he whispered, 'I love you, Sophie; more than I thought humanly possible.'

Desire spread through her body. She whispered, 'Then make love to me.'

He looked into her eyes. 'Are you absolutely sure?'

'Yes.'

Then it happened.

After preparing her with more foreplay he grabbed a foil packet and applied the protective barrier. Slowly, he entered her, holding her gaze as he did so. It hurt at first, but after stretching her out with a few gentle thrusts, the pleasure built until it overtook the pain.

'Wow. That was… *wow*.' Sophie couldn't even find the words to describe her experience. It was mind-blowing. She curled up against Derrick's heaving chest. She thought oral sex to the point of passing out was incredible but that had a lot more to do with the number of orgasms that Derrick kept drawing out of her over an extended period. But feeling him inside her was something else. The intensity of her climax was beyond anything she'd ever felt.

He turned on to his side and kissed her gently. 'You were amazing, Sofia.'

They kissed again, this time with renewed vigour. Before she knew it, another condom was in place and he was inside her again. Just like that, her afternoon was gone.

෨ඏ

With the uni semester finished, Dominic decided to take Owen up on his invitation. He still hadn't plucked up the courage to talk to Tegan about his suspicions, but he figured afternoon tea would be harmless enough.

The Edwardian terrace apartment that Owen called home was far from luxurious, but it had a certain old-world charm to it that Dominic admired. The abundance of potted plants and colourful sculptures that furnished the front porch and balcony also added a lot of character.

When Owen opened the door, he smiled brightly. 'Hey man. It's good to see ya. Welcome.'

'Thanks.' When Dominic stepped inside, his senses were immediately overwhelmed by the mix of smells. He detected oil paints and their solvents, sawdust, clay, and some sort of incense. And there was stuff everywhere. It wasn't like the mess of a hovel, but more the clutter of a busy mind.

'Here, grab a seat.' He cleared away some newspapers so that Dominic could sit on the antique sofa that matched the era of the house. 'Would you like some tea? I don't entertain much, so I don't have any coffee or milk I'm afraid.'

'Tea would be great, thanks.' Dominic looked around the front living room while his host ducked out to the kitchen to make their drinks. It was a small space and he was amazed at how much had been crammed into it. The entertainment unit, also Edwardian, held an old CRT television and a record player that was attached to a stereo that looked like it was made in the '70s. There were no appliances that Dominic would consider modern for the twenty-first century.

'Here you go,' Owen returned, handing him the tea. He also placed a sugar bowl on the minute coffee table.

After adding a couple of sugars to his tea, he questioned Owen on the music system. 'Is that a functional vinyl player?'

'Yeah man. It's great. Better quality sound than CDs. I have a small CD player in the bedroom, but this's what I use when I want to appreciate music.' He sat down in the armchair directly in front of the television.

'What sort of music do you like to appreciate?' Having just spotted the bookshelf, Dominic was in awe of what looked like an extensive record collection.

'Pretty much anything and everything. I got some new stuff like modern folk, trance, trip-hop, pop, R&B, even a little hip-hop, but I also love prog rock, jazz, world music, and classical.' He gestured toward the shelf. 'Why don't you pick something to listen to?'

Dominic put his tea down, then stood up and carefully manoeuvred around the stacks of books. Once he reached the shelf, he flicked through the options. He was relieved to find they were grouped by genre. 'Wow, this is an impressive collection.'

'Thanks man. Along with sculpture and painting, it's one of my great passions.'

Looking through the pop music, he pulled out something that caught his eye. 'Oh my God! You've got Cher's greatest hits. Can we put this on?'

Owen gave him an odd look for a moment, then grinned. 'Yeah, sure.'

He turned towards the stereo, then froze.

'Sorry, but I have no idea how to work this thing.'

'Oh right, sorry. My bad. I shouldn't have assumed.' He stood up and took the LP from Dominic, brushing his hand lightly in the process.

Dominic sucked in a sharp breath. It was the lightest of touches, but the contact left his skin electrified. Once the music started and Owen was seated, Dominic made his way back to the sofa and resumed his tea. After listening to the first track he understood what Owen meant about the sound quality. 'It definitely has a warmer sound than the digital version.'

Owen simply nodded in agreement as he looked at Dominic with intense curiosity. But then he spoke again before the silence got too awkward. 'So, what other pop music do you like, Dom?'

'Well, Kylie Minogue, Madonna and Britney Spears are definite faves.' He noticed that Owen's grin was expanding. 'What? What's funny?'

'Oh nothing…. It's just that… never mind.' He stood up then. 'So, you still want to see the art?'

'For sure.' Dominic finished his tea, then followed Owen.

He was impressed by Owen's work, from the abstract paintings in vivid colours, to the beautifully painted clay sculptures and intricate wood carvings. When they reached the studio, which was clearly designed to be the master bedroom, Dominic was gobsmacked. It was the only bronze work he had seen thus far and it was a series of male bodies in very sensual poses. 'Wow, you've done some stunning work, Owen.'

'Cheers man. I'm glad you like it. You know, most of my straight friends can't stand these.' He was looking at Dominic expectantly as his hand swept the room.

'Well they must all be uncultured Luddites.' He was sensing some strong chemistry between them.

'Clearly.'

Dominic's phone alerted him to a text message. He looked at Owen. 'Mind if I…?'

'Nah man, go for it,' he smiled.

Yep, there was definite chemistry. Dominic decided he was going to have to talk to Tegan that night. He looked at the message. It was from Tegan, who was hoping to catch up for dinner. He quickly sent an affirmative, then noticed the time. 'Oh crap, it's four already. I've got a date with Tegan tonight, so I betta get moving.'

'Yeah, of course. Thanks for popping 'round.' He led Dominic back downstairs. When they reached the front door, he looked into Dominic's eyes. 'You know, Tegan's a pretty lucky girl.'

Dominic blushed. 'Um, thanks. See you again soon?'

Owen beamed. 'Count on it.'

Chapter Ten

Sophie sat in the plush couch of the rumpus room, watching intently as the band set up their music gear for rehearsal. She was feeling pretty good about life. Exams had gone okay and things with Derrick were great. They'd had a date the night before and she was still revelling in the afterglow of amazing sex. She also had an upcoming holiday in Italy to look forward to. 'I'm gonna a grab a cider. Did any of you guys want a drink?'

Silas the singer and Chris declined, but Luke and Stefan both asked for beers.

When she handed a drink to Stefan, he gripped it with both hands, ensuring that his left hand enclosed hers. Holding her captive this way, he took a moment to lock eyes with her. 'You're looking well today, Soph. Glowing, even.'

'Um, thanks. I guess I am feeling pretty good.' She returned his licentious grin, despite her better judgement.

As if content with her reaction, Stefan released her hand. 'Thanks for the drink.'

'Welcome.' She held her bottle towards his. 'Cheers.'

He clinked her drink, still maintaining his gaze. 'Cheers.'

'You ready Stefan?' Luke beckoned him.

Sophie returned to the couch and settled in to enjoy the show. She loved watching the guys rehearse and made a point of doing so whenever time allowed. Their music was good, and it was more in line with her preference for prog metal over other sub-genres.

By God, Stefan looked hot playing guitar in his jeans and Karnivool t-shirt! *Damn it!* How did she think this would be a good idea? She was beginning to see a lot more trips to the confessional in her future. When Stefan glanced up and caught her gawking at him, he grinned, and she practically creamed herself.

After several more glances and an hour of rehearsal, the guys took a break. Stefan collapsed on the couch next to Sophie and stretched his fingers. 'Man, I'm out of shape after a few weeks without any practice. And my playing sucked.'

'I didn't think so. You guys sounded good,' Sophie protested, looking directly at Stefan.

'Nice of you to say, Sophie, but we were all shit,' Silas argued. 'I'm gonna go grab a coffee.' He walked out.

Then Chris excused himself, 'I need a smoke. Joining me Luke?'

'Yeah in a minute. Gotta reply to a text from the missus.' Luke grabbed his phone and started texting as Chris stepped outside.

Stefan turned his head and looked into Sophie's eyes, sending another jolt of desire charging through her nervous system.

'Fuck's sake! Would you two get a room already!' Luke exclaimed, as he threw his phone down and walked outside.

Sophie's skin instantly burned, and she suspected her face had turned crimson. Her heart was also pounding furiously, trying to escape its cage of bones.

Holding the eye contact, Stefan grinned. 'He's gotta point, hasn't he Sofia?'

Shit! 'You know I'm with Derrick, right?' *What the hell? Was that my best defence?*

'I know, but I don't hear you denying it.' His gaze travelled down to her chest and he picked up the masquerade pendant around her neck. 'And I can't help but wonder that you've been wearing this daily for some time now, despite Derrick.' His eyes returned to hers, but he still held the pendant, his hand lightly touching her throat.

She was dangerously close to giving in to some powerful urges. 'Stefan, we shouldn't.'

'Believe me, Sofia, I know we shouldn't, but do you deny that you want to?'

She said nothing. To deny it would be a lie and to admit it aloud…

'Because I want you, Sofia. I've wanted you for years. Do you want me?' He let the necklace fall from his grasp, then moved his hand to grip her chin. His thumb brushed across her bottom lip.

She whispered a reply: 'Yes.' *Wait, what? Did I just say that aloud? Fuck!*

Stefan smiled. 'Thank you, Sofia.' He pulled away at the sound of the door. 'Did you want another drink, Soph?'

Looking up, she saw Silas walking through the door. 'Yes please.' She watched Stefan leave, her mind reeling, heart aching and vagina throbbing. What the hell was she gonna do? In several hours the rest of the band would be gone and they would be alone together upstairs.

After handing her another cider, Stefan returned to his guitar. The rest of the guys reassembled and resumed their practice. This time the twins' glances were more frequent and lasted longer. And they were both smiling with the knowledge of a shared secret and a mutual attraction.

୨୦୧

Sophie lay in bed watching the storm through the

window. A sudden clap of thunder and the room lit up, then the sound of rain bucketing down. She looked at the clock: 2AM already. Maybe he wouldn't come to her after all. A moment later, she saw someone open her balcony door, the chill air touching her hot skin. Her heart started racing. The door-lock clicked, and the room became a sauna. He was upon her in a flash. Stefan was with her at last. She smelt his sandalwood cologne, layered with the familiar scent of his spicy shower gel; tasted his salty lips as they kissed hers; felt the stubble on his cheeks scratch her skin. She welcomed the touch of his calloused fingers as they explored her body, starting from her face and gradually working their way down. As they reached their destination, her senses blurred, then...

She awoke frustrated and unsatisfied. Why wouldn't her dream reach the climax? She looked at the clock: 3AM. She was relieved and disappointed that Stefan didn't make a move with her earlier that night. After dinner, they played *Halo 2* and things felt completely normal between them. Well, almost. Every touch was electric, every hug superheated. But he eased up on the bedroom eyes and didn't broach the topic during conversation.

Her sex ached for some attention, so she grabbed the vibrator. Since the air had been cleared, she was no longer worried if Stefan heard the buzzing noise. She almost didn't need any visualisations. It was a powerful tool, and very effective.

ℰℛ

Stefan couldn't get to sleep that night. Having his suspicions confirmed excited and terrified him. He knew he should resist the urge to take things further, but knowing the feelings were mutual made it that much harder.

He was suddenly aware of a buzzing noise. What the hell was that? It sounded like his electric shaver. He got up and inspected his bathroom. Nothing in there was running. He walked out into the gaming room to inspect the devices out there. Then it dawned on him. The sound was coming from Sophie's bedroom. He grinned. Listening closer at her door, he could hear heavy breathing and even a little moaning. The conclusion he drew was incredibly arousing.

Returning to his room, he decided to follow suit. He gripped his hard cock, imagining the hand to be Sophie's. Knowing that she was orgasming a short distance away, most likely because of him, helped facilitate his fantasy. It was probably the closest they could get to the real thing.

ℰℛ

'Hey Soph,' Candice said, walking through Sophie's open door. She'd agreed to help the girl pack because she needed to clear her mind.

'Hey Candice. Did you want a coffee before we get on with it?' Sophie looked vibrant, Candice thought. Must be all that sex with Derrick.

'No thanks. My stomach's been a little unsettled.' She headed straight up the stairs.

Following her up the stairs, Sophie sounded worried. 'Oh, okay then. Are you sure you're up to this?'

'Yeh, although I'm still not sure how I can help. I've never packed for an overseas trip.' She looked at the mess of clothes strewn across Sophie's bed and asked if the holiday was a few weeks or a few months.

Sophie smiled apologetically. 'Honestly, neither do I. I really just wanna catch up. It's been a while and I am about to go away for a few weeks.'

'Ah, okay.' That was a bit out of left field. Was Sophie genuinely interested in some sort of friendship? Candice had never had a real friend before. Most people just used her for something or other, then moved on. It had hurt at first, but people's motives soon became apparent to her and she was able to shield herself. After a while, she started treating people the same way, men in particular.

'So, I tried out that vibrator for the first-time last night.' She was folding some clothes and sorting them into piles as she spoke. 'It worked a charm. Thank you.'

'Good. I'm glad you liked it.' Sitting down in Sophie's study chair, she sighed. Her own toys had become her only bedfellows of late.

'Hey, Candice, can I confide in you about something?' The folding had ceased, and she sat on her bed looking at Candice expectantly.

'Yeh of course.' She was good with secrets, never feeling the urge to gossip.

'It's about Stefan...'

Candice suddenly needed to rush to the bathroom and throw up her breakfast.

Sophie cried from the open doorway, 'Oh God, Candice! Are you okay?'

After flushing the toilet, she turned around, still sitting on the floor. 'I think I might wait here a little longer, in case there's more.'

'Can I get you anything? Should I call a doctor?' It sounded like she was panicking.

'No, I'm sure it will pass soon enough.' *Oh joy!* No sooner had she spoken!

Once the worst of it subsided, she picked herself up off the floor and washed her face.

Sophie still looked worried. 'I think you should see a doctor.'

'I don't need a doctor, Soph. I've already seen enough of the bastards.' *Damn it!* She was hoping to avoid this topic.

'Why, what's wrong?' When Candice didn't

reply, her anxiety appeared to increase. 'You're scaring me Candice. What's wrong?' She grabbed the chair. 'Here, sit down.'

'Relax, Soph. It's just morning sickness.' She braced herself for the reaction.

'Oh shit! You're pregnant? Really? Wait, is this good or bad news?' Sophie sat back on the edge of her bed.

'It wouldn't be news at all if I could find a doctor willing to sign-off on a termination. Apparently, I'm too healthy and there is no threat to my life beyond the normal risks of pregnancy and childbirth. As it stands, *I'm stuck with this thing for now!*' She pulled a peppermint out of her pocket and popped it in her mouth.

'I guess that makes it bad news. Shit. That's so unfair. Shouldn't it be your choice?'

'Yes, it absolutely should be my choice. If I have this baby, my future career prospects are royally screwed. And I'll be yet another single mother bringing another poor soul into this fucked up world.' Even the mint wasn't enough to hide the bitter taste in her mouth or her soul.

Sophie frowned. 'Does the father know you're pregnant? Surely he should be helping you through this?'

Candice shook her head.

'Wait, do you know who the father is?'

Crap! She feared the conversation would

evolve to this. 'Yeh, I know.'

The frown intensified. 'And, who is the jerk?'

Candice flinched. 'Soph, you know I've had a dry spell recently. There was only one guy for several months.'

Sophie's complexion paled as she put the facts together. 'No, it can't be!' Her voice was barely audible. 'But I know you guys used a rubber.'

'Condoms can break, Soph.' Candice started crunching the mint to calm her nerves.

'Weren't you on the pill?' Was Sophie seriously turning this around on her now?

Candice could hardly blame her. The issue had suddenly become a lot more personal for her. 'I had troubles with the previous pill, so I'd just started a new one. I wasn't on it long enough yet.'

Sophie stiffened. 'You have to tell him Candice.'

'Absolutely not. I can deal with this alone, like the rest of the problems in my life.' She didn't see the point in ruining someone else's life.

'This is Stefan we're talking about! You don't need to go through this alone.' Tears started to trickle down her face.

'I don't want to burden him, Soph. Please don't tell him. I will deal with this, okay?' Why was Sophie crying when Candice hadn't shed a single tear over the matter?

Sophie threw her arms around Candice and

sobbed. 'Okay, but you still don't need to go through this alone. Please let me help. If the kid can't know its father, it can still have an aunty.'

Candice hesitated at first, but then let her arms enfold Sophie. 'Okay.'

෪෨

Wow. She was gonna be an aunty. As soon as Candice left, Sophie collapsed on the couch in the gaming room. The tempest of emotions rushing around inside her was overwhelming. She considered calling Derrick about going to her sleepover early. He was good at clearing her mind.

'Hey Soph, how'd the packing go?' Stefan was standing above her.

Sophie jumped. *What the hell? Where'd he come from?* 'When did you get home?'

'A few minutes ago. Sorry, did I startle you?' He sat close beside her. Very close. He looked into her eyes. 'Were you thinking about me again?'

She blushed. There was no denying that he'd been at the centre of her thoughts.

He grinned. 'Well shit. You were thinking about me.' He placed a hand on her knee.

Oh God!

'Were they sexy thoughts?' His hand started sliding upward.

Sophie jumped up. 'You know what Stefan — not everything has to be about sex!'

His eyes narrowed. 'Oh? Were they more romantic thoughts, 'cause…'

'Stop it Stefan! We can't do this. It's too wrong.' The tears escaped.

'Oh God, Sofia. I'm sorry. Here.' Pulling her down into his arms, he comforted her. He gently kissed the crown of her head. 'I love you Sofia. I know I love you more than a brother ought to, but it is still love. Anything that injures you, pains me. I don't want to hurt you or push you into anything you aren't ready for…. If you're still struggling to come to terms with what you feel, I can wait.'

Sophie looked up into the eyes of the man she loved more than anything. 'The problem is that I know exactly how I feel about you and that terrifies me.' It felt like her heart was about to leap up out of her throat.

Stefan sucked in a breath, then stroked the side of her face with his callused fingers. 'Why does it frighten you?'

'Because what I want is a mortal sin.' She shuddered, thinking about her dreams of hell.

'Surely you don't really believe that church nonsense anymore. Do you honestly think a loving God would condemn people for the true expression of love? I don't think there's anything fundamentally wrong with what I feel for you.'

She hadn't thought of it that way before. 'Maybe not, I dunno. But what I believe doesn't matter because it's also illegal.'

He pressed his forehead against hers. 'I'm all too aware of that. Section 44, part 4 of the *Crimes Act 1958.*'

Horrified, Sophie pushed away from him. 'Jesus, Stefan. If you know the law that well, why aren't you trying to resist this?'

Stefan's jaw dropped. 'You don't think I'm trying? I've been struggling with my desires for about five years now. If I wasn't trying, I would have rushed through your door last night when I heard you masturbating, and I would've fucked your brains out.'

It was Sophie's turn to be gobsmacked. She stood up, fuming. 'And now we're both gonna have to keep fighting temptation before you ruin anymore lives.' *Oh crap!* She didn't mean to blurt that out!

'What the hell does that mean, Sofia?' Standing to face her, he scowled.

'Nothing. Forget I said anything.' She started moving to the stairs, but Stefan grabbed her.

Spinning her around to face him, he asked, 'What did you mean by ruin more lives?'

'I didn't mean anything. I was just angry. Ow, you're hurting my arm Stefan!' As soon as he released his grip, she fled downstairs.

He cried out after her, 'Where are you going?'

Shouting as she ran, *'Derrick's house! He's still my boyfriend you know!'* She passed through the front door, slamming it behind her.

ഇൽ

'Derrick?' Sophie was struggling to hold back her tears when the call connected. Discovering that he wasn't home yet came as blow because she really needed his embrace. In her rush, she'd also forgotten a jumper and it was icy cold outside.

'Sofia? God, what's wrong? Where are you?' Just hearing his voiced eased her tension a little.

'Your house. Will you be home soon? I…' She chocked back a sob.

'Hang on, Soph. I'm just out at the shops. I'll be right there.'

'Okay, thank you.' She tried to calm her breathing.

'Love you and see you soon, okay?'

'Okay, love you too.' She let the call disconnect. Then it occurred to her. Derrick would want to know why she was upset. *What am I gonna tell him?* She began to panic. *Did I make a mistake rushing over?* She should have gone to Dom's house. Slumping back against Derrick's front door, she slid down to sit on the front step. It was too late to change her mind.

When the Lexus pulled into the driveway, Derrick didn't bother parking in the garage. At the sight of Sophie, he stopped directly in front of the house. He ran to her, then scooped her up in his arms. 'My God, Sophie! You're freezing! Let's get you inside.' He unlocked the doors, then lay her down in the front lounge room. After fetching a blanket, he wrapped her up and held her tight.

'Thank you, Derrick.' Looking at him, a shocking realisation began to dawn. He looked as gorgeous as ever, but she found herself admiring his beauty objectively, as if he were a model or a sculpture.

'So, what the hell happened Soph? Why were you collapsed and almost hypothermic on my front porch? You should have called me from your… wait.' His body tensed. 'Stefan didn't do anything to hurt you, did he?'

She shook her head adamantly. She decided to pretend that Candice's news had been the sole cause of her distress. 'No, at least not directly. It involves Candice, but I can't go into details because I promised to keep it secret.'

'Okay, if you're sure. Did you still want to stay tonight?' He looked worried.

'Yes, of course. I hope my being early isn't a problem?' Sophie was leaving for Italy the next day and she wanted to make the most of her time with him before she left.

'No problem at all. My folks are always happy to have you for dinner. Did you want to

watch a movie or something in the meantime?'
Standing again, Derrick picked her up.

'Sounds good.' Sophie let him carry her to
the family room where they snuggled together,
watching an episode of *Poirot*.

ഔഈ

Sophie lay naked upon Derrick's bed, waiting for
him. When he returned from the bathroom, he was
only wearing boxer-briefs. Only a few days ago the
sight would have been a huge turn on for her, but
this time she only felt a slight tingling.

He stood at the end of the bed and grinned at
her. 'Mmm, that's a rather brazen declaration of
what you want.'

'What?' Then she realised what he meant.
'Oh right. I hope I'm not being too presumptuous.'

Kneeling between her legs, he ran his fingers
along her bare skin. 'Not at all. I love your body,
Soph, and I love what you do to mine.' Then he was
on her, kissing her passionately.

Why did she feel so numb? Not even his lips
pressed against hers was exciting anymore. As he
went down on her, she closed her eyes and tried to
focus purely on the feel of his tongue licking her,
penetrating her. It felt nice, but the usual heat was
gone. Then an image entered her mind and she
moaned loudly as she exploded. Stefan! She tried to
block the visualisations from taking over, but the

more she tried, the more she failed. Logically she knew Derrick was the one pleasuring her, but in her mind, it was Stefan and it felt incredible.

Several hours and countless orgasms later, Sophie sat in bed awake and guilt stricken. Derrick was sleeping soundly next to her, oblivious to the real reason they just had the best sex of their relationship thus far. She felt as though she'd cheated on him. More importantly, she realised that while she still loved him, she was no longer in love with him.

Her phone vibrated on the bedside table. A message from Stefan: MAMMA WANTS TO KNOW WHEN YOU'LL GET HOME. WE STILL HAVE STUFF TO ORGANISE BEFORE WE GO.

It was just after 1AM. Given the need for an early morning, she figured Stefan was having difficulty sleeping too. She sent a reply: I'LL TRY TO GET HOME BEFORE 9. I NEED TO TALK TO DERRICK ABOUT SOMETHING IMPORTANT BEFORE I LEAVE, BUT HE'S ASLEEP NOW.

Another message followed soon after: SORRY, I WASN'T EXPECTING SUCH A QUICK REPLY. I FIGURED YOUR PHONE WOULD BE ON SILENT. I HOPE I DIDN'T WAKE YOU.

She sent her response: 'IT'S OKAY, YOU DIDN'T WAKE ME. I CAN'T SLEEP, NO THANKS TO YOU :P

His following message made her blush: SERVES YOU RIGHT! THOUGHTS OF YOU ARE WHAT'S

155

KEEPING ME UP ;-)

DAMN YOU STEFANO! I WAS ALREADY FEELING GUILTY ENOUGH BEFORE :P *And damn this flirting.* She was feeling aroused again.

The speed of Stefan's response was impressive. OH? WHAT GAVE YOU THE GUILTS BEFORE?

She almost giggled as she typed, I JUST HAD THE BEST SEX BECAUSE I WAS IMAGINING THAT DERRICK WAS YOU.

WELL SHIT! NOW I REALLY AM HARD. I HOPE YOU DIDN'T CRY OUT MY NAME. Stefan was such a devil!

She paused to picture Stefan's erection. *Damn. Best not to comment directly on that one.* LOL. I DON'T CRY OUT NAMES OR WORDS DURING SEX. THAT'S SO CLICHÉ.

She almost came in response to his next message: 'I BET I COULD GET YOU CRYING OUT ALL SORTS OF WORDS.

Her initial instinct was to type, OH REALLY? YOU'D HAVE TO GET ME IN BED WITH YOU FIRST ;-)

Sophie considered this response carefully. If she sent it, there was no going back. What she felt for her brother was so wrong and encouraging him was such a bad idea.

…

She hit send.

CHALLENGE ACCEPTED ;-) Stefan's response

was exciting and terrifying.

Well on that note, I'm gonna go have a cold shower. Buona notte, Stefano. She was seriously considering a shower, probably not a cold one though. It was close to zero degrees outside.

Enjoy the shower. I know I'm gonna enjoy visualising you in it while I pleasure myself. Buona notte, Sofia. Then a quick follow up came through: PS. Best if we both delete this message thread.

Prudent advice. She hit delete, then got up and went to the bathroom.

ॐ

The moment Derrick opened his eyes he was greeted by Sophie's beautiful eyes staring at him. 'Mmm, morning bella.'

But then her first words were so unbelievable that he had to pinch himself. 'I think we should break up.'

He sat up suddenly, almost fainting from the sudden blood rush. 'What the fuck, Soph? That's an extremely cruel joke to play first thing in the morning.'

'It's not a joke, Derrick. I'm sorry.' There were tears in her eyes. She was also completely dressed.

Shit. She was serious. 'But why? I thought things were great between us.' He couldn't remember the last time his heart was beating so hard.

'They were, but I realised something last night. I don't think I'm in love with you anymore.' Her words stung like a million wasps.

'So, was that before or after the earth-shattering sex? Because that didn't feel like a sympathy bone to me.' He wondered if that sounded as bitter as he felt.

'If you must know, it was during. Then I spent all night thinking about it. I'm sorry Derrick, but I just don't feel the same way about you anymore.' Her eyes downcast as she spoke, she fidgeted nervously with the quilt cover.

'But how? Why? I don't understand.'

'Neither do I. Maybe years of having my feelings ignored by you tempered my feelings and it took me this long to work it out.' There was bitterness in her tone too.

'I don't buy it. There's gotta be more to it.' He was contemplating other possibilities. Remembering Luke's response in that game of Things, he wondered if there was someone else.

'Well there's not. It's over Derrick.' With that she stood up and bolted out the room.

He felt completely shattered. While he was usually the one to end relationships, he had been dumped by a couple of girls before, but it never felt like this. And he knew it was because he had never really been in love with anyone else but Sophie. He decided then that it was a love worth fighting for.

Chapter Eleven

'I'm so sorry Tegan. I don't know what's wrong with me.' Dominic felt ashamed, humiliated. He lay next to Tegan's beautiful naked body after yet another failed attempt at sex.

Looking up at the ceiling, Tegan replied, 'I'm beginning to think I'm the problem.'

'What? Why?' He wondered if she was trying to hold back tears.

'Have you ever felt aroused by me?'

On the verge of tears himself, he couldn't speak. His silence was the only answer she needed.

'I didn't think so. You just don't seem to be all that into me.'

'That's not true, Tegan. It's just that… I don't have much sex drive.' It wasn't a lie: he still couldn't bring himself to masturbate.

Turning onto her side to face him, she sighed. 'Or you just haven't found the right stimulus. Remember when you told me you thought you might be bisexual? What makes you think that?'

Dominic considered his answer carefully. When he first told her about his suspicions, he left Owen's name out of the conversation. 'I guess it's because I find male bodies beautiful too.'

There was a sudden spark in her eyes. 'What if we try a threesome with another guy sometime?'

It was an intriguing idea, but also terrifying. 'I dunno, Tegan.'

'I do. I think it would be fun. Who knows, maybe it will ease the tension enough for you to get turned on.' She began stroking his hair tenderly.

'If you really think it will help, then I'll try it.'

෨෬

'Isn't it a pity that we couldn't get seats closer to dear Mamma and Papà?' Stefan was watching Sophie attentively as she reached up to stow her overhead luggage. He was surprised and impressed that she'd opted for a mini skirt as travel attire.

She shot him a glance. 'Such a pity.'

'Tell me Soph, did you have the mile-high club in mind when you chose that skirt?' He could even see her black lace panties when the pink plaid skirt lifted during her stretch.

After taking her seat and buckling in, she turned to him, grinning. 'I said you'd have to get me into bed first, not an airline toilet cubicle.'

Damn! She was good at this. He got the

impression that she was treating their flirtation like a game, letting her competitive streak shine. And Stefan was loving every minute of it. 'I see how it is. You're just gonna drive me to distraction in the meantime.'

'After what happened last night, it's only fair.' She grabbed the safety instructions booklet for the Airbus they were sitting in and started reading.

Relaxing into his business class seat, he recalled their text messages from the night before. He was getting hard again just thinking about them. But then take-off put an end to his brief reverie.

Once they were cruising at about forty-three thousand feet, Sophie turned to Stefan and dropped a bombshell. 'I broke up with Derrick this morning.'

'Wait, what?' *This was a game changer.*

'After what happened with my mind wandering during sex, I realised that I just don't feel strongly enough for him anymore. So, I broke it off this morning.'

Knowing she was single would make it much harder to avoid temptation. 'Geez Soph, I didn't think you were being serious in that text about the guilts. I thought you were just teasing me.'

'Nope, every word I sent you last night was true. Well, except the cold shower… which was actually pretty hot.' She gave him an inquisitorial look. 'Am I to infer that your messages weren't truthful?'

Smirking, Stefan leaned in close. 'There were varying degrees of truth to all of them and those degrees are climbing as we speak.'

'Much like the temperature on this damn plane.' She removed her cardigan to reveal a skimpy camisole.

'Yeah they always set the heaters too high and for some reason it feels even hotter this time. But now I'm curious. All that talk about resisting temptation yesterday afternoon; do you still feel that way, or have you thrown caution to the wind?'

Grinning, she leaned in and put a hand on his thigh. 'That's for me to know and you to find out. It wouldn't be a challenge if I told you.' Yawning, she started to lower her seat. 'Sleep deprivation is catching up now, so I'm gonna call it a night.'

Stefan put his own chair back, then turned onto his side to face Sophie. 'You know, this is almost like being in bed with you.'

'Almost. Pity it's also a public space.' Covering her legs with the blanket, she snuggled up against Stefan.

'Yes, it is a pity.' He put his arm around her. Having a sleep debt of his own, it wasn't long before he drifted off to sleep.

༄ༀ

Breathing in the fresh country air of Toscana revived Stefan, as did the magnificent vista. He spent most of their long journey from Melbourne drifting in and out of sleep and the two-hour drive from Bologna had been a blur. It had been a few years since their last visit to the Pacini family estate in Lucca, but nothing had changed much. The house itself was at the top of a hill, providing a panoramic view of the *vigneto*, with the main town some distance away on one side and an old medieval castle on another.

'*Ah, Stefano e Sofia! Sei cresciuti così tanto.*' Nonna rushed out of the house to greet them with hugs and kisses.

Nonno took a bit longer to reach them, having broken his hip a couple of years back. '*Ehi, Stefano, sei un uomo ora.*' Then he pulled Stefan into a bear hug.

'*Sì Nonno,*' Stefan replied.

They moved inside and took their luggage to their rooms on the third floor. Stefan felt a spark of excitement when he observed Sophie's hand on the door of the room next to his. A spark that was ignited when she looked across to him.

After exchanging a mischievous grin, Stefan spoke. 'They're making this too easy.'

'*They* might be, but I won't.' With that, she walked into her room and shut the door.

He burst into his own room, desire surging

through him. After throwing his suitcase in the closet, he collapsed on the bed. It was a few hours until dinner and Nonna had told them all to take their time unpacking and resting first. He considered going next door and showing Sophie his raging boner, but even if she welcomed him into her bed, it would be safer to wait for the cover of night. And nightfall was only hours away. The heat of his body intensified. He was desperate for some relief, so he squeezed himself, thinking about what he would do when he snuck into Sophie's room later that night.

He was close to reaching his climax when he heard Sophie's voice. 'Couldn't wait for me, hmm?'

He flicked his eyes open. Sure enough, Sophie was there. She was a vision standing just inside his room, wearing a pink and yellow summer dress. He quickly withdrew his hand.

Grinning, her eyes settled on the sight of his erection. 'No need to stop on my account.'

'Would you like to come over here and help me?' It took all his willpower not to fly across the room and pin her up against the door.

She gave him a penetrating stare. 'Tempting, but I'm not going to make it that easy for you. I think I'll just watch for now. Please… continue.'

'My God, you're audacious, Soph.' When his comment was met with silence and her continued stare, he resolved to finish what he started. At least this time, he had the real deal to look at.

ഗ∞രു

'Wait, is that a bed you're in?' He walked into the room grinning and sat next to Sophie. 'Oh look, now I'm in it too.' It was around midnight when he stole into her room, wearing nothing but a pair of red satin boxer shorts. He still wasn't used to the seasonal contrast of the Tuscan summer after coming straight from a Melbourne winter.

Sitting up, Sophie put her manga aside and grinned, 'Yes, but you didn't get me into it.'

'Geez Soph, with technicalities like that you should be going into law, not science.'

Sophie bumped his shoulder with hers. 'I told you I wouldn't make it easy.'

The body contact combined with the sight of her in a black satin slip with red lace trim was driving him crazy. 'What were you reading?'

'*Cowboy Bebop*.' She picked up the comic and handed it to him.

He flicked through it. 'Nice. I loved the anime.' Handing it back, he locked her gaze. 'I still can't believe you went to see *Star Wars Episode III* without me—and with Derrick no less.'

Laughing, she put a hand on his bare knee. 'Are you still bitter about that? You didn't even like the other prequels.' The light touch of her fingertips tickled.

On the brink of savagery, he looked at her fiercely. 'If you keep your hand there much longer, Sofia, I'm going to have to pin you down and fuck you senseless.'

The humour in her eyes fled, but she held his gaze. And her hand persisted. They remained locked in this contest of wills for a full minute. Then as Stefan moved closer, she quickly withdrew her hand. 'I'm sorry, Stefan... It's late and I'm tired... I think you should go.'

With the spell broken, he sighed. 'Fine.' He stood and walked to the door. With his hand on the knob, he turned and smiled. 'But now that I'm clearer on the rules, it will be game on tomorrow, so you better be prepared.'

Sophie grinned. 'Oh, I will be.'

ഒരു

Now that Sophie was a few years older she could properly appreciate the beauty and history of Florence. She thought of Dominic. He would be like a kid in a candy store surrounded by so much Renaissance art and architecture. Not to mention the fashion.

The morning had been spent touring the museums and churches with the family group, then they all enjoyed a pizza lunch. Shopping was the plan for the afternoon, so the group split up, leaving Sophie and Stefan at large in the city together.

'Ooh, perfume. I need some of that. I forgot to pack mine.' Sophie stepped inside the store.

'*Buongiorno.*' The female shop assistant greeted them as they entered.

'*Buongiorno. Possiamo guardare e provare?*' Sophie figured it was okay to browse and sample the perfumes, but she knew it was important to be polite in Italy.

'*Sì, per favore.*' The shopkeeper smiled and stepped back to give them room to inspect the merchandise.

Stefan followed closely behind, speaking softly in her ear. 'Any particular reason you want to be smelling nice?' When she looked at him, he was giving her a cunning look.

She smiled coyly, then started spraying some tester bottles. 'Well there is this one guy who likes to visit me in the night. I call him my mysterious stranger.'

He started browsing through the men's cologne. 'Oh really? And when did he start visiting?'

Good question. She thought back to the first time she'd had that dream. It would have been Carnevale five years ago. By God! How did she not see it earlier? 'For about five years.'

Stefan shot her a glance, but then resumed the flirtatious line of questioning. 'So how would you describe this mysterious stranger?'

'Well he's about yea tall.' She put her hand next to the top of Stefan's head. 'And has a goatee.' Finding a sweet, musky fragrance, she applied it to her wrists, then questioned Stefan. 'I like this one. What do you think?'

He moved close and took her hand to smell it properly. 'Mmm, very nice. A lot like your usual, just a little sweeter.'

Wow! His familiarity with her perfume was telling.

Stefan started trying the men's products. 'I think I might get something. My supply is getting low.... But do go on. You were describing this mystery guy.'

Sophie purchased a bottle of the perfume, then joined Stefan. 'Well, he also has calloused fingers.' Then she moved close to his ear to whisper the next bit: 'And wears sandalwood cologne.'

'Oh? You mean like this?' He spritzed his arm, then presented it to her.

'Exactly like that.' The scent caused some serious stirrings between her legs.

He looked her in the eye. 'Interesting, because this is the stuff I use for nice occasions. I should stock up while I'm here because I think I'm gonna be needing a lot more of it soon.' He winked at her, then approached the lady behind the counter. Once they were back outside, Stefan continued talking. 'They were some interesting features of mine that your subconscious chose.'

'So bold of you to assume that you and he are the same!'

'Come on Soph. It's pretty obvious. Why else would you have thought I was him at the ball? You've been crushing on me for about five years now, haven't you?' Grinning at her, he moved in close, pulling her into a partial embrace. 'Tell me, can you recall the first night you had that dream?'

Looking straight into his eyes, she told him, 'The night you gave me this.' She put a hand to the pendant that was resting against the top of her sternum.

Looking down at the piece of gold jewellery, he gasped. 'Intriguing.'

'Oh? And why is that?' She was expecting him to make a smart-arse comment about how obvious the timing was.

'Because I gave you that necklace on the day that I realised something. I woke from my first ever wet dream that morning. Can you guess who it was about?' He started fingering the pendant. His touch was extremely stimulating.

And it was a mind-blowing revelation. Damn! His flirting had levelled up to full seduction mode. 'I think I have a pretty good idea.'

'Shall we continue shopping?' Stefan offered her his arm.

Linking her arm in his, she replied, 'Yes, we

should.'

Sophie spotted a tourist shop with postcards and decided she ought to get some to send her friends. 'Hey Stefan, let's stop here.' She broke from his hold and walked inside to look at the postcard stands.

Stefan walked up behind Sophie and hugged her. 'Ooh, postcards. Hey, should we get one for Derrick? What do you think would be suitable?' Still maintaining the embrace, he spun the racks around until he found a picture of Michelangelo's *David* sculpture. 'Hey, this would be perfect! I could send it with a message that reads "Sorry to hear my sister dumped you because she wants my dick instead of yours."'

She gasped. 'Stefano! That's a terrible idea.' But then she giggled. She took the postcard from him and read the inscription. 'Hey maybe we should go to the *Galleria dell'Accademia* and see this thing for real.'

'You know if you want to see large-scale full-frontal nudity you only need ask. I'm sure I can pull off the same pose as David.' He looked at the picture then tried to imitate it. 'What do ya think, hmm?'

Sophie looked at Stefan, then at the photo for comparison. 'I dunno Stefan, you're wearing too much clothing for me to see any likeness.'

'Fine, buy the postcard and I'll pose again for

you when we get back to Lucca.'

Sophie giggled. 'Fine, I'll buy it if you promise to pose *completely* nude for me.'

'So long as there are no cameras around when I do, it's a deal.'

Sophie finalised her purchases. As soon as they stepped outside, Sophie remembered what Stefan had said about sending the David card to Derrick and she burst into laughter.

Stefan eyed her with curiosity. 'What? What's so funny?'

When she was able to compose herself enough to speak, she leaned against Stefan for support. 'I was just imagining Derrick's reaction to your hypothetical postcard message.'

Grinning, he pulled her into a strong hug. 'Yeah, it would be priceless for sure.' A few minutes later, he linked arms with her again. 'Where to next?'

Sophie couldn't really think what else she wanted to do. 'I dunno, that way.' She pointed to the large bridge crossing the Arno river.

As they traversed the Ponte Vecchio, a jewellery store caught Sophie's attention. 'Oh my God, those rings are gorgeous! They look a bit elvish, don't you think?'

When he stopped to look, he moved his arm to grip her waist. 'Yeah actually they do. Which one catches your eye the most?'

After browsing the range properly, she pointed out a ring with intricate gold swirls that was embellished with several small diamonds. 'That one's definitely a favourite.'

'Good choice. You should try it on.' He grabbed her hand and pulled her toward the door.

She broke free of his grip. 'No, Stefano. I don't want to waste their time.'

'They're not exactly busy. Come on.'

She conceded and followed him inside.

The jeweller smiled and greeted them as they entered. *'Buonasera. Come sta?'*

Stefan replied, *'Molto bene, grazie e buonasera signore anche a te.'* Then he gestured toward Sophie and continued speaking to the jeweller, *'Questa bella signora vorrebbe provare uno degli anelli nella finestra, per favore.'*

Sophie blushed when he referred to her as beautiful and she wondered if the jeweller thought she was Stefan's girlfriend or if he could pick the family resemblance. They moved to the window display and before long, the ring was on her right hand. It was a perfect fit. She admired it for a minute, then handed it back. *'Grazie, signore.'*

'Lo comprerò.' Stefan pulled his wallet out.

She gasped. *'Che cosa!* No, Stefano!' She was shocked. They didn't even know how much it cost, but she was sure it was very expensive.

He paid no heed to her objections and

purchased it with his credit card.

As they were leaving the store, the jeweller looked at Sophie. *'Bellissimo anello per bella fidanzata.'* Then he winked at her.

So, he did think she was Stefan's girlfriend. Figures. No brother in his right mind would do a thing like that. Once they were out of sight of the store, she stopped and turned to face Stefan. 'I can't believe you just did that!'

Standing in front of her, he took her hands in his. 'What's so unbelievable? Derrick bought you diamond jewellery not so long ago.' After retrieving the ring from his pocket, he put it on her finger, then kissed her hand. *'Bellissimo anello* for the woman I love.'

It felt like she was about to melt, or float, she couldn't tell. Stefan was still holding her hands and looking into her soul. Flirting she could handle because she could give as good as she got and it wasn't like she intended to let it go anywhere. But she didn't know how to respond to romance, especially not with Stefan. All she could do was whisper, 'Thank you, Stefano.'

She sensed him moving in to kiss her, but then his phone rang. 'It's Mamma.' He took the call. *'Sì mamma, ci vediamo lì.'* After hanging up, he took her by the hand. 'Come on, it's dinner time. They're all waiting for us.' Then he led her away.

ഔര

It was already dark when they got back from their day in Florence, so Stefan excused himself for the night and went straight to his room. After putting his shopping away, he retrieved a bottle of sandalwood cologne. He was still applying some when there was a knock at the door.

When he opened it, he was met by the most breath-taking vista. Sophie was leaning up against the doorframe with her right arm. She wore a transparent black chiffon negligee and her only other attire was two pieces of gold jewellery and a small black G-string. In her left hand, she held the *David* postcard.

She handed him the picture, then entered the room. 'Now it's your turn to pose. And as you can see, I'm not hiding a camera anywhere.'

He quickly closed the door then sat on his bed. 'I can see that. You're really not hiding much at all.' Stefan's body was going into overload: racing heart, heavy breathing, surging hormones, blood rushing to his cock. He put the postcard on his bedside table, then removed his shoes and socks. Standing up, he moved close to Sophie. 'Should I undress myself now, or would you like to do the honours?'

'Hmm, when you put it that way, how can I resist?' Her hands went straight to the hem of his t-shirt, pulling it up and over his head. She pressed her hands against his chest then started moving them south, running her fingers through the thick mat of hairs that grew on his torso. 'You have a lot more hair than *David*.'

'Is that a problem?' he asked.

'No, just an observation.' Her hands were at his belt. She unbuckled it with ease, then unfastened his jeans. The moment his fly was down, his erection burst forth, barely contained by his cotton boxers. She pushed his underpants along with his jeans halfway down, then knelt on the hard wood floor to finish undressing each leg.

Oh God! The sight of her kneeling before his naked body sent his mind reeling!

She pulled his leather belt from the waistband of his jeans, then stood up and handed it to him. 'You can use this in place of the sling he holds in his left hand. You'll have to pretend there's a rock in your other hand. And Rome is South-East from here, so I guess your eyes will have to face that way.' She pointed towards his walk-in closet.

'I'm impressed by how much you've thought this through, Soph.' He walked back to his bedside table to double check the reference picture. After studying it a moment, an idea occurred. He left the postcard on the table and moved to the foot of his bed. Assuming the pose such that his body was facing the bed, he turned his head to face the closet.

'How's that? Have I got it right? You should check the photo for comparison.'

Sophie sat on his bed and looked at the postcard, then at him. 'That's pretty damn close, although *David* doesn't have a raging boner.'

Turning to look at Sophie, Stefan grinned. 'Oh look, I got you into my bed.'

'Well shit! I guess you did.' She lay down and rested her head on the pillow. 'Now what are you going to do about it?'

Suddenly a loud crashing noise and running feet preceded Mamma's cry: *'Stefano, vieni presto!'*

'Fuck! What was that?' He quickly threw on a pair of shorts.

Sophie sat up, startled. 'I don't know.' She made a move to leave the bed.

'No, don't Soph. It might not be safe. Wait here, okay?' He kissed her on the forehead, then ran out into the hall.

℘ℭ

The sight of Nonno unconscious on the floor still haunted his thoughts. When he first arrived on the scene, he found Mamma arguing with Papà about lifting the fallen man. Papà's first instinct had been to rush in and help the frail old man, but he twinged and yelped with back pain, abandoning his attempt. Nonna on the other hand was a blubbering mess, crying and howling over her collapsed husband as though he were dead.

But then Nonno came to when Stefan knelt beside him and the commotion that followed might have been comical had it not been so serious. Stefan was the only sensible person there. He'd always thought his ability to cope in a crisis was uncanny. It was as if a switch in his brain turned off all the unnecessary emotions, allowing him to focus on what needed to be done; but the feelings would all come flooding back in the aftermath.

The crashing noise they had heard was the result of Nonno slipping in the hallway, sending his walking stick flying down the stairs. Without his walking aid, he fell and knocked his head on the floor. He was a stubborn old man, insisting that he was perfectly fine, despite the fact he looked concussed and couldn't stand up without Stefan's help.

When Mamma suggested an ambulance or driving him to hospital, he blatantly refused to allow it. Stefan offered to get Sophie, but Nonno complained about all the fuss, not seeing the need to wake the poor girl if she was tired. Stefan felt a pang of guilt when he didn't admit he knew she was awake and probably worried. Deep down a part of him was still hoping to pick up where they'd left off when he got back to his room.

In the end, Nonno conceded to visiting a doctor in town the following day as a compromise, sending everyone else off to bed.

Stefan promised to sit with him, but first he needed to put on more clothes. So, he ran back to his room. After reassuring Sophie that everything was okay, he promised to return as soon as possible because they still had unfinished business. Then he settled in for a late-night vigil with his dear old Nonno.

By the time Stefan returned to his room, Sophie was asleep in his bed. He briefly considered waking her to continue what they'd started, but she looked so peaceful, and he was exhausted anyway. Carefully lifting the bedsheet, he climbed in next to her and tried to rest.

Chapter Twelve

Sophie woke to find Stefan's sleeping body still fully clothed and wrapped around her. Poor guy. He must have been exhausted after staying up to nurse Nonno. Her heart melted when she looked at him, thinking of all the times he had nursed her. She gently kissed his cheek. Then desire suddenly surged through her as she remembered how close they had come to consummating their love. The realisation that she had been willing to take things that far struck her. *When did I reconcile my feelings for Stefan with any notions of impropriety?* Nothing about their intimate escapades of the previous night felt wrong at the time, nor did they upon further reflection.

There was a soft knocking at the door, then Mamma popped her head in. Sophie panicked a little, but at least the bedsheet covered the fact that her night gown was not PG-rated. The sight of Sophie and Stefan in bed together was common enough, so Sophie relaxed when Mamma didn't even raise an eyebrow.

Seeing Stefan asleep, Mamma whispered to Sophie, 'It's okay, don't-a wake him. The rest of us are heading out now. We have many errands to run, so probably won't-a be back before five. You stay. Look after your brother.' She smiled warmly.

Sophie could barely contain her excitement. The whole house to themselves, all day. *Look after Stefan you say?* Giving Mamma the straightest face possible, she whispered, 'Okay. I will. Thanks, Mamma.'

The door closed.

Her mind started racing with all the possibilities. *Should they stay in bed all day?* There was a part of her that relished the idea. *Or should they make full use of the house and have even more fun?* Sophie had to admit she was getting a huge thrill out of playing hard to get. And she could tell Stefan was loving it too. The perfect plan suddenly came to her.

She carefully eased herself out of bed, then found her phone.

ฅଓ

Disappointment was the first thing Stefan felt when he opened his eyes, finding himself alone in bed. He sat up and checked the time on his phone. It was already ten in the morning. *Damn it! Why didn't Sophie wake me?* Then he saw the message from her:

I'M SINCERELY SORRY YOU LOST YOUR CHANCE IN BED WITH ME, BUT A NEW DAY DAWNS AND IT'S GAME-ON AGAIN. ON THE BRIGHT SIDE, YOU GOT THROUGH THE FIRST STAGE. CONGRATULATIONS! TO PASS THE NEXT STAGE, YOU'LL NEED TO GET ME WET IMMEDIATELY BEFORE YOU GET ME COMPLETELY NAKED. BUT YOU'LL HAVE TO FIND ME FIRST. ;-)

PS. WE HAVE THE ESTATE TO OURSELVES TODAY. ALL DAY. :P

He smiled. *That's my girl.* Always the gamer. As Stefan showered, he contemplated his options. She hadn't specified how wet, or where. But then he figured his chances of getting her completely naked immediately after throwing a glass of water on her would be slim. Then he grinned, recalling that Nonno had had the pool cleaned specifically for their holiday.

Once he was dressed in his board shorts, Stefan grabbed a quick bite to eat before setting off on his treasure hunt. It reminded him of the days they'd played hide-and-seek in this house as little kids. He was tempted to call out, but then decided for the more high-tech approach and sent a text: READY OR NOT, HERE I COME ;-) His phone buzzed a few seconds later with her reply: OH, I'M GOOD AND

READY. HAPPY HUNTING.

He wondered if she was using any of her old hiding spots. Or would that be too easy? Well he had to start somewhere, so he decided to cross them off the list. After looking through the house under every bed, in every walk-in closet and broom cupboard, and behind every curtain, he had ruled out her old haunts. He decided to try his luck and sent her a message. DO I GET ANY CLUES?

THINK OF ALL THE PLACES WE COULD DO IT. Sophie replied.

NOT HELPING! I'D DO YOU JUST ABOUT ANYWHERE AND NOW IT'S EVEN HARDER TO THINK. And he was getting harder.

I NEVER SAID THAT SEX WAS IT, BUT I'M SURE THAT'D BE FUN HERE TOO. :P

Right then. She had to be in one of the activity spaces. Stefan decided to start with the pool area. Even if she wasn't there, he could scope it out for later. No sign of her, but the pool was the perfect temperature. Then he tried the billiards room. He couldn't find her there either. *Damn it.*

Oh my God, that clever girl! He ran back inside the house, then made his way down to the basement. Stefan found Sophie gaming on one of the computers in their old playroom. She looked up and smiled. 'Took your time.'

The first thing he noticed was that she was dressed in a skimpy bikini. So. Fucking. Hot! Then he pulled a chair up beside her and saw that she was playing the original *Doom* computer game. 'Wow, that's a blast from the past.'

She paused the game and looked at him. 'Ain't it? I remember spending hours on this when we were kids. Wanna have a go?'

He put his hand on her thigh and looked at her hungrily. 'At that or at you?'

She grinned. 'Either.'

He leapt out of his chair and moved towards her suddenly, but she pushed back using the wheels of her own chair, laughing as she fled.

৪ও৫

Starting to tire after being chased for about half an hour, Sophie ducked into the loungeroom and collapsed on the couch to catch her breath. The footsteps were close. Stefan was still hard on her heels. *Shit!* She quickly covered herself with a blanket and surrounded herself with cushions.

He entered the room and looked around for a bit. Stefan's voice was right beside her ear. 'Hmm, that cushion pile seems to be breathing.' Then he was upon her, pulling the blanket away. 'Gotcha!'

She giggled as she attempted to wrestle out of his hold, but he was too strong for her. She tried to wriggle free. But just as she got into a sitting position, he shifted his weight and straddled her, pinning her arms against the back of the couch.

He was grinning wildly. 'Where do you think you're going, hmm?'

'Well shit. I think you really did catch me.' She bit her bottom lip.

Stefan's gaze intensified as he continued to press his body against hers.

Sophie returned his stare and the air between them electrified. A strong yearning surged through her body. She felt dangerously close to giving in to him in that moment. His lips looked so tempting. And she could smell the sandalwood cologne.

He must have been reading her mind, because Stefan's lips suddenly kissed hers.

…

Sophie's heart skipped a beat.

…

Then she yielded, allowing his salty lips to devour her and their tongues to coil together. The feel of his goatee scratching her chin felt even more arousing in reality. And his calloused fingers gliding along her skin sent shockwaves of passion down to the core of her womanhood.

Pausing for air, Sophie gasped. 'I think we just broke the law.'

His reply came amidst kisses that he planted along her jawline and neck, 'Well… I'm not… clued in… on Italian… incest laws… but… as far as… the state of Victoria… is concerned… it's not a breach… unless there's… some form… of sexual penetration.'

She groaned pleasurably as his lips touched her skin. 'Mmm... aside from the obvious... what constitutes sexual penetration?'

The kissing ceased and he looked at her with lustful abandon. 'Well to start with, if I were to put any object or a part of my body in here.' He tapped her lightly on the backside. 'Or inside here.' His hand firmly gripped her pubis. 'For any reason that isn't medical, or hygiene related, that would be sexual penetration.'

Sophie gasped. Her body quivered under the pressure of his hand. His fingers were skirting around the edges of her bikini briefs.

'It would also be a crime if I stuck my dick in here.' Stefan's tongue was suddenly probing her mouth and their passionate kissing resumed with his hand still pressed between her legs.

After a few minutes, Sophie paused to ask, 'So would it be illegal for me to hold your dick with my hand?'

'You know, I don't recall seeing anything about that. My guess would be no.' He returned to kissing her neck.

'Hmm, interesting.' With that, she reached inside his shorts and grabbed hold of his hard cock.

His whole body convulsed, and he cried out, 'Oh God, Sofia!'

She pressed her lips to his ear. 'You know, you still haven't completed stage two.'

'Mmm, you have a point there.' Suddenly, he picked her up so that her legs were straddling his hips and carried her off.

Once she realised where he was taking her, she giggled. 'Clever thinking Stefano, but you already got me wet.'

He stopped next to the pool and grinned. 'Oh, believe me, I know. But I thought this would be still be fun.' Placing her on the floor, he pushed her into the water, then dived in after her.

She swam to the edge of the pool where she could gain a foothold. When Sophie broke the surface, she observed her bikini top floating a few metres away. Kudos Stefano! She didn't even notice him unclasp the strap. Next thing she knew, there were hands gripping her legs and tugging at her briefs. She squealed and giggled as Stefan emerged above the surface, holding the last of her attire in his right hand.

Throwing the briefs aside, he encircled her with his arms. His body pressed against hers. 'Stage two cleared. Is there a third stage?'

Grinning, she replied, 'Yes.'

Stefan was still wearing his boardshorts, but they did little to hide the feel of his erection pressing against her naked flesh. He looked at her fiercely. 'What do I need to do for stage three?'

She took a deep breath before replying, 'Make me cry those words.'

He inhaled sharply, then his hands were upon her breasts, stroking them and squeezing her nipples. His left hand remained there, as the right slid down between her legs. His calloused fingers rubbed at her clit vigorously, making it swell— making all her womanhood swell.

Sophie groaned loudly. She desperately needed to come.

After a few minutes, Stefan asked, 'Do you want me to penetrate you?'

Her reply was immediate, without restraint, *'Yes, please yes.'*

He removed his shorts, then hoisted her up, aligning their bodies. 'Are you ready to commit incest, Sofia?' His prick pressed at the precipice.

'Yes, I'm ready.' She screamed. She had never felt more ready for anything in her life. What was so wrong with this anyway?

'Are you sure you're ready?' His eyes were boring into her.

'I'm sure. Please fuck me, Stefan!'

'Stefano! Cosa diamine stai facendo?' Mamma's sudden, angry voice made Stefan jump back, releasing his grip of Sophie. The moment Mamma recognised Sophie; her visage was one of complete shock. 'Sofia? Oh, good heavens no!'

୫୦ଔ

The three of them sat beside the pool, Sophie and

Stefan both wrapped in towels. The pool water dripping from Sophie's hair combined with the first of her salty tears, blurring her vision.

Mamma was looking at them both, sighing in disbelief and it took several minutes for her to find her voice. 'I cannot believe this! How... how long has this-a been happening?' her hands gesturing at the two of them.

Sophie felt mute. She looked to Stefan for support.

But he didn't see her. His eyes were downcast. When Sophie didn't reply, he spoke. 'This was the first time, Mamma. I swear. And we didn't even...'

'What in tha devil's name possessed you to-a do such a thing?' She sounded furious.

'Love, Mamma. Love is what possessed us. It had nothing to do with any devil nonsense.' Stefan's tone sounded a little bitter, but he was controlling his temper well.

Mamma slapped him across the cheek. 'Stefano! Do not speak-a such heresy.'

Unable to contain her emotions anymore, Sophie cried, 'Please Mamma.' Then she wept and wailed without restraint.

Mamma flew at Sophie, scooping her into an embrace. 'Oh, dear child. My dear babies—what have you-a done!' After a few minutes of comforting and hushing Sophie, she went on. 'If anyone else were to-a find out… No! I must protect you both. Sofia, you will-a go stay with Bianca in Venezia until we-a go home.'

Stefan looked up and pleaded, 'No! Please Mamma!'

Even through her tears, Sophie could see the pain in his eyes; hear it in his voice; feel it in her soul.

'I'm-a sorry Stefano, but this be for your own good. For both of-ya sakes. Think-a yourselves lucky Papà did not find you.' Mamma stood up, lifting Sophie with her. 'Now get yourselves cleaned up, then you best start packing, Sofia.'

ഇൽരു

Every part of Sophie's body and soul ached as she stepped out of the car at Lucca train station. She didn't get any sleep the night before, and that wasn't just because of Mamma hogging most of the bed.

She heard Stefan ask, 'Please, Mamma, give us a minute to say goodbye.'

'Fine. I'll wait here.' Then Mamma sat back inside the car.

As Sophie reached for her suitcase, Stefan's touch stopped her. 'Here, let me get that.' He pulled the suitcase out of the boot, then took Sophie's hand to walk her up to the platform.

Standing alongside the tracks, Sophie looked

into Stefan's eyes, then her tears returned.

He pulled her into his arms to soothe her with his tender words. 'Hey, it'll just be a couple of weeks. We'll be home together again soon.'

Clutching his shoulder blades tightly through his t-shirt, she breathed in as much of him as she could. 'We've never parted for more than a couple of days before, Stefano. It feels like having a limb torn off and half my soul ripped out.'

Stefan sighed. 'I know. I feel it too. I'm just trying to look on the bright side. I promise to call you often, okay?'

'Thanks.' She looked into his eyes, tears streaming down her face. 'I love you Stefano. I love you so damn much.'

He tucked a strand of hair behind her ear. 'I love you Sofia, more than anything.' Then he kissed her, gently at first, but with increasing passion.

Their lips remained locked until the train arrived. Sophie hesitantly climbed the steps onto the locomotive, then retrieved her suitcase when Stefan handed it up to her. Once aboard, she rushed to her seat so that she could see Stefan again.

He was waiting just outside her window. Sophie gazed upon her beloved twin with her hands on the windowpane. He stood less than a meter away, but the cold glass and steel that divided them made the distance feel like they were galaxies apart. She was suddenly overcome by a horrible sinking feeling, fearing that this might be the last time she would see the love of her life.

Then the train jolted forward, and Sophie wept violently as Stefan's face faded from view.

৩০০৪

'Who wants more wine?' Owen asked, walking over to the box of drinks that he'd brought to Tegan's house.

'Sounds good, thanks.' Dominic beamed. He was loving the wine and the company. With Tegan's parents away for the weekend, they had the place to themselves.

'I think we should take the next bottle to the spa,' Tegan suggested as she moved toward the back door.

Returning, bottle in hand, Owen followed her. 'Brilliant idea, Teegs.'

Dominic stood up, baffled by the sudden decision that was apparently made for him. Not that he minded the idea of a spa in that moment. When he stepped outside, Dominic was startled to find the other two stripping off all their clothes. *My God! Was this how they always did spas? Outrageous!*

Tegan, completely naked by this point, walked up to a stunned Dominic. 'Come on handsome. You aren't afraid of a little skinny dipping, are you?'

'Not afraid exactly.' He carefully placed his

wineglass onto the outdoor table. Owen had jumped into the water already and was looking at him with inviting eyes. *So, this must be Tegan's plan for a threesome.* He felt panic rising, but Tegan kissed him, and the feel of her lips helped ground him. She undressed him then led him to the spa.

Owen popped a bottle of bubbly, then skulled a mouthful straight from the bottle. Moving in close to Dominic, he handed him the bottle. 'Cheers!'

Dominic blushed, then took the bottle. 'Cheers. And thanks.' He drank two mouthfuls, then handed it to Tegan. This spa was not as large as the one attached to Sophie and Stefan's pool, which meant they were all in arm's reach of each other. *Very cosy!*

'So, Dom what did you think of Owen's artwork? Isn't he just so talented!' Tegan's arm was around Dom's waist and her hand was stroking his backside.

He looked directly at Owen to give his praise. 'I loved it all. So many vibrant colours and the sculptures are so beautifully shaped.'

Owen smiled at him. 'Thanks man. It's good to find people who appreciate it.'

Dominic was suddenly aware of toes between his legs. He was startled at first. But then he relaxed into it, enjoying the suggestive look in Owen's eye and the thrill of it. The sensation of another man's body touching him there was titillating.

After another round with the sparkling wine, Tegan moved into kiss Dominic's lips and Owen flanked him, kissing his neck. *Oh God! This is definitely doing something for me.* Tegan moved back and let Owen kiss Dominic on the mouth. And it had all the fire and passion that he expected from a kiss: the taste of wine on his lips, the feel of his strong tongue probing his mouth; all incredible. Then Dominic was suddenly aware that Owen had pressed him against the edge of the spa. In this position, one of the jets was squirting pressurised water on his back passage. It was exhilarating! And he was getting hard.

Owen whispered in his ear, 'Did you want to take this inside?'

Dominic groaned pleasurably. 'Mmm, yes.'

Then the three of them went to Tegan's bedroom. While kissing Tegan, who lay on the bed, he became acutely aware of Owen's hands on his backside. His fingers started poking and prodding while applying some sort of lube and Dominic felt a sudden jolt of pleasure. Within minutes Owen was completely inside him and all sense of the world was lost.

Chapter Thirteen

'It's over, Dominic,' were Tegan's last words, before she hung up the phone.

Dominic felt completely blindsided. He thought their previous night had gone well. *Wasn't a threesome exactly what she wanted?* And it worked. His sex drive had awoken, and he was finally able to give Tegan what she needed.

His phone buzzed with a text message, startling him out of his pensive mood.

It was from Sophie: I WISH INTERNATIONAL ROAMING WASN'T SO EXPENSIVE! I REALLY NEED TO TALK TO YOU.

He quickly typed a reply: YEAH, DITTO. TEGAN JUST DUMPED ME! OVER THE PHONE NO LESS.

THAT BITCH! WHAT REASON DID SHE GIVE?

Love the snark, Soph! Dominic was really missing his best friend. APPARENTLY I'M TOO GAY.

Sophie responded, asking, WHAT KIND OF LAME EXCUSE IS THAT?

He thought about it for moment before

replying, PROBABLY A TRUE ONE. OWEN'S THE BOMB IN BED BY THE WAY :P.

:O. WOW. I WANNA HEAR ALL ABOUT IT WHEN I GET HOME.

He was looking forward to a big debrief session with her. WHY DID YOU NEED TO TALK?

Sophie's next text came a few minutes later. MAMMA CAUGHT ME AND STEFAN ABOUT TO HAVE SEX.

Dominic's jaw dropped. *My God!* Deciding a phone call was essential, he dialled her number. 'Jesus Soph, are you okay?'

'Not really.' It sounded like she was crying.

'What happened?' He panicked, imagining the worst.

Her voice was shaking as she spoke. 'After days of sexual tension building between Stefan and me, it all came to a head yesterday when we had the house to ourselves, or so we thought. We were in the pool when Mamma walked in to find our naked bodies wrapped around each other. Apparently Nonna wasn't feeling well, so they came home early.'

'My God! So, what did your mum do?' He shuddered to think of Francesca's reaction.

'Completely flipped her shit. Then instead of my room, she's sending me to Venice.'

He tried to stifle a laugh but failed.

'What's so funny?' Sophie asked defensively.

'I'm sorry Soph, but your mum has some

pretty funny disciplinary ideas. Venice? Really? Can we please swap parents?'

It was good to hear her laugh at that, but then she sighed. 'I wish we could swap parents, then the love Stefan and I feel for each other wouldn't be forbidden.'

He joined in with his own sigh. 'Yeah, I'm sorry Soph. That really sucks.'

'I've gotta sign off. I need to swap trains. Thanks for the call.' At least she sounded more composed.

'Okay hun, no worries. Take care.'

'You too.' Then the line disconnected.

He put his phone on his bedside table, then thought about the mess that Sophie was in. It certainly put his own problems into perspective. He knew that even this short separation would be agonising for both twins.

ಬಂಡ

Sophie's cousin Bianca was a lot more fun than she expected. They hadn't seen each other since they were both young children. Her memories of those times were all dolls and tea parties, much to Sophie's disgust. But Bianca had grown into a successful hedonist who could charm the pants off absolutely anyone—and often did. From the moment Sophie's feet landed on Venetian ground, she was whisked away to a world of extravagant meals, expensive wines and late nights at jazz bars. While Venezia didn't have a reputation for much nightlife, Bianca knew all the good spots and how to keep the party going. *Who figured that marriage to a rich man could still be a career move in these modern times?*

This lifestyle was a welcome distraction for the first week. While it didn't take her mind off Stefan entirely, it helped fill the time between phone calls. And those nightly phone conversations were what kept her going, giving her something to look forward to each day.

Apparently, Bianca's house was always a forty-eight-hour party zone on weekends, so Sophie wasn't quite prepared for Stefan's call on Saturday night. One of Bianca's rich bachelor friends was trying to chat Sophie up when her phone rang. She looked at her mobile, then made her apology to Lorenzo before talking into the phone, 'Ciao Stefano.'

Lorenzo shot her a look then asked, *'E 'il tuo amante?'*

Giggling she replied, *'Sì, scusami.'* Then she walked off to her bedroom. 'Sorry about that, Stefan.'

'Wait, did you just tell some guy that I'm your boyfriend?' Stefan's tone was teasing.

'Kinda. But then he was hitting on me, so it was an effective way to get him to leave me alone.'

She made it to the safety of her room before adding, 'Besides, it's not far from the truth.'

She heard his sharp intake of breath. 'God, I so want it to be the absolute truth.'

Sophie was in bed by this point. Closing her eyes, she let Stefan's voice wash over her, imagining that he was there with her. 'Me too.'

'But since I'm also your brother, it'd be best if you don't go telling too many people that your boyfriend's name is Stefano.' There was a serious hint in his voice.

'Yeah, I know. So, what did you get up to today?'

'Well it was market day, so we went into town and did some shopping. Nothing very exciting. Not like your day by the sounds of it. With all those parties, I'm surprised you have time to be taking calls from your brother.'

'Hey, it's not all fun and games here. I still get time to be miserable.'

'You know I thought Mamma was being harsh on you at first by sending you away rather than me. She's always been tougher on me. But now I see that I got the raw end of the deal after all,' he teased.

'Oh, poor Stefano!' She switched to a seductive voice before adding, 'I promise to make it up to you in ways you can only begin to imagine.'

'Mmm, now you've done it.' His voice was

deep and sexy.

Grinning, she feigned innocence. 'Done what?'

'What do you think?' It sounded like he was unzipping his fly.

'I haven't a clue. You'll have to be more explicit.' Sophie was getting wet just thinking about it.

'Fine, but you asked for it.' Stefan suddenly hung up the phone.

'Wait, Stefan? Hello?' *Shit.* A few seconds later Sophie received a multi-media message from Stefan. It was her first ever dick pic. She giggled with delight.

The phone rang again. 'Explicit enough for you?'

'Short of having the real thing here inside me, it's about as obvious as it gets.' She recalled those precious moments when Stefan's cock was pressed against her. It sent an exhilarating rush through her body. Laying back on the bed, she set her spare hand to work.

'When I get my hands on you Sofia, I am going to fuck you so hard that you won't be able to walk for days.'

'Oh God, Stefano. I almost came hearing you say that.' She wasn't lying.

He groaned. 'Mmm, good to know. Even though I already cleared the third stage, I'm looking forward to repeating that one over and over.'

'Since when did you pass?' Sophie gasped as she felt her climax approaching.

'Since I got you *begging* for me to penetrate you.' His words took her over the edge.

Oh God, Yes! Sophie moaned as she felt the sweet release.

'Wait, did you just...?' He sounded excited.

'Come? Yes. I couldn't help myself. And that begging doesn't count by the way. We weren't having sex yet.'

'Mmm, you amaze me Soph.' Then after a short pause, he continued, 'And I'd argue it does count. I just said I'd get you crying out all sorts of words. Sure, it was implied that I would have you in a heightened state of sexual arousal. You felt very aroused to me when I got you crying out words like "Yes", "I'm Sure." Oh, and my faves were "Please Fuck me, Stefan." Quite loudly too.' He sounded proud of himself.

'Well damn. You just beat me at my own game.'

'But I learnt from the best.'

Sophie sighed. 'I can't wait to feel your body against me again. Hey, one week down, just one more to go right?'

Stefan went silent.

She checked her phone connection. It looked fine. 'Stefan? Are you still there?'

'Yeah I'm here.' He sounded despondent.

'What's wrong?' She sat up worried.

He sighed loudly. 'I won't be coming home with you.'

Sophie panicked. *'What? Why not?'*

'The folks have arranged for me to study my next semester at the University of Bologna.'

'No way! That's so unfair! Why didn't you refuse?' *To be separated by a hemisphere and for so long was unthinkable!*

'I did, but then Mamma made me see reason.' He sounded very bitter.

Sophie shivered, wondering what Mamma had threatened him with. 'Argh! I can't believe her! Is she gonna try and keep us apart forever?'

'I challenged her on that myself. She said it was best that we had some cooling off time.' He paused for a moment. 'She promised to let me return home in December, but then we will have to prove that we can be trusted under the same roof during the summer. Otherwise she will probably ship me off somewhere else next year.'

Sophie burst into tears upon hearing this. *Was there really no hope for them?*

'I'm so sorry Soph. I did what I could. But you know how stubborn Mamma can be.'

She continued crying, not saying a word.

He tried to soothe her. 'I will still call you every day or night. We'll have to work around time zones of course, but I'm sure we can figure something out. And then I will be back in the summer and we will find a way to make it work.'

Sophie practically screamed at him, *'How can you sound so reasonable about this?'*

Stefan gasped, then after a painful moment of silence, he replied, 'Because I have to. It's the only way I know how to get through this. I love you Sofia and I miss you more than anything.'

Sophie sobbed as she spoke. 'I love you and miss you so much.'

℘℃

After the bombshell Stefan just dropped over the phone, Sophie wasn't about to get any sleep, especially with all the noise. She decided she needed some air, so she stepped out into the courtyard. If she were in a better mood, she would have spent some time admiring the large red and white neo-Gothic villa and its surrounds, but she couldn't seem to care at this point.

It was a warm enough night to sit outside, even in her short, black and gold party dress. Having pilfered a bottle of champagne on her way out, she settled in to numb the pain.

Hunched over the bottle, crying, she heard a familiar man's voice. *'Mi scusi signorina, stai bene?'*

She looked up and saw Derrick standing there, looking very suave in his tailored suit.

'Sofia? My God! What's wrong?' He pulled a chair up in front of her.

'Derrick? What... what are you doing here?' She felt a sudden pang of remorse for the way she'd dumped him. In hindsight, it *had* been cruel springing it on him like that.

'This is my cousin's house. I was staying at the family estate on the mainland last week and now I'm about to spend the last week of my holiday here.'

Sophie was puzzled. 'Cousin?'

'Yeah, Alessio's my first cousin. He owns this place. Do you know him?'

She smiled a little. 'Yeah. He married my first cousin, Bianca. I guess that makes us related somehow.' The irony was not lost on her.

'Well I'll be damned! Small world, huh? So, are you gonna tell my why you were out here drowning your sorrows all by yourself?'

'I'd rather not talk about it. But now that you're here, I don't need to drink alone.' She offered him the bottle.

'Sure, why not? He drained his current glass, then poured a drink. 'Where's Stefan and your folks? I didn't see them inside.'

Sophie tried to hide the pain from her face. 'Still in Tuscany. It's just me out here staying with Bianca. We've been having some girl time. I'll be here for the next week too.'

There was the brief hint of a sly grin before he put on a straight face. 'I guess we'll be staying under the same roof for the week then.'

'I guess so.' She looked at her glass pensively, thinking about how she was going to survive the next semester of uni without Stefan. The tears came flooding back.

Derrick took the glass out of her hand, putting it safely on the table along with his own, then embraced her. 'Hey, it won't be that bad will it? There's like fifteen rooms in this house, I'm sure I can stay out of your way,' he jested.

'Ha, very funny!' She sobbed. Sophie gripped him tight and wept in his arms for a while.

He gave her some silence, just holding her and stroking her hair. It felt like one of Stefan's more platonic hugs.

She looked up and tried to compose herself. 'Thanks, Derrick. I needed that.'

He smiled. 'The hug or the cry?'

'Both, but I was thanking you for the hug.' Looking into his eyes, Sophie forgot herself in a moment of weakness and kissed him.

And Derrick welcomed the renewal of their old passion. But this was unlike any of their previous kisses. It was fierce verging on violent, lust in its purest form. Before she knew it, he was carrying her through the house and up the stairs. He bumped into numerous walls on the way as they continued kissing each other. Given what everyone else in the house was doing, no one batted an eyelid at them.

Their bodies crashed together on Derrick's bed. Limbs flailed everywhere in their feverish attempts to undress. As Derrick bit and sucked at Sophie's neck, she dug her nails into his back and dragged them down as far as she could reach. He made a vicious growl in response and gazed upon her savagely for a moment before attacking her nipples with his teeth. Then he drove himself into her with all his force, making Sophie scream from her very core as she came and came again.

ഇരു

It was late morning when Sophie first stirred. As soon as conscious thoughts were possible again, she sat bolt upright and panicked. 'Oh, fuck!' She looked at Derrick's naked body next to her.

He was laying on his back, eyes wide open. And he was grinning. 'Yeah we did. And when did you become such an animal in bed, Sofia?'

Sophie double face palmed. 'Oh God, I'm sorry Derrick.'

'Don't be, that was damn hot. And I'm sure the scratch marks will heal soon enough.' He lightly dragged his nails along her back.

She blushed as she remembered her own nails on his back. 'I wasn't apologising specifically for… that.'

He raised an eyebrow. 'What are you sorry for then?'

'Leading you on.' Sophie couldn't understand how she'd slept with him again despite no longer being in love with him.

Derrick sat up. 'Don't worry about it, Soph. There was absolutely no pretence in the way you fucked me last night. That's not to say I wouldn't jump at the chance to get back with you if I could, but I can still enjoy sex without strings.'

Sophie relaxed. 'Wait, so you don't mind that I used you?'

He narrowed his eyes and gave her a smouldering look. 'Not with sex that good. Haven't you ever heard the term "friends with benefits?"'

Those eyes were extremely arousing. 'Yeah, I've heard the term, but I didn't understand it properly before.' She was amazed at her own ability to partition her heart and sex drive.

'Come on, let's get some brunch. I know a great place. You'll love it. I'm just gonna grab a shower first.' With that he jumped out of bed and headed into the bathroom.

Sophie needed a shower too. She briefly considered going to her own ensuite. It would have been the sensible thing to do. But she was hungry.

The sight that greeted Sophie as she opened the glass door was breathtaking. Hot, steaming water cascaded down Derrick's perfectly toned body as he rinsed his hair.

He opened his eyes in response to the intrusion, then his lip curled into a grin. 'Is there something wrong with your own shower, Sofia?'

She stepped into the cubicle. 'There is actually.'

He let the door slam shut before asking, 'Oh? What's the problem?'

Pressing her hands against Derrick's chest, she gave him her bedroom eyes. 'It's just not hot enough.'

Derrick grabbed her and pushed her up against the wall. 'Well aren't you just full of surprises.'

The sensation of the cold tiles against Sophie's skin in contrast to Derrick's heat was exhilarating. She clawed at the cheeks of his backside.

He bit her neck in response, then nibbled at her earlobe. 'What do you want from me, Sofia?'

Sophie moved her right hand onto Derrick's swelling cock. 'I want you to make me come.'

Clenching his teeth, Derrick sucked in a deep breath. He hoisted her up, letting her legs straddle him. 'And why do you want my dick inside you?' Sophie could feel one of Derrick's fingers pressing at her back passage.

She moaned, 'Mm. Because I'm horny as

hell.'

'And?' His inquiring eyes asked for more as his finger started to probe deeper.

It was titillating. Sophie groaned loudly.

Derrick looked at her expectantly. His thumb started rubbing her clit.

Words… were… becoming… hard… 'Because… it feels good… when you fuck me.'

'And?'

What more did he want to know? Closing her eyes, she searched her soul for the core reason. She trembled as she forced out her reply, 'Because I want to forget my pain.'

Clearly satisfied with her answer, Derrick thrust himself inside her with incredible force. And Sophie felt her cares slipping away as she let out a deep, guttural growl.

ഇഐ

As Sophie finished changing in her room, she heard her message tone.

It was Dom. GUESS WHO HAS A BOYFRIEND NAMED OWEN?

She smiled as she sent a reply. IS IT YOU? IT BETTER BE YOU COS I'M ALREADY GONNA SLAP TEGAN FOR DUMPING YOU OVER THE PHONE.

LOL, YES IT'S ME. :D

Sophie imagined Dom probably did have a big stupid grin on his face. THAT'S AWESOME NEWS!

NOW GUESS WHO KIND OF, ACCIDENTALLY, HAD SEX
WITH HER EX!

WAIT, WHAT? IS DERRICK IN VENICE TOO?

YEP. I BUMPED INTO HIM LAST NIGHT. THEN HE
BUMPED INTO ME ON HIS BED, THEN AGAIN IN THE
SHOWER THIS MORNING. *By God! What's wrong with
me? When and how did I become so sex-crazed?*

:O. ARE YOU GETTING BACK TOGETHER? WHAT
ABOUT STEFAN?

IT WAS JUST SEX WITH DERRICK. NOTHING
MORE. I STILL LOVE AND WANT STEFAN, EVEN IF I CAN'T
HAVE HIM. The pain of knowing she wouldn't see
Stefan again for five months was still too much to
bear, so she decided to hold back on that news for
the time being.

SCANDALOUS! WELL, HAVE FUN WITH YOUR
VIVACIOUS VENETIAN! I HAVE A DATE WITH A
BOHEMIAN BABE NOW :P.

Grinning, she heard a knock at her door.
'Come in.'

Derrick walked in as she was putting her
shoes on. Glancing around her room, his eyes
settled on the postcard on her bedside table. He
briefly inspected the photo of the sculpture. 'An
interesting choice of pornography.'

'That's not porn, Derrick. It's art.' Memories
tried to force themselves upon her, but she pushed
them aside and stood up.

'That's a good one, Soph. I'll have to

remember it if I ever get busted with porn.' Smiling humorously, he held the door open for her.

It was a warm, sunny day as they walked along the paved streets and alleys of Venice. And Sophie felt happy, talking and laughing with Derrick. It felt good to have her life-long friend back; better still since she was free of her old fixation with him.

After about twenty minutes of walking, Derrick suddenly stopped. 'Here we are.' He was looking at the entrance to Caffè Florian.

Sophie was gobsmacked. She'd heard of this place—read about it even—but she never imagined that she would have the opportunity to dine at one of the oldest coffeehouses in the world. She followed him inside, speechless, as she took in the beauty and splendour of the eighteenth-century gilded wall panels.

A very friendly, middle-aged waiter greeted them as they took a seat. *'Teodorico! Buongiorno, benvenuto. Come stai amico?'*

Derrick looked up and smiled. *'Buongiorno, Giuseppe! Sto molto bene.'* Then he gestured to Sophie. *'Questa è Sofia.'*

Giuseppe smiled at her. *'Buongiorno, Sofia. Piacere di conoscerti.'* Then he gasped and looked back to Derrick. *'Sofia?'*

Derrick nodded. *'Sì.'*

Sophie blushed, wondering what Derrick

had said about her. She tried to maintain her composure as she spoke to the man. *'Buongiorno, Giuseppe.'*

'Non mi hai detto quanto fosse bella. Vergognatevi, Teodorico!' Giuseppe winked at her, then took their orders. *'Cosa posso portarti?'*

As soon as he walked off, Sophie challenged Derrick. 'What the hell have you told him about me?'

He looked directly into her eyes. 'Just that we've been friends forever, then we dated, but I screwed up my chance with you.'

Staring at him sceptically, Sophie got the impression there was more to it.

'Don't worry Soph. I didn't tell him any graphic details.'

Sophie sighed. 'Fine, keep your secrets.' She had plenty of her own besides. The arrival of food and coffee soon put an end to that train of thought, and she became engrossed in the taste sensations of a gourmet breakfast.

%)CR

'Mi stupisci, Bianca! Non posso credere che tu abbia sedotto ogni membro del gruppo jazz!' Sophie was laughing hysterically as she enjoyed a nightcap with Derrick and her hosts in their lounge room. They'd just spent the night at a jazz club where Bianca had incited a fight between the band

members who all thought she was their girlfriend. The best part was when she introduced her husband, who knew about all her extra marital affairs, to the poor musicians who were ignorant of her open marriage.

Her shrieking came to an end the moment her phone rang. She looked at the device on the coffee table and saw Stefan's name on the screen. *'Mi scusi, devo prendere questo.'* She answered the phone as she walked to her bedroom. 'Ciao Stefano.'

'You seem to be in good spirits.' He sounded melancholic.

'I was just having a laugh with Bianca. You wouldn't believe what she did!' Sophie burst into the story of her cousin's outrageous liaisons.

Stefan chuckled a few times during the retelling. When she concluded, he remarked, 'You're right, that is pretty unbelievable.' Then he sighed. 'I'm glad Bianca has been good company for you in my absence.'

Feeling a slight pang of guilt, Sophie reassured him, 'Yes, she has been very entertaining, but no one could ever fill your shoes, Stefan.'

'Well you know what they say about men with large footwear.' It was good to hear him jest.

Sophie giggled. 'Yes, I guess you do have big feet.'

'You've been drinking lots tonight, haven't

you?' Stefan asked. 'I can tell by the way you're laughing.'

'There's no hiding anything from you, is there?' Sophie's heart rate suddenly increased. 'Speaking of which, there's something you ought to know.'

'Hmm that's a frightening segue.'

Tensing up, Sophie continued. 'Derrick's in Venice now, visiting family.'

'Did you give him my postcard?' he joked.

'Not exactly, although he did find it on my bedside table.' There was no longer any humour in her tone.

'Do you seriously keep that thing on display?' After a few seconds, Stefan sounded alarmed. 'Wait, what was Derrick doing in your room?'

Sophie trembled. 'I'm sorry Stefan. He found me crying after our phone call last night. I was in a dark mood.'

His level of anxiety increased. 'What happened, Sofia?'

'I… I fucked him.' Sophie knew this would be difficult news to break.

'*Jesus*, Soph! What the hell? I… I thought you were over him?' Stefan's pain was evident.

'I was—*I am*. It was just sex, Stefan. I'm in love with you, not him.'

'And what a way to show it!' He sounded

angry.

Sophie couldn't hold back the tears any longer. 'I'm sorry Stefan, but it's not like we're married. We aren't even a couple.'

'You needn't remind me. But I thought we could at least stay true to each other.' And so bitter.

'It's unfair to deprive each other of sex for five months, Stefan.' Sophie was getting furious.

'I've waited five God-damned years for you Sofia! I think I can manage another five months.'

'But five months without any physical contact? All while teasing each other over the phone. Besides it's not like you abstained *all* these years. You fucked Candice, remember?' It was still heart-breaking to think of the aftermath from that one night.

Stefan exhaled heavily. 'You're right, I'm sorry. That whole incident was quite unexpected. I was in a dark place too. I've never wanted anyone but you, Sofia.'

Her rage subsided as her heart melted. 'I know, Stefan. I love you.'

'I love you too, Sophie…. I need to go now but I'll call you again tomorrow, okay?'

'Okay, good night.' After hanging up, Sophie felt utterly miserable. With sleep out of the question, she decided to seek solace with a friend.

ഇൠ

Thoughts of Sophie regaled Derrick's mind as he settled into bed. If the previous night's sex had been an anomaly, he wouldn't have entertained hopes. But the way she came to him in the shower. Derrick knew he was still under her skin. *Perhaps I could use this to my advantage.*

A sudden, violent knocking at the door tore him away from his machinations. He jumped up to find Sophie sobbing on the threshold of his room wearing nothing but a black satin slip. She rushed into his arms. 'Please make the pain stop.'

Hadn't she just been on the phone with Stefan? Curious timing. 'What's wrong Soph? Is your brother okay?' He started gently stroking her scantily clad back with his fingernails.

She shot him a panicked look. 'Why would you think this involves Stefan?'

'Well he did just call you, didn't he?' He slowly moved his hand toward the hem of her slip.

'Oh right. Makes sense. The thing is Derrick…' She sucked in a sharp breath as his fingers found her thighs. 'Stefan won't be coming home this semester. He is going to study at the University of Bologna.'

'Isn't that exciting news? I thought you'd be happy for him.' Derrick could feel his body stir with desire as his fingers caressed her soft skin, working their way towards her most sensitive area.

'I am, but at the same time I'm sad to be

separated for so long. He's not just my brother, Derrick… He's my twin. We've never spent this much time… apart.' She suddenly dug her nails into the bare flesh of his back.

The pain felt exquisite. He never imagined he would be receptive to such masochistic delights. It occurred to Derrick that Sophie was grieving for highly inappropriate reasons. While disturbing, the thought troubled him little. She was in Derrick's arms at this point and that was all that mattered. 'Yes, I see now how that could be upsetting for you.'

She was already yielding to his touch, so he took her to the bed and fucked her until she blacked out.

ಬಿಞ

Cracks of light beaming in through slits in the shutters provided soft illumination as Sophie awoke. Not ready to face the day, she rolled over and nestled into warm, welcoming arms. For the first time since leaving Tuscany, she felt at peace.

Derrick kissed her on the forehead. 'Morning, sleepy head.'

She looked into his smiling eyes. 'Is it still morning? I was hoping to sleep right through the day.'

'Would you like my help forgetting the sun too?' Derrick looked like a dark angel in the ambient glow.

'Mmm, yes.' Sophie leaned and pressed her lips to his. They enveloped each other and continued kissing for almost an hour before things progressed. While fervent, the sex wasn't violent. It wasn't fed by grief, anger, or frustration. Instead, it felt like healing salves, closing the wounds in her heart.

After drifting in and out of sleep amidst fits of passion, Derrick and Sophie managed to pass the daylight hours without stepping beyond the bedroom door. As the last rays of natural luminescence dropped below the window, Derrick turned to Sophie and smiled. 'That was one hell of a way to spend a day.'

'Agreed.' Her stomach groaned. 'But God damn, I'm hungry now.'

'I heard that, and I think mine's about to join the chorus. Let's grab a pizza, or maybe ten.'

Sophie jumped out of bed. 'Hell of a way to work up an appetite too.'

When they headed downstairs there was a note from Bianca in the kitchen. It was essentially her agenda for the day, just in case either of them needed her. But she also hinted they should take their time alone together. Sophie sighed to herself. She hadn't told her cousin about recent history with Derrick, so it probably looked like romance was brewing. Well, Bianca could think what she liked.

At least suspicions weren't directed towards Sophie's true love.

After a short walk, they found a delightful *ristorante* with alfresco dining by the Grand Canal. Sophie was captivated by the colourful Murano glass lanterns that embellished the railing along the water's edge.

They were shown to their table by an amiable waiter. *'Buona sera signora e signore. Per favore siediti.'* Handing them the wine list, he asked, *'Ti piacerebbe iniziare con un vino?'*

Derrick took the menu, *'Sì, grazie.'* Then he looked at Sophie. 'Did you want to choose a bottle of red to share?'

'Sure, why not.' She flicked through the options, then asked for a Vin Santo Rosso, the one type she knew thanks to Nonno's *vigneto*.

Hearing their language, the man commented. 'Is English your first language? You both look Italian and speak so naturally that I thought you were locals. Where are you from?'

'We are both Australian-born Italians,' Derrick explained. 'My family are *Veneziano*, Sofia's parents come from Lucca.'

'That's good, that's good. I can practise my English. I get you that wine now. *Un momento.*' He walked off.

Sophie smiled. 'Well he's nice. And it's good to find a place where they don't know you for a change.'

Derrick gasped. 'Oh no! My celebrity status has been compromised.'

They both chuckled.

When their friendly attendant returned, he remarked as he poured their drinks, 'You make a good couple.'

Sophie blushed, 'Oh! No, we are just friends, *solo amici*.'

'Oh, *mi dispiace*.' He also appeared embarrassed.

Derrick reassured him. 'Don't worry. It's an easy mistake. We've been friends forever.' He looked at Sophie as he spoke, a subtle glint in his eye.

After making their food orders, Derrick gazed at Sophie a moment. 'I've noticed a lot of sudden changes in you lately, Soph. Ever since you rocked up to class looking hot. It's like you're a different person. I'm just wondering what triggered your changes.'

Sophie gave some thought to her recent developments before answering. 'You know, I don't know if there's been any particular catalyst. I think this new side that you're seeing has always been there, but I've kept it buried under layers of social and religious intolerance. Mamma has always preached the importance of chastity and sex was rarely discussed in our household beyond that. I guess if anything has prompted my awakening, it has been university life.' She paused a moment, then added, 'And meeting Candice. She's opened my eyes a lot.'

'Yes, I suppose you were always more devout than me. How do you feel about the church these days?' Derrick looked up as the pizza arrived. 'Grazie.'

The distraction of food gave Sophie time to contemplate her reply. After devouring half her pizza, she reduced her eating speed enough to talk. 'I think there is a lot of church doctrine that I disagree with and I can't help but think how hypocritical they are, if you consider that Jesus was the basis of the Christian faith and he was all about promoting social justice and tolerance. But there is so much they won't tolerate, such as homosexuality. Then take their stance on sex in general. We are taught that to enjoy any form of sex is a sin because it is a sacred act reserved for the purpose of procreation. But this denies our fundamental nature as human beings. I guess I just find it hard to reconcile my views with those of Catholicism anymore.'

'That sounds like a pretty big crisis of faith there, Soph. It's no wonder you've been so distraught lately.' Derrick suggested.

'I guess you could call it that. To be honest, I don't know what I believe now, but I don't think I

221

want to go to mass anymore.' She finished the last of her pizza, then chased it down with the wine.

'Did you want dessert?' he asked.

Sophie shook her head. 'No thanks. I'm full.'

'I'll just go fix the bill.' He walked to the counter.

Jumping up, Sophie followed him. 'I can cover my half.'

'Don't worry about it, Soph. I got this.' He handed over his card before she could stop him.

This irked Sophie a little since they weren't dating anymore. But then she shrugged it off as old habits.

'Shall we go for a walk?' He asked as they left the restaurant.

'Sounds good. I could probably use the exercise after all that food.'

They were crossing the *Ponte degli Scalzi* when Sophie became enamoured with the view. Leaning against the bridge, she whistled. 'This place looks magnificent from here at night.' Illuminated buildings of all shapes and sizes stretched out along the Grand Canal, reflecting white and yellow light on the water. The iridescent ripples of water created by this effect looked magical.

'Very romantic, isn't it?' Derrick spoke directly into her ear.

She hadn't even noticed him coming up behind her, placing his hands on the concrete railing to flank her. When she turned, Sophie was encompassed by Derrick's arms. He looked intently into her eyes.

Sophie gasped. 'Derrick? What…'

His face was almost touching hers. 'Tell me honestly that you don't feel something more than lust or the love of friendship with me. Tell me there isn't a trace of that spark and I will step away.'

'I…' Sophie felt like a rabbit in headlights. She didn't know what to say.

'Tell me Sofia.'

'I… I can't.'

His response was immediate, pulling her into his arms and kissing her vehemently.

Chapter Fourteen

"Tank!" By Yoko Kanno started playing across the room from Sophie's phone just as Derrick was going down on her. Startled, he looked up at her suddenly. 'What the hell is that?'

'My new ringtone.'

'Geez, Soph. Talk about manic.' He moved up the bed to face her directly, pinning her arms to the bed. 'What's that song from anyway?'

'An anime show I like.' She had recently changed it over from the *Halo 2* theme since reading the *Cowboy Bebop* manga even though she saw the anime a while ago.

'I liked your old tone better. Less of a mood killer. Who would be ringing you at one in the morning anyway?' His lips moved to her neck.

'Shit. Is it that late already? That's probably Stefan.' Sophie moaned as the feel of Derrick's nibbling teeth sent chemical signals rushing through her body.

His mouth pressed against her ear as he spoke. 'Your brother? Really? At this time?'

'Yes, really. This is the time we've been talking on the phone every night this last week.' When the phone rang out, the song started again.

'Well I'm sure he can manage one night without you.' Derrick was studying her closely.

Sophie wondered if he suspected anything. It'd be best to play it cool, not look too eager to answer. 'Yes, I'm sure he can.' Attempting to ignore the phone, she drew Derrick down so that she could kiss his mouth. But it rang a third time, then a fourth.

Derrick pulled back from her suddenly. 'Argh! How long is he gonna keep trying?'

'I dunno. Maybe I should get it. Might be important.'

Sighing, Derrick sat back to let Sophie up. 'It better be.'

When Sophie retrieved her mobile, she could see that it was her brother. 'Ciao Stefan. Is everything okay?'

'Christ, Sofia. About time. You had me worried. I'm okay, well aside from the fact that I can't be with you right now. Are you okay?' Stefan sounded anxious.

'Yes, just busy. Now's not a good time to talk.' She looked at Derrick who was sitting on the bed, still naked. He was watching her with curiosity.

'Why, what's going on?'

'I'm with Derrick.' The line went dead the moment that name left her mouth. 'Shit! Stefan? Are you there? Hello?' Panicking, she tried calling him back. It went straight to voicemail. *Oh Stefan, that must have been such a blow!* She resolved to try him again the next day. Looking back to Derrick she faked a shrug. 'Hmm, I think his battery went flat.'

'Shame.' He was smiling as he advanced upon her.

As Sophie went to put her phone away, she noticed that one of the missed calls was from Candice. 'Just a sec Derrick, there's a message from Candice.' They had kept up with daily message correspondence, mostly to reassure Sophie that her friend was okay, but also to update each other about life in general (except for the whole incest bit).

'You have one new message: Hi Soph, Candice here. I guess you must be asleep by now, sorry. I just wanted to talk to you about this clinic I found. If I can get the funds together in time, I should be able to get that procedure. I wouldn't normally ask, but I don't know who else to turn to for this cash. Could you call me back as soon as possible? Thanks.'

'Jesus Candice!' Sophie cried as she hung up. What sort of clinic had she found?

Derrick was holding Sophie by this point. 'What's wrong Soph? What has Candice done?'

Tears were forming when she looked into his concerned eyes. 'Can you promise to keep a secret? And I mean do not tell a soul?'

'Yes, of course.'

'Candice is pregnant.' She paused to read his reaction.

'Yes, I guess that's a pretty shit situation for a smart girl like her.' He didn't seem that surprised or appalled.

Sophie continued. 'Stefan's the papà, but he doesn't know she's pregnant yet and Candice doesn't want him to know the baby is his.'

His jaw dropped. 'Well fuck! That changes things. When did he knock her up?'

'April, so approaching three months now. She wants to get rid of it but can't get any doctors to sign-off on the proper procedure. Now it sounds like she's found some dodgy backyard facility and needs help finding funds for it.'

'Seriously? I thought she'd know better! You aren't gonna give her the money, are you?' Derrick looked dumbfounded.

'I don't know. I need to call her and discuss it.' She dialled her friend's number.

'Hi Soph. I didn't think you'd call back so soon. What's the time there?' Candice sounded like her usual self.

Sophie felt relieved. 'Just past 1AM. Sorry I missed your call. I've been fooling around with Derrick.' She noticed her lover's expression change to one of amusement as she spoke.

'Right, of course. Did you get my message?'

'Yes. Have you investigated this clinic properly? Cos you know the risks of unsafe abortions, right?' Sophie replied.

'I know the risks, and yes, of course I've done my homework, Soph. They showed me the place and it all looks clean and properly equipped. The only thing standing between me and freedom of choice is three grand.'

'Three thousand dollars? My God! Talk about extortion. Are you sure this place is safe?' Sophie could see Derrick shaking his head in disbelief.

'I'm sure. And of course it's extortion. It's the black market, Soph.' Candice sounded so blasé, as though illegal dealings were part of everyday life.

But then Sophie suddenly realised just how little she knew of Candice's life. Maybe her parents had normalised crime for her. It was a terrifying thought. 'Fine, I'll get you the money. When do you need it?'

Derrick shot her a stupefied look then mouthed something that looked like 'Are you serious?'

'Friday. It's the only day they have free

before the procedure becomes too risky.'

'What? Really? I was hoping to at least be there with you. I fly back that day and won't get a chance to see you until Saturday.' The whole situation was giving her a bad feeling.

'I'll be fine Soph. Should I text you my bank details?'

'Okay. I don't like the sound of any of it, but okay. I promised to help you through this mess, after all.' Sophie signed off with Candice, then hunched over to rest her head in her hands.

'I can't believe you agreed to that Soph.' Derrick put his arms back around her.

She sighed. 'I know, but I have to help her. And she seems so certain. I'm just gonna go borrow Bianca's computer to do some Internet banking. Please give me a few minutes.' She threw a robe on, then just as she headed for the door, he stopped her. 'Please don't make this any harder for me, Derrick.'

'Do you even have enough money?' he asked.

'It'll probably put a big dent in my savings, but yes I have the means.' She looked into his eyes, silently pleading with him to let her pass.

'Fine.' He stepped aside.

ഇരു

Whilst Derrick was out having lunch with family, Sophie took the opportunity to contact one of her own relations. Sitting on the edge of her bed, she grabbed the phone from her side table. But when she called Stefan, she was immediately greeted with his voicemail again. *Damn it!* She decided to try Papà.

'Ciao Sofia. Is everything okay?' Even in holiday mode he sounded irritable.

'Ciao Papà. I'm okay. Just worried about Stefano. I can't get through to his phone today. Is he with you?'

'*Sì*. He broke his phone. I'm taking him into the city tomorrow to get a new one.'

Images of Stefan throwing his phone invaded her thoughts. 'Oh. Can I talk to him for a minute, please?'

'*Un momento.*' He put the phone down. All she could hear were muffled voices.

'Sofia?'

Her heart sank when Papà's voice returned. 'Yes?'

'Stefano said he's busy, but he'll call you once he gets his new phone.'

'Okay, *grazie Papà. Ciao.*'

'*Ciao Sofia.*' The line went dead.

Shit! Stefan is really pissed with me. The thought alone made her sick. *What the hell am I doing with Derrick anyway?* She'd left him because she realised how much she loved and wanted Stefan; feelings that were still as strong as ever. *So why couldn't I tell Derrick that I only wanted to be friends, or friends with benefits as he put it? Is it possible I am in love with them both?*

Pushing Derrick out of her mind for the time being, she lay back on her bed to think about Stefan. Memories of their life together flooded her mind. Recent events, like their first kiss and their talk during band practice, were at the forefront. But then she delved deeper into their history. Playing together as children and the way he would nurse her whenever she tripped. Always so loving and caring. All the times they snuggled on the couch or fell asleep in each other's beds. The erotic dreams that started following Carnevale. The rain had just started that night when Stefan rushed over to protect her with an umbrella. Holding her shivering body tight. The embrace felt as electric as the atmosphere. *Gosh! No wonder my dreams started with a storm.*

With these recollections occupying her thoughts, she drifted back to sleep. And dreamt of Stefan coming to her in the night.

෨෬

Having to wait an extra day to get a replacement phone was probably a good thing. It gave Stefan a chance to cool down a little after his last call to Sophie. It was amazing how easily Derrick could incite his rage. Hopefully Sophie was ready for him this time.

'Ciao Stefano.' She sounded anxious

'Is this a suitable time for you, Sofia?' He hoped his tone didn't sound too bitter.

'Yes. I'm alone and I've been waiting for your call.'

A small comfort at least. 'I'm sorry for… uh… hanging up on you the other night. I just couldn't believe that you would blow me off to fool around with Derrick.' He could feel his temper escalating again, so he focused on his breathing.

'It wasn't like that Stefan. I lost track of time, then got worried that Derrick was becoming suspicious of our late-night calls. I was trying to play it cool.'

'Shit. I didn't think of that. And he was probably already on to us before we came to Italy.' First Luke, then Mamma and possibly Derrick. Too many people were uncovering their secret.

'Why do you say that?'

'Because of what he said when I punched him. I haven't told you the full story from that night yet.' He gave her the unedited version this time.

She whispered her reply. 'Damn it! Give me a sec, I need to check something.' After a minute she returned. 'It's okay. I just wanted to ensure he wasn't listening in the corridor or the room next door.'

'Wait, so he's still at the house?' Deep

breaths.

'Oh, right. I guess I forgot to mention. Derrick is staying in the house because Allesio's his cousin.'

Stefan relaxed, then sniggered a little. 'So, you guys are related now? Man, that's just too funny. I can see why you were suddenly attracted to him again.'

She shrieked. 'Stefan, you insolent man!' Then she laughed.

He loved that sound. 'Geez, I feel like such an idiot for jumping to conclusions. I totally flipped my shit because I thought you were in bed with Derrick again and wanted to fuck him instead of talking to me. Hence the broken phone.'

'Oh wow! Did you actually throw it in a fit of rage?' Her laughter continued.

'Yep. Guilty as charged.' It was pretty funny in hindsight.

Once composed, Sophie's tone became more serious. 'I'm sorry Stefan. I should have handled things differently. The truth is, I was in bed with Derrick that night, but I really did want to talk to you. It's just that walking out of his room to take your call would have seemed suss.'

'Jesus, Soph. Have the two of you been hooking up daily?' His left hand was clutching his pillow, the grip tensing.

'Yeah, kinda. I'm sorry Stefan. But we

already spoke about my needs and such, so I don't want to go into that again. Please try not to think about it if it makes you angry.'

'Easier said than done, Sofia. The thought of that creep's hands instead of mine on your body…'

'Well focus on imagining your hands on my body instead. Those long, calloused fingers of yours touching my naked skin, exploring every part of me.' She was employing a very sexy tone.

It was an incredible picture. 'Wow, you are extraordinary. I can feel blood rushing somewhere now.'

Sophie continued with her seductive voice. 'Good, cos I want you to grab hold of that delicious dick of yours while I talk you through something.'

He did exactly that. 'Are you touching yourself too?'

'Yes. I want to come with you Stefan. Now close your eyes.' She began telling him the minute details of her dream.

Knowing that she was pleasuring herself while delivering her narrative was extremely arousing. And becoming privy to her innermost fantasies was thrilling. Such an intimate feeling.

'That's where my dream ends every time, just before you bring me to climax. So, I need you to tell me the rest.' She was breathing heavily by this point.

'Well, after enjoying the feel of your soft,

succulent insides with my fingers, I decide I want to taste your juices. So, I kiss your mouth once more before moving down to your other lips. I feast on you, sucking, licking, probing until I can drink you.'

She moaned. 'Mmm! That feels fantastic.'

'And you taste delightful. I'm so hot and hard. I want to make love to you, Sofia, and your body feels ready. So, I press my cock against you and ask, "Do you really want your brother inside you?"' He paused for her answer.

'Yes, Stefan. By God, Yes. I want you. I need you.' Even in her impassioned state, she sounded genuine.

'I penetrate you, driving myself deep.' He lost the ability to speak as the intensity of his desire suddenly increased.

But he didn't need words anymore: his panting and groaning answered in kind, as they both orgasmed together.

After catching her breath, Sophie broke the silence. 'Woah, that was intense. I can't wait for the real thing with you, Stefan.'

'Same here, Sofia. On that note, I'd like to go to sleep dreaming of more mind-blowing sex with you.' This was the best he'd felt for over a week and he wanted to savour it.

'Okay, good night, Stefan. I love you.'

'I love you too, Sofia.'

ℰᏣ

The journey home was excruciating for Sophie. While it was good to have Derrick with her, he could do little to ease her anxiety over Candice and even less over the fact that she was flying to the other side of the world without Stefan. When they finally made it back on Melbourne soil, she was an exhausted wreck, but still insisted on visiting Candice before going to bed.

Having sent their luggage home with his parents, Derrick pulled her into his arms. 'I'm coming with you then.' He was as bleary-eyed as Sophie but remained adamant about helping her.

She forced a smile. 'Thanks.'

After their taxi dropped them at the West Melbourne address that she had insisted on getting from her friend, Sophie looked at the dingy, old terrace share house and sighed. A party appeared to be in full swing. 'How's the poor girl supposed to rest and recover with all this noise?'

Stepping over a pile of maggot-infested rubbish on the porch, Derrick gagged. 'I can't understand how people live in such squalor.'

Sophie's knock at the door was answered by a woman in her mid-twenties. Her blonde hair was streaked with bright pink and tied into lots of little loops. Just about anything that could be pierced on her face was. 'Ah yous must be some of Andy's clients, just a sec…'

Sophie cut in: 'Actually, we're here to see Candice. Is she home?'

The woman let them in. After leading them into the kitchen, she hollered up the stairs. 'Hey Candy! Ya got some rich cunts here to see ya.' Turning back to Sophie, she added, 'Just give 'er a sec.' Then she walked off.

Glancing around the rancid room, Sophie noticed numerous items that she assumed were drug paraphernalia. There was one other woman in the room who eyed them suspiciously from the stove as she heated something in a spoon. *My God! Did Candice use any of this stuff?* She'd never seen evidence of the girl being stoned or high.

'Hey, Soph. And Derrick? What's he doing here?' Candice stared at him cautiously.

'Well currently, I'm acting as Sophie's bodyguard while having all of my senses assaulted.'

Sophie glared at Derrick, then turned back to Candice. 'It's okay, he knows and has sworn to secrecy. We came straight from the airport to see how you're recovering. How was the procedure? Are you feeling okay?'

She waited for the other woman to finish her cooking, then replied, 'I didn't go through with it in the end. I got halfway there this morning, then I was struck by an uneasy feeling about the whole thing, so I turned around and came home.'

'Oh, thank God!' Sophie heaved a sigh of relief, then threw her arms around Candice. 'I was so worried about you.'

Candice hesitated at first, but then brought her arms up to return the hug. 'I've decided to keep the kid.' She whispered, 'I'll return your money too.'

Refusing to let go, Sophie could feel tears streaming down her face as she spoke. 'Please keep it. You'll need it when the baby arrives. And I mean it when I say that I'll help you through every step of the way by whatever means possible.'

She pulled herself free of Sophie's hold. 'Thanks, Soph. Now get going before I start crying. My risk is much higher with all these damn hormones. Plus, you look wrecked.'

'Fine, I'll go. Will I see you at uni on Monday?'

'Yes, of course. I plan to finish this semester, then I'll apply for leave.'

'I'm glad you've thought this through. See you again soon.' Sophie smiled as Derrick took her hand and led her back outside. She really was going to be an aunty. And somehow, despite her emotional mess and complicated relationship with Stefan, the thought of helping Candice with this child brought her a sense of joy that trumped it all.

Chapter Fifteen

L ife without Stefan was a difficult adjustment in the beginning, but a full-time study load helped to occupy Sophie's thoughts and before she knew it, two months had passed. During this time Sophie and Derrick's relationship became official again and while Stefan didn't like it, he agreed that it was an effective cover-story.

It was the start of mid-semester break when Sophie rang Stefan for advice. 'Ciao Stefano.' Busy schedules didn't always allow for daily calls, but the twins were able to contact each other several times a week.

'Ciao Sofia. I'm so glad to hear your voice after what I had to go through recently.'

'Why, what happened?'

'My flat mate brought a couple of girls home last night. He tried to set me up with one of them, but I just wasn't interested. So, he ended up sleeping with both and made a hell of a noise while he was about it. I couldn't get to sleep for ages and the sound drove me to distraction because I kept thinking of you.' He sounded exhausted.

'Oh man, that sucks. While I wish you could have gone for it and worked off some of that sexual tension, I'm also kinda flattered that you're still only interested in me.'

'I'll manage, especially if we keep up with the weekly phone sex. So how are you, my love?'

Sophie's heart leaped at those words. 'Okay, I guess. I still haven't got a cosplay sorted for Manifest though, and it's next weekend. I've just been too busy with uni. Any ideas?'

'Well if you're going for an anime character, I bet you could pull off the bandaged Lucy from *Elfen Lied*. You'd just need the right wig.'

Sophie rolled her eyes. 'You would think that, wouldn't you? And if you were here, I'd probably do that one just for you. But I was thinking of something a little less revealing.'

'You know I'll remember that next time we go to an anime con together. How about Faye Valentine then? I know you love that show and she has slightly more skin covered.'

'Hmm, that's not a bad idea actually. I'd still need a wig though, 'cause I'm not cutting my hair that short.' She started jotting down some notes for the costume.

'Fair point. I do love your beautiful long hair. You better send me lots photos. I hate that I can't be there with you.'

'Me too. And yes, I will inundate you with pictures. So, did you feel like some Xbox Live now?'

'Yes please. I could use the relaxation.'

ꗥꛯ

The rest of Sophie's week was spent frantically sewing between online gaming sessions and conversations with Stefan. Then the convention weekend arrived.

Dom ran to embrace her, then stood back to inspect her outfit. 'Wow Soph, that cosplay's um… impressive. What there is of it, anyway.'

'Thanks… I think. Come on, let's line up.' They joined the back of the queue. 'It feels weird being on campus in the middle of holidays.'

'Yeah, I suppose it does. Okay, time for our obligatory standing-in-line selfie.' Dom huddle up next to her with his camera.

Before breaking their pose, Sophie grabbed a shot of them with her phone. 'I promised Stefan lots of pics, so I'm gonna send him this now.' After forwarding the message, she put her mobile away and sighed. 'I really wish he could be here now. As much as I love you Dom, this event won't be the same without Stefan.'

He smiled apologetically. 'Yeah I know. Although if he were here, I bet he'd have a pretty hard time keeping his hands off you with all that

241

bare flesh showing. Speaking of which…'

Sophie drifted off, imagining the fun she could have teasing her brother dressed the way she was.

'Soph?' Dom's voice pulled her back.

'Oh right. Sorry, Dom. You were saying?' She tried to focus her mind.

'Are you okay? You seem really out of it.'

'Yeah. I was just thinking about him. With Derrick away, Stefan and I've been in constant communication this week. I guess I didn't get a lot of sleep either.'

'I can only begin to imagine how hard it must be for you guys. I guess you won't want to hear about my week with Owen.' He was grinning.

'Hey, just cos I'm not getting any, doesn't mean I'm gonna begrudge my friends enjoying it.'

'It's okay, I'll tell you the details later. There's something else I need to share with you first.'

'Oh?' They picked up their passes, then started walking through the main hall full of excited *otakus*.

'I've been doing some research and I think I have a possible solution for your Stefan dilemma.'

Sophie became hyper-alert, stopping suddenly in front of a cosplayer posing for a photo. 'What? Really?'

Dom apologised to the others on her behalf, then pulled her aside. 'It would mean moving to the other side of the world.'

'Go on. I'm listening.'

'Well the idea occurred to me following the announcement that gay marriage was recently legalised in Spain. Apparently, incest between siblings is not a crime there either.' He showed her his findings. 'So, if you can work out a way to live there…'

Sophie shrieked and grabbed her friend in a bear hug. 'Oh my God, that's fantastic news! Thanks Dom. I hadn't even considered the possibility that it would be lawful anywhere. I can't wait to tell Stefan about this. What's the time?' She looked at her watch, then did a quick mental sum. 'Damn. There's a chance he's asleep already since he didn't reply to my last message.' She sent him a quick text, PLEASE CALL ME ASAP WHEN YOU WAKE UP.

Stefan responded immediately, his worried voice greeting her the moment she picked up. 'Are you okay Soph?'

'Ciao Stefano. I'm super excited.'

'Geez Soph. I was asleep, but the notification tone woke me. I thought something was wrong when I saw that message,' he yawned.

'I did say it could wait till you woke up.' Hearing his voice again triggered the flutters in her stomach.

'Well you've got me now, so tell me.'

'I've found a way for us to be together, like properly together.' It felt unreal reading the words on the printouts from Dom.

She could hear his sharp intake of breath. 'What do you mean, Sofia?'

Jumping in with her explanation, she felt like she was about to burst. 'If we moved to Spain, we could be a legitimate couple. Obviously, there would be a heap of logistics to work out first, but could you imagine it? Being able to openly love each other?'

'It sounds like a dream, but I'm a little lost. Why Spain?'

She lowered her voice. 'Because incest is okay there, Stefan. We could have a sexual relationship and being twins wouldn't matter according to their legal system.'

His tone became hopeful. 'Seriously? How did you discover this?'

'Absolutely. Dom did some research for us. We can talk more on the technicalities later, but I had to let you know there is hope for us yet.'

Stefan didn't like the fact that more people were in the loop, but at least he trusted Dom. 'That's the best news I've heard since… since discovering my feelings for you were mutual. I can't believe I never thought to look into that option.'

'Isn't it awesome? I'd better get going now. There's a screening of something I wanna see starting soon, but I'll call you when I get home tonight.'

'Okay. I love you Sofia.'

'I love you too. Ciao Stefano.'

ഇരു

'So, Spain, huh?' Stefan was overjoyed by Sophie's news. He'd spent the night contemplating the possibilities before eventually drifting back to sleep. As soon as he awoke, he got online and started his own research to confirm what she had told him. It was at the forefront of his mind when she rang him.

'Yeah, I almost couldn't believe it at first. We'd have to learn more Spanish but knowing fluent Italian should help there. In theory, we could even do it in Italy so long as we didn't cause public scandal, but I suspect Mamma would make things too difficult for us there.'

Thinking about how much Mamma had interfered with their relationship thus far, he had to agree. 'Good point. You know one good thing has come of this exile of mine: I'm adapting to the European lifestyle and learning to live away from home, so that ought to help with the transition too.'

'Yeah, I guess that will take some adjusting for me, but at least I'll have you. So, I guess the next step is to work out things like residency laws, a place to live, and of course the biggest issue will be money.'

'True. If we do this, I doubt our parents will be on board with the idea. We will have to make our own way. I've got some investments that will help. We could use your savings to put together another portfolio and…'

'Shit! Oh God, how could I forget?' She suddenly panicked.

'What is it Soph? What's wrong?'

'There's one slight complication with this plan. I've promised to help a friend with something important. I wonder if we could…' Her voice trailed off to silence on the other end of the line.

'If we could what, Soph? What are you talking about?' His heart sank. It sounded like she was having seconds thoughts. Just as he was getting his hopes up.

'I'm sorry Stefan. There's something I'm gonna have to look into before committing to anything.' So much doubt in her voice.

'Don't tell me this involves Derrick.' If that jerk…

'What? No. This is a… family matter, but something I can't tell you about. Not yet.'

'What the hell are you talking about Soph? Is something wrong with Mamma or Papà?' His anger suddenly turned to fear.

'No, nothing like that.'

'Then what? You're being cryptic Sofia.' His head starting spinning as he thought of the possibilities. *Grandparents? Aunts or Uncles? Cousins? Who could be in trouble? How?*

'I'm sorry, I can't say anymore. Look, I'm sure it'll be fine. We'll find a way to be together, okay? I promise.' She softened her tone, but it wasn't any more reassuring.

'I dunno, Soph. You've got me worried now.' *What family matter could possibly be more important than their own reunion and future happiness together?*

'Please trust me. I will sort this out. I've gotta go now, but please don't lose hope.'

'Okay. I love you Sofia.' *It wasn't okay, but I can't really argue.*

'I love you Stefano.' Then she was gone.

He threw his phone on the bed out of frustration. *Damn it! What the hell was going on?* He needed to clear his mind, so he got ready to go for a walk. Just as he did, his mobile rang. Unknown Australian number, curious. 'Hello, Stefan speaking.'

'Hi Stefan, it's Candice here.' It was her usual nonchalant tone.

'Candice? Uh, hi. You haven't just spoken to Sophie by any chance?'

'No. Why?'

'I just had a very strange conversation with her is all. Anyway, what's up Candice?'

'I figured it was about time I told you that I'm pregnant.'

Okay, weird that she would… Fuck! Did she just…

Candice went on talking despite his silence. 'It's okay, I don't expect anything from you, I just thought you should know that I'm gonna have the kid and he or she will be carrying your genes. But like I said, I don't expect anything from you.'

'Jesus, Candice! What? How? We had sex like once and with protection. How do you know it's mine?'

'Because you were the only guy for several months either side. Look, I'm not calling to argue or demand anything. I just wanted to tell you.'

Family matter. Sophie's words suddenly occurred to him. *Shit!* 'Did Sophie know about this?'

'Yes, but I made her promise not to tell you. She's already insisted on helping. She wants to be a good Aunty apparently, so I don't need you to be an active parent. I just felt guilty for hiding the truth for so long. I think it's these damn hormones…'

Stefan could still hear her talking in the background, but he couldn't make out the details. His head swam with confused thoughts and emotions. As far as he knew, Sophie hadn't told Candice about their feelings or plans for Spain, so she had no reason to be manipulating them. But Sophie had already promised. *Oh God, Sofia, no wonder!* How was she planning to fulfil her promise to them both? Rage suddenly swelled. *Why the hell didn't Sophie tell me I had a baby on the way! How could she think keeping Candice's secret was more important than telling me what was at stake?*

'Are you there Stefan?' Her increased vocal volume reeled him back to the conversation.

'Yeah, sorry. Just in shock. Thanks for being honest. I want to help somehow, but I need time to process the news. When are you due?' *This is too much for me to deal with after Sophie's call. I really need that walk.*

'Twelfth of January. Sophie told me you'll be home by then, so you can come along to the birth if you want. I'm sorry for springing it on you like this. I did look at other options, but our stupid conservative government have their heads too far up the arse of the Church to given women much choice.' She sounded angry for the first time ever. 'Damn there I go with the unchecked emotions again. Sorry.'

'It's okay. I totally get where you're coming from.' The air was becoming stifling.

'Well that's all for now.'

'Okay. Take care, Candice.'

'You too. Bye.'

This is fucking huge! I am going to be a papà! Even though Candice didn't expect anything from him, he still felt obligated to help somehow. *But what the hell can I do? This is also likely to blow my plans with Sophie out of the water.* Stepping outside, he decided a jog was in order.

ஐ෬

After a late Sunday night, Sophie awoke to Derrick's soft kisses. She guessed it was probably early morning. Mamma must have let him in before heading out.

'Good morning, sleeping beauty,' Derrick smiled as she opened her eyes.

She groaned. 'Yuck, that's so corny!' But then she pulled him down to kiss properly. Before long they were both undressed and enfolding each other's bodies completely. Sophie was glad to have Derrick back, even if she knew things couldn't last much longer.

'Good heavens Sofia! Have you-a no sense of propriety anymore?' Mamma suddenly appeared at the door.

Obviously not gone yet. *Oops!* She glared at the mother of all interruptions as Derrick dashed to cover himself.

'Well at least you're with-a Derrick this time.' She walked out, slamming the door.

'Damn that woman,' Sophie smiled coyly at Derrick. 'Sorry about that.' She tried to pull him back into her arms, but he resisted.

Adopting an inquisitorial look and tone, he asked, 'What did she mean by at least you're with me this time?'

Sophie paled. 'Well you know she loves you. She's probably still happy we're back together, even though she just witnessed us committing a sin in her eyes.'

'Yes, I get that. But what did she mean by *this* time? Who did she catch you with *last* time?'

Shit! Sophie started thinking of ways to skirt around the truth. She knew that Derrick would pick a blatant lie too easily.

'Oh my God! You fucked him, didn't you?' There was a look of distaste in his eyes.

Dread filled Sophie to her core. 'What? Who are you talking about?'

'Stefan. Your God damn brother! It all makes perfect sense now. I mean I'd figured you had some inappropriate feelings for each other. You always seemed too close; then there was the ball and the way you reacted to being separated. But now I get it. The reason for his exile. It's cos you did it, didn't you?'

The pit of her stomach lurched, as though she was going to be sick. 'Not exactly.'

'Then what exactly, Soph? Enlighten me.'

She closed her eyes. She couldn't bear to see those judging eyes upon her. 'Mamma caught us before it got that far.'

'Jesus Christ! How far did things get? Did you guys kiss? Were you both naked?' His tone was terrifying.

Keeping her eyes closed, she hunched over to rest her forehead in her palms. 'Yes and yes.' Then the tears came.

She heard Derrick sigh, then his arms were around her. 'I'm sorry Sofia. I didn't mean to upset you. I was just shocked is all. It doesn't change how I feel about you.'

She tried to respond between sobs. 'But how could you love me? Knowing what I did—what I almost did…? What I still want to do…? I'm in love with him, Derrick.'

He looked at her, his disbelief plain to see. 'Are you saying you still intend to…? Oh wow! I…. What about us, Soph? Does our relationship mean nothing to you?'

'Of course you mean something to me, Derrick. I still love you. It's just….' She knew this day would come eventually, but not this soon; too late to hold back now. 'I love Stefan more.'

He let go of her and stood up. After pacing the room for a few minutes, he sat on the bed again. 'You know incest is a crime, right?'

'It is here—yes, I know. But not everywhere in the world…' Before she could explain her plans, Derrick cut in.

Grabbing her, his grip was firm to the point of painful. 'The point is that you can't legally have each other here, so you can have me instead.'

'That's not what I was…'

'I wasn't implying anything about your motives Soph. I'm offering myself to you. I am so damn in love with you—so fucking obsessed with having you—that I'm willing to overlook any past and future transgressions of yours. Be mine and I'll let you have your fun if you keep the whole disgusting thing with Stefan away from prying eyes.' He looked at her fiercely, lust evident in his eyes; but other passions were emanating from them too.

She couldn't believe what he was saying. 'I…' She couldn't think of the right words.

'Do you still love me, Sofia?'

'Yes.'

He pounced, pinning her to the bed. 'Do you want me to stop?'

'No.' The desire she felt for him was far too strong. So, she yielded as he took her with the sort of savagery they had not indulged in since Venice.

Chapter Sixteen

'I want to take you out for dinner,' Derrick announced as soon as he'd caught his breath.

'What, now?' Sophie looked at him in bewilderment. They'd just spent most of the day having crazy, wild sex and she wasn't even sure if she could walk again yet.

'Yes. Well, as soon as we can get showered and dressed. This may have been presumptuous of me, but I already made plans for us and I'd like to get there before sunset.'

He wasn't wrong, Sophie thought, considering how close they came to breaking up that morning. But she felt a little better about things by this point. 'Okay, fine. Let's get moving now then.' She headed straight for the shower.

'Mind if I join you?' Derrick stood behind her, sliding a hand around her waist as she adjusted the taps from outside the cubicle. He pecked her shoulders with small, gentle kisses.

Sophie giggled and squirmed a little under his light,

ticklish touch. 'Sure, but if you keep that up, we won't get to see much sunlight.' Once the temperature was right, she turned and pulled her bodacious boyfriend under the water. After kissing briefly, Sophie looked into his eyes. 'You know, I still can't believe you want me despite everything.'

Shielding her from the stream so that droplets trickled around his face, Derrick gazed upon her longingly. 'I know it doesn't make any sense, but that's the thing about love: it defies logic. I love you, Sofia, and tonight I'm going to prove it to you.'

'Now I'm intrigued. Where are we going?' Her mind started racing. What could he have planned?

His lip curled slightly as he smiled. 'It's a surprise.'

'Can you at least give me some sort of dress code guidelines?'

He pondered her question a moment. 'Hmm. Probably something warm and you'll definitely want long pants. Other than that, the degree of formality's entirely up to you.'

'Most curious.' She thought about her wardrobe options as she bathed and settled on wearing dress pants and one of her nice cardigans.

Once she was dressed, Derrick looked at her. 'Perfect. I need to run home to change and collect a few things. I'll come back and collect you in twenty minutes.'

'Okay, sounds good. Should give me time to put on some makeup.' She kissed him goodbye, then got to it. As she finished up, she opened her jewellery box to retrieve her three favourite pieces of gold. The bracelet from Derrick was essential she decided, and she never went anywhere without her masquerade necklace. Having adorned herself with those, she rolled the ring around in her fingers. Vivid memories of her time in Tuscany with Stefan came flooding back. She hadn't worn it around Derrick before, having been too afraid of arousing suspicions. But that wasn't a problem anymore. If Derrick really did want her as he'd said, then he would have to accept everything Sophie and Stefan felt for each other. With that in mind, she slipped the ring onto her right hand.

Sophie glanced across at her phone and noticed it was still off. Oops! After turning the device back on, a message came through from Candice: Just thought you should know that I told Stefan about my pregnancy last night. He took it okay; I think. Oh God, that's huge, Candice! She wanted to call Stefan straight away, but there was a good chance he wasn't awake yet and Derrick would be back any minute. Damn it! It would have to wait until she got home. She threw her mobile in her bag, then ran downstairs to meet Derrick.

'Are you okay? You seem a little distracted?' Derrick asked as they drove alongside the Yarra River in a westerly direction.

She was, despite her best efforts to focus on the

lovely scenery outside. The river was buzzing with life on a fine spring afternoon, but all Sophie could think about was Stefan. How did he really feel about impending fatherhood? She sighed and looked at Derrick, whose eyes were still on the road. 'I just got a message from Candice. Apparently, she told Stefan about the baby. I'm worried about him and how he took the news.'

'Yeah that probably would've been a shock for him... I imagine you're also worried about... how this will impact on his feelings for you.' His tone was uneasy as he broached the topic.

It was true though, which was nagging at her. 'I'm sorry if this is still a bit much for you to process. But yeah, I was thinking that. I'll admit that honouring Candice's secret wasn't the only thing preventing me from telling Stefan myself.'

'It's okay, Soph. It'll probably just take a little while for me to become comfortable with the whole situation. And I'm sure there's nothing to worry about with Stefan.'

Sophie noticed they'd crossed the river and were passing the Melbourne Cricket Ground. Her interest started to pique again as she considered their possible destinations. It wasn't long before Derrick stopped, parking the Lexus in front of the Fitzroy Gardens. When he pulled a picnic basket out of the boot, she realised his intentions. 'I take it we're dining alfresco tonight.'

'An astute observation, my dear.' He smiled at her, then took her hand is his as they made their way over to the lush green paradise. 'Do you recall coming here as kids? I used to love this place, especially when I got to play here with my best friend.' He squeezed her hand.

A mix of emotions surged through Sophie as he spoke. There was no denying that she still felt a strong bond with Derrick. Eighteen years of solid friendship compounded with a crush that lasted almost half that time wasn't something easily forgotten or ignored. 'Yes, I remember this place fondly.' Her eyes lit up as they passed a familiar sight. 'Especially that Tudor Village and the Fairy Tree. It felt like such a magical place back then.'

They walked until they reached the lake and dolphin fountain. Derrick set out a rug on the lawn, along with a large spread of cold meats, cheeses, pâté and fruit, among other tasty treats.

Sophie took a seat. 'Wow, this an amazing selection of food Derrick. Thank you.'

'You haven't even seen the best of it yet.' He pulled out a bottle of Moët champagne, then poured her a glass.

She grinned. 'Mmm, yum. I love that stuff!'

'I know.' He gave her a cheeky look. 'I'd like to toast to us. I know things have become… a bit more complicated, but I love you Sofia. And I want to keep showing you that for as long as possible. So, cheers to us!'

Clinking her glass with his, she felt a few small tears escape. 'Cheers.' After sipping the delicious bubbles, Sophie kissed Derrick. Their lips moved together slowly and with a tenderness that brought a few more tears. How can this man be so gentle and romantic this soon after the ferocity of their earlier passion?

After enjoying their feast, Derrick looked at her strangely. Sophie detected a hint of anxiety, but he was hiding it well. 'Have you thought much about what I said this morning?'

'What do you mean?'

'When I offered myself to you. I asked you to be mine.' He shifted his position so that one arm was by his side but kept his left arm close behind her.

'I haven't really had much of a chance yet. You distracted me for most of the day after that. But I think I kinda answered when I gave myself to you.' She eyed him lustfully.

He returned her gaze. 'Not entirely what I meant. I... I want more Sofia. I know your heart can't entirely belong to me, but I want as much of it as you can spare.' He retrieved something from his pocket, keeping it clenched in his tight grip. 'I'm completely in love with you, Sophie, and I need you to believe me because... (He suddenly revealed the sparking diamond he was holding). Because I want to spend the rest of my life with you, as your husband.'

What the hell? Was he for real? Sophie was utterly astonished. 'I... uh... I'm sorry Derrick, but I don't know what to say.'

'How about Yes? Or at least a maybe.' His eyes were intense.

Marriage had never even crossed her mind. 'Don't you think we're a bit young to be getting married? We haven't even finished our first year of uni.'

'I'm not suggesting we rush into the wedding planning, Soph. I'm happy to wait until after graduation before settling down. I'm just asking you to commit to the idea.' He extended his right hand forward to present the ring to her.

'I don't know, Derrick. I need time to think on this. And I've got to talk to Stefan about it.' If it weren't for Stefan's child on the way, she probably would've said "No". But Spain was probably nothing more than a dream, especially if Candice didn't want to move with them.

'So, is that a maybe?'

'I guess it is. I'm sorry I can't give you more than that, Derrick.'

He took her hand and placed the ring in her palm. 'Please take this while you think. Then you can give me your answer either by returning it, or hopefully by putting it on your left hand.' This was when he noticed the other diamond ring she wore. 'Hey, I haven't seen this before. Is it new?'

Blushing, Sophie took the ring from Derrick. 'Kinda.

I got it in Tuscany.'

'But you've only just started wearing…. Oh. It's from Stefan, isn't it' Lifting her hand to inspect the ring more closely, he gasped. 'I don't think you have anything to fear from Candice and that baby coming between the two of you.' He released her hand. 'I just hope that you consider my proposal properly, from all angles.'

৪০৫৪

Dominic was pleasantly surprised when he was summoned by the doorbell. It was Monday afternoon and he'd spent most of the morning resting after a full weekend of pop culture. He greeted Owen with a wide grin, 'Hi sexy,' then pulled the man into his hallway to kiss him passionately.

'I take it your parents are out.' Owen looked around cautiously, understanding Dominic's reasons for not yet telling his family about their relationship.

Leading his boyfriend by the hand, he walked into the kitchen. 'An astute observation. So, what brings you out here today? I didn't think I'd get to see you again till Wednesday night.'

'My plans for the afternoon fell through, so I decided to surprise you.'

Dominic beamed. 'Naw, you're the best. Can I get you a drink?'

'Something cold would be great.'

He opened the fridge to inspect the options. 'Well there's beer, cider, Moscato — or soft drink.'

'I'll go the beer. Thanks Dom.'

After handing Owen an ale, Dominic grabbed a cider for himself, then took him up to his bedroom. 'Fancy a movie?' He gestured to the shelf of DVDs beside his entertainment unit. Where Owen had spent a small fortune collecting music over the years, Dominic had invested in a collection of arthouse and foreign films, along with a few good Hollywood blockbusters.

Owen browsed the selection, then picked out House of Flying Daggers. He looked at the box briefly before asking, 'Is this by the same guy that made Hero? I've heard it's s'posed to be good, yeah?'

'That's right. It's absolutely gorgeous and with a stronger plot in my opinion. I'd be down for that if you're keen.'

'For sure.' He smiled as he handed the case to Dominic.

They settled in to watch it, snuggling together on Dominic's bed. It felt incredible to have this wonderful man's arms around him.

When the end credits started to roll, Owen looked at Dominic intently with a cheeky grin. 'A very enjoyable movie, thanks in part to your wandering hands. I'm not sure how much of the plot I followed though.'

Dominic blushed. His hands had developed a mind

of their own and he found one of them between Owen's legs. 'Oh, sorry.'

There was hunger in his eyes. 'Don't be.' Owen pounced, then kissed him deeply. The taste of beer was strong on his breath, but Dominic didn't mind. He wanted this man; needed him to fulfil his desires. As the heat increased, Dominic decided that clothes were no longer necessary, discarding them all to the floor. The feel of Owen's rough fingertips gliding over his skin drove him wild.

Owen groaned into his ear. 'Mmm, I want you now.' Dominic pressed his lips to his lover's once more, then turned over to surrender his body to Owen.

'What the hell?'

Dominic looked up at his father's voice, paralysed by terror. He was vaguely aware that Owen scrambled to cover them both with the quilt, pulling Dominic into his protective arms.

'Get away from my son, filthy faggot! I'm calling the police.'

Owen gasped. 'With all due respect sir, Dom was fully consenting, so nothing criminal happened here.'

He looked to his son, wide eyed. 'Is that true, Dominic?'

Dominic lowered his head in shame. 'Yes, father.'

'By God! How could you? After everything your mother and I have done for you. Is this how you show us your gratitude? I will not tolerate sodomy in my house. And I refuse to acknowledge a homosexual for a son, so you'd best straighten up or get the hell out.' He slammed the door.

Dominic was numb with shock.

'Are you okay, Dom?' Owen's voice sounded distant. When Dominic looked up, he saw the man's eyes staring at him with concern. Words were too hard to muster, so he shook his head.

Owen held him close. 'It'll be okay. Did you want to come back to my house?'

'I… I don't know.' His father's words kept rolling through his mind. If he went with Owen, he knew it would mean the end of all family ties.

'You're not gonna let that tyrant push you around, are you?'

'He's still my father, but if I go… if we go… I… I won't be his son.'

'Come on, Dom. You don't need a dad like that.' Owen was looking at him expectantly.

Dominic didn't know what to do or say. He looked back at Owen blankly.

'Fine. I'm outta here anyway. You can either stand up to your old man and come with me or stay here and kiss our love goodbye.' He stood up suddenly and dressed.

Remaining speechless, Dominic watched as Owen finished getting ready. He was torn. His heart desperately wanted to follow the man he loved, but also knew that life would be nigh impossible without the support of his family.

'So, what's your decision, Dominic?' Owen stood over him with pleading eyes.

'I… I'm sorry.'

'Well, I guess this's it.' He turned and left the room. Oh God! What have I done? Dominic couldn't believe he just let Owen walk out of there. But then Owen's reaction was a bit harsh. How could Owen drop such an ultimatum on him when he was still in shock from being discovered by his dad? He felt his heart breaking and his soul shattering.

𝕤ℭ

Sophie sat in her room and compared the two diamond rings as she thought about the men who had bought them for her. Derrick had proposed to her with a classic, solitaire diamond of generous size set on a gold band. It was conventional and bold, much like Derrick himself. The Tuscan ring from Stefan, on the other hand, was artistically styled and unique, both traits she could easily attribute to her brother. Two very different diamond rings from two very different men, yet both symbolised their givers' intense love.

She sighed as she set Derrick's ring down on her dressing table, then picked up her phone to call Stefan.

'Sofia.' So abrupt! He sounded annoyed, or possibly angry.

Her anxiety increased. 'Ciao Stefano. How are you? Candice told me she rang you.'

'Yeah she did. Why the hell didn't you tell me? And don't give me the excuse that Candice begged you to keep it secret. That's not good enough.'

Damn it! He was pissed. She could feel her own rage increasing. 'Well for one thing, it wasn't my place to tell you. I thought it was important to respect her decision. But if you must ask for the main reason I hesitated, then you don't know me as well as I thought!'

'Wha… what do you mean?' His tone had eased to one of concern.

'What's my greatest fear, Stefan?' She shuddered. It was bad enough be apart for several months, but to be separated longer still… possibly permanently. She could feel emotion swelling in her eyes.

'Yeah, but what's that…? Oh God, Soph. I'm sorry.' He sighed heavily. 'I guess I really screwed things up for us huh. I mean Spain's much less viable with this baby on the way. I can't exactly abandon my child. Man, that still sounds so strange!'

'This is pretty well exactly what I feared. I was hoping to talk to Candice about the possibility of moving overseas with us, but that means telling her our secret. Plus, I don't know how she'd feel being a third wheel. Geez, how did things get so complicated, Stefan?'

Sighing again, he responded, 'I dunno. I still don't

know what came over me that night.'

'Well it's not like I'm any better. I'm probably worse, in fact. Which brings me to some Derrick-related news.'

'Judging by your tone, I'm guessing it's not something amazing like you broke up and won't ever see him again.' Stefan became noticeably worried.

'I thought things were about to go that way at one point today.'

'Oh?'

She continued reluctantly. 'He knows all about us now. I'm sorry Stefan, but I couldn't lie to him when he questioned me so directly.'

'Shit! What did he say? Did you make him swear to secrecy?'

'I didn't need to. Given what he proposed, he's just as keen to keep it under wraps as we are.' Why couldn't she just get to the point?

'Wait, so he didn't flip out over us almost having sex?

'No, he didn't. He didn't exactly like it, but it didn't send him packing. He also knows we're in love, but that doesn't change how he feels about me.... He frickin' well proposed to me, Stefano. Diamond ring, romantic picnic, the whole shebang. It was bizarre.'

'What the actual fuck? He proposed to you after finding out about us, knowing that your heart lay elsewhere. That man is unreal. How did he respond when you turned him down?' He was on the verge of laughter by this point.

'That's just it, Stefan. I haven't given him an answer yet. I told him I need time to think on it and to talk to you.'

'You aren't seriously considering this madness, are you?' The amusement vanished from his voice.

'Why not? It would make an ideal cover for us if we can't move to Spain with the whole pregnant Candice situation. He said he'll let us carry on if we keep the affair discreet.' She could hardly believe she was contemplating the idea.

'Are you insane? There's a myriad of reasons for why not, but the ones that stick out to me most are how young you are and more importantly, the fact that you don't love the guy. Call me old-fashioned, but I still think marriage should be about love.'

'I already pointed out the age thing, but he said the wedding could wait till after graduation. As for your other point, I kinda do still love him.' There, it was out. The truth she'd been too afraid to tell Stefan since her realisation in Venice.

'What? How do you kinda love someone? Do you love Derrick, or not? Which is it Soph?'

'I do—okay? I'm sorry… but I still love…'

'You know what? I can't deal with this right now, Soph. This whole fucking mess is too much for me. Maybe you should just go marry that twat and I'll move in with Candice. At least then we won't be living under the same roof and I'll be less tempted to break the law by fucking my own sister!' The pain in his voice was unbearable.

Sophie burst into tears. 'But Stefano...'

'It's time we faced reality, Soph. This dream of us being more than normal siblings isn't going to work. We never should have crossed over into such forbidden territory.'

'How could you say that Stefan? We can't just ignore how we feel!'

'I can and will. It's the only way. I have to go now, Soph. Good night!' The line was suddenly quiet.

'Stefan?' She looked at her phone. He'd hung up on her! The sobbing intensified with the agony of despair. While the twins had had their fair share of fights over the years, past disputes never felt so horrid or crushing. Sophie wondered if this was what it felt like to be dumped. Stefan's words felt final. Was there really no hope for their love after all? She considered calling Dom for support, but it was after midnight. Instead, she lay down and wept until exhaustion overcame her.

Chapter Seventeen

Sophie woke to the sound of her phone ringing. She felt a little dazed after the anguish of the night before. Not recognising the number, she picked up. 'Sophie speaking.'

An urgent voice greeted her. 'Hi Sophie. This's Ruby, Candy's flatmate. I didn't know who else to call, but I remember you visiting her and being like the only person she trusts. So, I found ya number in her phone.'

Panicking, Sophie asked, 'Why, what happened? Is Candice okay?'

'I dunno yet. She's in hospital. I found her collapsed at the bottom of the stairs this morning. And the blood—oh God, there was so much blood.'

'Shit! Which hospital did she go to?' That can't be good, Sophie thought.

'We're at the Royal Melbourne emergency.'

'Okay, I'll be right there.' She hung up the phone then quickly dressed. She thought about calling Stefan but decided against it. He was probably asleep and there was little he could do at this stage. So, she rang Derrick.

'Good morning my love, have you got an answer—'

Breaking him off before he could finish asking that awkward question, 'Candice has been rushed to hospital. Can you please come with me to see her?'

'Oh, is she okay?'

'I don't know yet, but it doesn't sound good.'

'I'll pick you up in five then.' Even Derrick sounded worried.

'Thanks. See you soon.' After hanging up, she grabbed a quick coffee, then waited out the front.

When Derrick arrived, he ran to her, throwing his arms around her shaking body. 'Are you okay?'

It wasn't a cold day, but Sophie felt a slight chill all the same. 'I'm really scared, Derrick. I need to see her; I need to know that both her and the baby will be okay.'

'I'm sure they will pull through. Let's go.' He helped her into the car, then took the driver's seat.

They remained silent for the journey, both lost in thought. Sophie was dreading the possibilities, for both her and Stefan's sake. Despite the poor timing and complications posed by the imminent birth of this kid, she or he would still be family and Sophie had already fallen in love with her niece or nephew. Candice had also become one of her closest friends and she feared for the girl's well-being.

When they reached the hospital, they rushed into the emergency department to meet Ruby. The girl with pink and blonde hair jumped up to greet them. 'Hi Sophie. Thanks for comin'. I'm still waitin' for news.'

'Thanks for calling me, Ruby.' They all sat down together.

About twenty minutes later, a doctor approached them. Looking at Sophie and Derrick, he asked, 'Are you Candice's family?'

Sophie stood up. 'Sort of. I'm Sophie, the aunty of her baby. This is my boyfriend Derrick.'

'I see. Is the baby's father here?'

Sophie tensed. 'No, Stefan is in Italy. Is Candice okay? What about the baby?'

The doctor frowned. 'I'm sorry. There were complications with the pregnancy. Candice had a severe case of what is known as a placental abruption. We were unable to save mother or child.'

'*What? No!*' Sophie burst into tears.

Derrick pulled her into his arms, then asked the doctor, 'Do you know what caused the complication?'

'I'm afraid not. It is a rare condition, especially in someone so young with no prior history or known risk factors. Do any of you know her parents?'

Sophie replied between sobs, 'No…. Her mum… died years ago… she broke all ties… with her abusive dad.'

'I see. I guess that makes you her next of kin, Sophie. Did you want to see her?' The doctor offered her a sympathetic smile.

'Yes please,' Sophie replied.

The doctor led the way. Ruby chose to remain in the waiting room, but Derrick joined Sophie, comforting her every step of the way.

When they reached the bed where Candice lay, the sight of her cold, permanently sleeping body came as huge shock to Sophie. She sucked in a breath, then let out a cry. *'Oh, dear God! Candice!'* Throwing herself on the girl's corpse, she wept frantically.

Some unquantifiable time later, Derrick pulled Sophie up to let the hospital staff take Candice away. 'Come on. I think the doctor is waiting for you.' He held her close, practically carrying her as they moved forward.

After pushing through some paperwork, Sophie asked Derrick to take her home. Every step she made, every word spoken since learning of her friend's demise, felt surreal. It was like she was watching someone else's tragic life unfold. The only thing that kept her grounded was the deep despair she felt.

Mamma was home when they returned. She was alarmed by Sophie's state. 'What's-a happened? Are you okay Sofia?'

Unable to answer, Sophie just cried harder as she collapsed on a couch in the family room.

Still holding Sophie, it was Derrick who explained.

'Oh. I had my suspicions about that girl's growing tummy. I suppose this is-a God's way for punishing her for the sin of lust.' She looked upon Sophie with concern. 'It's still not too late for you, Sofia. I'm sure God would welcome you with loving arms if you would just repent.'

Furious, Sophie glared at Mamma. '*Would you just shut up!* You don't get it, do you Mamma? That was Stefano's child. Your own God-damned grandson died with her!'

Mamma gasped. 'What? Oh, dear Lord. I... I'm sorry Sofia.' She attempted to sit and console Sophie.

But Sophie stood up and stormed off to her room, slamming the door shut behind her. Then she threw herself on the bed and tried calling Stefan. No answer. *Damn it, Stefan!* She tried again and again, all with no success.

Derrick walked in a few minutes later. 'I rang Dominic. He's coming over shortly.'

She looked at him, despondent. 'I... I can't

reach Stefan. He still won't talk to me after… after I told him…'

When she didn't continue, Derrick asked, 'What did you tell him, Sophie?'

'I told him about your proposal… and that I still… I still love you.'

He sat down to embrace her. Holding her face, he looked into her eyes to speak. 'I'm sorry Soph. I didn't want to be the cause of such pain for you.' He kissed her softly on the mouth, then held her tight again.

ॐ

It was four in the afternoon when Stefan's phone rang again, but this time it was an unknown Australian number. He hesitated at first, thinking this could be another of Sophie's attempts to talk to him. She'd rung him several times that day, but he just wasn't ready to talk to her again. Then a sudden pang of anxiety kicked in as he realised how late it was back home, so he answered. 'Hello, Stefan speaking.'

The unexpected and unwelcome voice of Derrick chastised him. 'Would you stop being a tool and ring your sister? She's completely beside herself and neither Dom nor I can calm her down. Listen.' He moved the phone into range of Sophie's cries.

Stefan's heart broke at the sound of his sister's wailing. He'd never heard her quite this distressed before. It was devastating. *What could have her in such a state?*

Derrick spoke again. 'As much as it pains me to admit it, I know how much she loves you. While your whole incestuous relationship sickens me, I know it means the world to her. You're the only one with any hope of soothing her. So, if you still give a damn about her, just get over yourself and talk to her.'

Stefan almost couldn't believe what he was hearing. Derrick's recognition of Stefan and Sophie's love clearly ate at him, but the man was more concerned with Sophie's welfare than his own. 'Okay, put her on the phone.'

Her sobbing voice greeted him. 'Stefano?'

His heart melted at the sound. 'Yeah, it's me. What's wrong Sofia?' he asked her softly.

'It's Candice! She's… she's dead!' The intensity of bawling increased again.

He was gobsmacked. 'Oh, Fuck! I'm so sorry, Soph! I know you loved her. And that baby too. Wha… what happened?'

'A pregnancy complication. Some rare condition known as a placental abruption. Now she's gone.' Sophie's crying continued, but it was easing a little.

'Damn it! That's so unfair. I'm sorry. If it wasn't for me…'

'Please don't blame yourself Stefan. You

weren't to know. I'm sorry that you never had a chance to meet your son. The doctor told me the baby was a boy. He asked me if you'd like to name the kid; so, I told him I'd check with you.'

A son? His son? It all felt so strange. 'Oh Geez. Um, I guess I'll have to think on that a bit. I mean, of course I'd love to name the child, I just don't know what name. Something Italian maybe?'

'Yeah, I guess. Candice never mentioned any ideas for names.'

After a moment of thought, he asked, 'How about Gabriele? It's angelic, like his dear little soul now.'

'Sounds perfect.' Sophie's voice was much calmer. 'Rest in peace, Gabriele Pacini. I want to organise a funeral for them, Stefano. Will you help me?'

'Yes, of course. Whatever you need, Soph. I'll start looking into flights and get over there ASAP.'

'Really? You'll come home? What about Mamma?'

'To hell with her. This is more important, Sofia. I'll deal with Mamma. You just focus on plans for the service. I'll be there to help you and comfort you soon.' The thought of confronting Mamma terrified him, but he wasn't going to let that stop him; not when Sophie desperately needed him.

'Thanks Stefano. I love you.'

'I love you too, Sofia. Try to get some rest

now, okay.'

'Okay. Good night.' Then she was gone.

Wow. The news of Candice and his son dying was hard to bear, but the grief he felt was mixed with so many other emotions. Strangely, the one that prevailed above the others was hope. He was going home to Sofia at last. And her love for him was still stronger than anything she felt for Derrick. That much was clear by Derrick's resolute tone.

₧₨

Having already booked his flights, Stefan decided to ring his parents to let them know he was coming home. The first phone call was easy enough since Papà still didn't know about what had happened in Tuscany. He even offered to pick Stefan up from the airport and cover the fares.

Mamma didn't take the news so well. 'I understand your reasons, Stefano, but I'm also worried that you will both be-a tempted.'

'I don't think you need to worry, Mamma; Sofia is too grief stricken. We both have a lot to worry about for the time being. Even when we have recovered from our loss, I promise to try hard to win your trust. Neither of us want to get in trouble with the law.'

She sighed. 'Okay, but I will be-a watching you closely. And you will have to-a move into the guest room so that you are not too close to Sofia's room.'

'Whatever it takes. I must start packing now, but I'll see you soon. Ciao Mamma.'

'Ciao Stefano.'

Stefan arrived home late Thursday night. After greeting Mamma and dumping his luggage in his new room, he made his way upstairs. He was weary from travel, but he needed to see his sister more than anything. He found her on the gaming couch, curled up and crying in Derrick's lap. The sight of them together splintered his heart a little. But he pushed the pain aside as he took in the view. Sophie wore a red cardigan, short red and black plaid skirt, and black stockings. Even in her current state, she looked incredibly hot. Dom was also there—appeared exhausted and depressed.

Sophie looked up as he approached. '*Stefano!*' She flew into his arms.

He whispered a soft greeting, 'Ciao, Sofia.' Savouring the feel of Sophie's warm body pressed against him, he was filled with a sudden rush of desire. He moved his hands to cradle her face and looked into her sorrowful eyes. 'I've missed you so much!'

'Me too.' She pressed her lips to his.

Stefan was a little startled at first, given the present company, but his hunger for her outweighed his doubts. He responded by kissing her fervently. She tasted salty from tears, but her mouth still felt as soft and her movements were as feisty as he remembered. Stefan was only vaguely aware of Dom taking his cue to leave.

It was probably just as well Derrick seemed determined to stay because Stefan might have broken his promise to Mamma on the first night otherwise. Instead, he took his spot on the corner seat of the couch and cuddled Sophie. Glancing across to Derrick, his look was met by a green-eyed glare. He didn't really care how Derrick felt, but he did wish the atmosphere between them could be less awkward.

'Sorry, Stefan. I'd leave you alone, except Sofia already asked me to stay tonight to help her avoid temptation.' His tone was spiteful.

'It's okay, Derrick. I understand.' Stefan pressed his mouth to Sophie's ear and whispered, 'I don't want to rush things either, my love. Especially not when you are so fragile right now.'

'Thank you, Stefan.' Sophie replied faintly, then yawned and drifted off to sleep in his arms.

ഇരു

Dominic closed his front door quietly and snuck through the house to avoid waking anyone. He could have stayed at Sophie's, but he felt superfluous there. Between Stefan and Derrick, her needs were covered. Dominic's needs, on the other hand, were far from met. With all attention on the

Pacini family's loss, he hadn't been able to tell anyone about his own crisis. He couldn't bring himself to add to their burdens.

Slumping down on his bed, he grabbed his phone and flicked through the photos of Owen. He missed his beloved bohemian and couldn't believe how stupid he'd been to just let the man go. *Why couldn't I fight to hold on to someone so dear?* Instead, he'd taken the coward's way out. He'd even agreed to letting his dad set him up on a blind date with a nice Polish girl.

He lay back sighing. *How long can I keep up the charade?* Having tasted life—the way it could be—denying his very nature would be much harder this time. He hated himself for what he'd done to Owen, and even more for what he would continue to do. There was only one way he could see things working.

ഇരു

'Have you sorted out the music yet?' Stefan asked Sophie as she worked through the funeral plans. They were sitting around the breakfast table, swamped in paperwork.

She sighed. 'No. I have no idea what to do there.'

'Do you want me to find some songs? I know the bands she liked.' Stefan had provided plenty of emotional support, but he hadn't done a lot to help with the service directly thus far and felt the need to do something productive.

She looked at him and smiled. 'Yes. That would be great, thanks Stefan. We need music for the Entry, Reflection, and Ending.'

'On it.' He grabbed his laptop and started looking through the discographies of Katatonia, Anathema, Nightwish and Evanescence.

Derrick returned with lunch a few minutes later. After putting the food on the kitchen bench, he walked over to stand behind Sophie and started massaging her shoulders. 'Come on, Soph. Take a break and eat something.'

She dropped her pen and closed her eyes for a moment of relaxation. When she stood up, she hugged Derrick, then gave him a short kiss.

It was still difficult for Stefan to process the sight of them kissing, despite logic telling him not to worry. He knew that Sophie loved him more than Derrick, but he also hated sharing her. Ultimately, she was going to have to choose and there was only one way that she could safely opt for Stefan.

Sophie pushed the papers aside and brought the food over to the table. 'I still can't get hold of Dom. I didn't think he had other plans today, but I wasn't in a very receptive state yesterday. Do you recall him mentioning anything, Derrick?'

Derrick was back in the kitchen, pouring

drinks. 'No, sorry.' He brought the beverages over, offering one to Stefan.

A little surprised, he accepted the beer. 'Uh, thanks.' Then sat down to eat the pizza quietly.

As they were finishing their meal, Sophie's phone rang. 'Hello, Sophie speaking… Oh, hi Amelia…'

Stefan guessed she was talking to Dom's sister.

Sophie's visage suddenly paled. *'He did what?... Oh God no!... where is he?...* I'll be right there. Thanks for the call.' Tears were forming in her eyes when she hung up.

Stefan jumped up and pulled her into his arms. 'What happened, Soph?'

Her reply came between sobs. 'Dom… tried…ending it.'

Both Derrick and Stefan responded in unison, *'What?'* Then Stefan followed up, 'You said tried. So, is he okay now?'

She nodded. 'Physically yes, but… he's still… under suicide watch.' She looked into Stefan's eyes. 'Can you take me to see him?'

'Yes, of course. Come on, let's go.' Stefan had become good friends with Dom over the years too and was just as concerned for the guy's well-being.

'What do you want me to do?' Derrick asked.

'Um, maybe just get some rest. We'll still have plenty more to do later.' She kissed Derrick goodbye, then grabbed her bag and followed Stefan to the garage.

It'd been a while since Stefan had a chance to drive, but thankfully it all came back to him easily. 'Where to?'

'The Royal Melbourne,' she sighed. 'Again.'

Even though Stefan hadn't been home at the time, he knew what Sophie meant. Once they were driving, Stefan asked, 'What did Amelia say? Do you know what he tried?'

'He tried to… hang himself from the ceiling fan. It didn't take his weight, so he crashed to the floor with it. Amelia heard the noise and found him on the floor tangled up with the rope and fan blades. She panicked and called their parents into the room.'

'Shit. Nasty business. Did she say why?'

'No. Dom's been very tight-lipped about his reasons. I feel like such a shit friend right now. I should have been there for him to help him through his problems.'

Stefan briefly placed his left hand on Sophie's knee to reassure her. 'You can't blame yourself for this, Soph. You've been under a tremendous amount of stress. Life has been shitty for all of us lately. We just deal with things in different ways. Unfortunately, in Dom's case, he didn't think to seek help before letting things get this bad.'

'Yeah, I guess. I wonder if it had anything to do with Owen. Surely he would have gone to Owen for help otherwise.'

'Owen? You mean Tegan's friend? I didn't realise they'd become good mates.'

'Oh right, you still don't know about that. I wasn't sure about telling you because it wasn't my place and Dom hadn't gone public. I guess you may as well know now. Dom's gay and he's been dating Owen.'

'Well that explains a lot. I should've guessed really.' He'd always wondered about the man's obsession with pop music.

They found Dominic in a secure mental health ward. Sophie rushed in to hug him. She was crying again as she asked him, 'Why Dom? Why did you do it?'

There was some faint bruising around Dom's neck, but nothing obvious. 'Hi Soph, Stefan.' He paused for a deep breath, then told them, 'Dad caught me with Owen…' The recollection was clearly painful. 'He told me to straighten up else he'd disown me… Owen wanted me to move in with him, but I couldn't find the courage to break ties with the family…. I tried to be straight, but I just couldn't. It's been eating away at me since then.'

Sophie looked shocked. 'My God, Dom! Why didn't you tell me about this earlier?'

'I didn't want to burden you more. You've had so much on your plate lately.'

Surprise turned to horror on Sophie's expression. 'And how did you think I would've felt if my best friend had died as well?'

He looked very sheepish. 'I... I'm sorry Soph. I guess I didn't think of that. I haven't been right in the head lately.'

Sophie hugged him tighter. 'Please don't ever do something like that again. You can always talk to me. Always. Even if it means waking me up in the middle of the God-damned night. Okay?'

He sighed. 'Okay.'

Stepping forward, Stefan added, 'And if you can't reach Sophie, you can always call me. You ought to know I'll always have your back.'

'Thanks guys.'

Chapter Eighteen

The day of the funeral was finally upon them. It had been a week since Sophie started the planning. The uni semester was back on, but she obtained leave for the day, as did Stefan and Derrick. Unfortunately, Dom was still in hospital. They weren't letting him out until he finished some intense psychiatric treatment.

The service was a modest affair in a simple funeral home with very few attendants. Sophie's parents came along, mostly because of their unborn grandson. Ruby and Stefan's bandmates were the only other people there to see Candice off.

Sophie managed to hold it together right up until the eulogy, when Stefan stood up to say a few words. The tears started to flow as he spoke, and she felt Derrick pull her into his arms. When Stefan returned to the seat on her left side, he also embraced her as 'Passing Bird' by Katatonia began playing for the reflection. This was her last goodbye to both Candice and Gabriele, so she let it all out.

When they moved into the lounge for refreshments at the end, Sophie noticed that Stefan's eyes were also red from crying: a rare sight for him. She was surprised and wondered what aggrieved him the most. The last time she'd seen Stefan cry was at Nonna Lombardi's funeral four years ago.

Stefan must have noticed her looking at him because he walked up and asked, 'How ya holding up?'

'I don't know. I'm not even sure how I'm standing up. My head aches and I'm completely exhausted. How about you?'

'Much the same really. That was a lot harder than I anticipated.'

Sophie moved closer and put her arms around him. 'I can see grief in your eyes. I'm sorry I never realised how much they meant to you too.'

Wrapping his arms around her in response, he whispered, 'Losing a son I never knew was difficult, yes; but the hardest part of today was seeing you so hurt. Your tears are my tears, Sofia.'

Gasping, she suddenly wished they weren't in such a public place. 'I want to go home now. Will you take me?'

'Would that I could, but Derrick drove us here, remember? Besides, Mamma is eyeing us suspiciously. She wouldn't take kindly to the two of us leaving alone.'

'Damn it!' she sighed. 'Well I still want out of

here, so let's grab Derrick and go. Mamma can't complain about us leaving with him.' She approached Derrick. 'Can you take us home, please? I'm not feeling well.'

Derrick looked concerned. 'Yes, of course.'

They said their goodbyes to everyone else then made their way home.

Sophie bee-lined for her bedroom, where she kicked off her shoes and slumped onto her bed. Both Derrick and Stefan followed her, standing in awkward silence. They appeared to be waiting for her to tell them what she wanted. Looking at them both, she spoke. 'I need to rest in your arms.' They both moved forward, then stopped as they realised the other was approaching her.

'Whose arms, Sofia?' Stefan asked.

'Right now, I need both of you... to just hold me.' She wasn't in the mood for anything sexual — he just wanted to be surrounded by their love.

Derrick took his place beside her, but Stefan stiffened and stood stock still a moment. *Was it Derrick's presence, or the invitation to my bed that made Stefan hesitate?*

She gave him a pleading gaze. 'Mamma can't complain about hugs, Stefano.'

He eased a little, then snuggled in on her left side. Turning to face Stefan, Sophie pressed her lips to his. The ferocity of his reciprocation startled her a little, but she welcomed and appreciated Stefan's love and passion. There was even a small spark of desire, but she still wasn't ready. As their kiss ended, she nestled against Stefan's chest, drifting off to sleep with Derrick's warm body pressed against her back.

ℛℬ

It was dark when Sophie stirred. Stefan was no longer in her bed, but Derrick remained. She rolled over to look at him in the dim moonlight shining through a crack in the curtain.

He smiled and ran a hand through her hand. 'Welcome back, beautiful. How do you feel?'

'Much better, but also hungry.'

'Me too. We did skip lunch and dinner.' He stood up and offered her a hand. 'Come on, let's go eat.'

They made their way downstairs and found Stefan raiding the fridge. 'Hey. Are you guys hungry too?' he asked.

'Starved,' Sophie replied. She helped her brother assemble a dinner of leftovers, then sat down. When she looked at the clock it read 11:30PM. Her parents were likely to be in bed by this time but not necessarily sleeping.

As their meal concluded, Stefan sighed. 'We need to talk, Sofia. I've been putting this off because of the funeral plans, but I don't think it can wait any longer.'

She looked at him anxiously. 'Why? What about?'

'I think we should go upstairs first. Will you excuse us for a bit, Derrick?'

'Yeah, whatever.' He walked off to the family room and put the television on.

Sophie followed Stefan up to the gaming room and sat with him on the couch. 'So, what's this about?'

He spoke softly to avoid sound travelling. 'Have you made a decision about Derrick's proposal?'

'No, not really. I haven't had much time to think about it.' She hadn't much time for any personal reflection beyond her grief.

'As I figured. With Spain a viable option again, I want you to know that I'm not okay with sharing you. I hate having to put you in this predicament, but I can't pretend to be comfortable about your relationship with Derrick. I want all of you, Sofia.'

She closed her eyes. *Why did he have to put this pressure on me so soon?*

Stefan continued. 'That said, even if you choose to run away to Spain with me, it's going to take some time to organise. I'm talking months, maybe even a year. In the meantime, we would have to be extremely careful to avoid temptation. One wrong step could see our plans shattered like glass.'

'What are you saying Stefan?' She could feel him moving closer to her.

His hands gently squeezed her shoulders. 'Whatever your decision, we can't afford to consummate our love. Not here in Australia. The risk is too high. But if you choose me, I promise to put things in motion as soon as possible. I'm not asking for your answer now, but the sooner you decide, the sooner we could be free to love each other completely if that's what you want.'

She shot her eyes open and looked deep into his. 'That's what I want more than anything. I love you Stefano. If I can't have both you and Derrick, then I absolutely choose you, no question.'

His eyes lit up as he exhaled sharply. Then he pulled her in for an ardent kiss. This time the urges were much stronger, but she worked hard to resist them.

Stefan suddenly jumped back, grinning lustfully. 'I'd better go to bed before this goes too far. Good night, Soph. I love you.' He leaned in once more to plant a gentle kiss on her forehead.

'Good night Stefan. I love you too.' As he started to make his way toward the stairs, she stopped him. 'Stefan?'

He turned to look at her. 'Yes?'

'Can you send Derrick up here? I should probably break the news to him now.'

Clearly trying to suppress the glee in his expression, he bit his lip. 'Okay. Just don't tell him about Spain. We should probably keep those plans a secret.'

෨෬

The soccer match on TV was only engaging a fraction of Derrick's mind. He was anxious to know what Sophie and Stefan were talking about— if they even were talking, that is.

About ten minutes later, Stefan entered the room, a smug grin on his face. 'Sophie wants a word with you.' Then he walked off to the repurposed guestroom and closed the door.

His heart was pounding as he made his way upstairs. Judging by Stefan's expression, he figured the talk wasn't going to be easy. Sophie's bedroom door was open and when he walked through it, he found her sitting on her bed looking at something in her hand. As he drew closer, his pulse quickened when he realised what she was holding. *This was it, the moment of truth.* Taking a seat next to her, he asked, 'Sofia?'

When she looked up at him there were tears in her eyes. 'I'm sorry, Derrick.' Taking his hands, she placed the ring in his palm, then closed his fingers over it. 'I can't accept your proposal.'

She was clearly struggling, and it pained him to see her suffering. He looked into her eyes. 'Oh

God, Soph! Are you sure you want to do this now? So soon after the funeral? I can give you more time to think it over.'

'I don't need more time. I've made my decision.'

He moved closer to put an arm around her. 'Then why do you look so torn up over it?'

She didn't move. 'Because I still care and don't like hurting you.'

'Why the sudden decision though? Was this Stefan's idea?' *It had to be. Stefan was the one who'd initiated the talk, after all.*

'Yes and no. He was willing to give me time, but he explained his sentiments on the situation, which makes my choice obvious. You know how I feel about him.'

A bitter taste was developing in his mouth. 'You've made them abundantly clear, yes. But do you still love me? Because if you do, you know I'm willing to share you.'

'I know that, Derrick, but Stefan's not. I can only have one of you and my heart belongs to Stefan.'

'Do you know how absurd that sounds? You guys are siblings for Christ's sake. You could never openly love each other. The law won't allow it. At least I could shield you from public scrutiny.'

'There's no point arguing your case with me, Derrick. I want Stefan, but he will only be happy if he can have me to himself.'

'That selfish jerk! Sorry Soph, but he's being unreasonable and unfair. If that kiss of yours escalated, I was willing to let it happen. You guys could've fucked with me right here in bed with you. Yet Stefan won't see the sense in what I'm offering.'

Her jaw dropped. 'Geez, Derrick. So much for being my chaperone. As for the law, Stefan and I have plans. I can't go into them, but we've found a way to be together.'

'What? How?' His mind started racing. *What could they possibly do to get around the law?* Then it dawned on him. 'Shit! You're leaving the country, aren't you? Where are you going?'

Looking down again, she shook her head. 'I can't say. Please don't keep asking.'

His heart started breaking at the thought of losing her completely. 'Have you thought this through properly? It would be a huge upheaval for both of you. Living away from all your friends and the rest of your family won't be easy. What about your studies?'

'We have both given this a lot of consideration. There were complications before… before Candice…. Well, it was less possible then, but now… now we just need time to implement our plans.'

'How much time? When are you leaving?'

'I don't know. Maybe a few months, possibly

a year.'

A tiny sliver of hope ignited. He still had time to win her over and to convince Stefan of his stupidity. He lifted her face to peer into those beautiful big eyes. 'And what of us, Sofia? Does our love mean nothing?'

'Please don't do this Derrick.'

Touching his forehead to hers, he asked, 'Do what?'

'Make this harder for me.'

'I'm sorry Sofia, but I won't let you get away that easy. If you don't want me, you'll have to push me away. If you're willing to give up on us, you'll have to tell me you no longer love me.'

She pulled away from him and shrieked, *'Just stop it! I want you to leave.'*

He recoiled in shock. She'd never spoken to him like that before. Slipping back into his shoes, he stood up and left silently.

Once he was safely within the confines of his own yard, he screamed out of rage, anguish and frustration. With no hope of sleep, he headed straight for the gym: the only way he knew how to vent.

This was where Papà found him, collapsed from exhaustion at six in the morning.

৪০৫

Smiling as Sophie entered the hospital room,

Dominic jumped up to wrap his arms around her. 'Ciao Bella!' It was the day after Candice's funeral, and he figured she still needed comforting. Her tired, red eyes were the first clue.

She hugged him tight. 'Your mood seems much improved.'

'Yeah, I'm feeling much better and the doctor reckons I'll be able to leave tomorrow.' He was getting a bit stir-crazy in the lockup ward and was keen to be free of its walls.

'That's awesome! You should come and stay at my place for a bit. I imagine things are still a bit tense with your dad.'

She wasn't wrong. 'Really? That would be a huge help.'

'Of course. Mamma loves having you over. It won't be a problem. Plus, I could use your help with a delicate matter.'

'Oh?' He was suddenly curious.

'Stefan and I have decided to make secret plans to move to Spain as soon as possible; but in the meantime, we need to behave. Do you think you could be my roommate and help me resist the temptation to break the law?'

'Oh wow! That's huge Soph. The two of you moving out on your own—and to a foreign country. I know I'm the one that found this option for you, but I didn't think you'd act on it so soon. Such courage! Of course I'll help.' It got him thinking.

'Thanks Dom,' she smiled.

'You know what? It's high time I embraced my homosexuality. I figure if you guys can do something so bold, I ought to be able to manage moving into my own apartment and finding the means to support myself. Once you leave that is. I have an important job until then,' he said, offering her a conspiratorial nose tap.

'Yes indeed.'

'So, I take it this means no wedding bells with Derrick?'

Sighing, she sat in the chair beside Dominic's bed. 'That's right. I broke it off with him last night. He didn't make it easy, either. Even after I told him that I wanted Stefan instead of him, he tried to seduce me.'

Dominic gasped. 'That beast! Did you give in to him?'

'Not this time. I've decided that Stefan means too much to me to risk sabotaging our relationship further. It was one thing when we were living apart, but I won't rub it in his face anymore.'

'That's fair enough. I'm proud of you Soph.'

Chapter Nineteen

Two full months had passed since Candice and Gabriele's funeral. After a few minor hiccups, life had settled into a pleasant routine for Sophie. It helped that she was able to throw herself into her studies: a welcome distraction from the constant cravings for an unsafe level of intimacy with Stefan. But with exams done and dusted, they had the summer holidays ahead of them.

Their plans for Spain had progressed well. While their parents were out at church, Stefan sat at the dining table with Sophie to show her how things were looking. He'd made some smart financial investments that secured nearly all the funds they needed for the move. 'I've even arranged for our university transfers. I still need to secure accommodation and part-time jobs along with an exit strategy. If we want to avoid being traced, it'd be best to fly to another state first, then I'm thinking we go to Italy and catch a boat to

Spain.'

Sophie could barely contain her excitement. 'Not a bad idea. So, when do we start at the Spanish uni?'

'September, so we have plenty of time. I'm thinking the earliest I can get us over there is March, which gives us half the year to settle in and find some employment. That leaves me three months to find housing.' He looked up from his paperwork and gave her a sly grin. 'But that's also another three months of keeping my hands off you.'

She sucked in a breath. 'I don't know how much longer I can resist you Stefan. Days like today are the hardest: being alone together. Especially now that I've worked out how to get around Mamma's security cameras.'

He raised an eyebrow. 'Oh? I know I shouldn't ask, but I'm far too curious.'

She couldn't believe she was even contemplating this, but desperate times call for desperate measures. 'Well there's one room she hasn't got surveillance on because it's usually occupied at night and she probably didn't think we would dare.'

'Which room is—' he grinned. 'Oh, you dirty girl! You aren't seriously considering using their bed?'

Giving him her bedroom eyes, she replied, 'I think you'd be shocked if you knew half of the thoughts I've had lately. Like the fact that Mamma is unlikely to suspect us of doing anything in this very room. She's got footage of us coming in here together countless times and never questioned it.'

Stefan didn't need more encouragement. Grabbing Sophie, he pulled her into a frantic kiss. After wiping the table clean of papers, he lay her across it, and they continued kissing. Sophie was thankful for the table's solid hardwood construction as their bodies ground together. His track pants did little to hide the extent of his arousal.

A wide grin formed on Stefan's face. 'Hmm. It would seem that dinner has been served.' He lifted her short skirt and whistled softly as he took in the view of Sophie's completely waxed bikini line, scantily clad in a black G-string. He slid a finger under the tiny garment and pushed it aside. Then his mouth was devouring her.

Sophie had just reached her first climax when they heard the front door slam shut.

'Shit!' Stefan jumped off the table and quickly gathered up the scattered pages on the floor.

Dom walked into the room just as Sophie took her seat. She let out a sigh of relief. At least it didn't matter if he suspected anything.

After a quick glance at each of them, he asked, 'Am I interrupting something?'

Stefan stood up, holding his stack of paper in

front of his erection. 'It's okay, Dom. We probably needed that intervention.' Then he walked out.

Dom shot her a look. 'Seriously, Soph? The dining table?'

Biting her lip, Sophie blushed under Dom's scrutiny. 'We didn't get past the foreplay, if that makes you feel any better?'

'Marginally.' He left the room, then returned holding a spray bottle of disinfectant and a roll of paper towel. 'Here.' He shoved them in her hands, then sat down to watch her clean the table. 'Your parents will be home with lunch soon. At least we can use the kitchen table for that.'

As if on cue, the garage door opened and Mamma walked in holding several pizza boxes. They all assembled for Sunday lunch, the one meal that Sophie's parents insisted on having everyone together for.

After eating his first slice of pizza, Papà looked at Sophie sternly. 'So, I had an interesting conversation with Paolo Vianello this morning. He had a lot to say about you and Derrick.'

All eyes were suddenly upon her. Gulping, she chanced a glance at Stefan, who looked suspicious. Although he shouldn't have worried because Sophie was no longer interested in Derrick. 'What did he say?'

'That you broke Derrick's heart back in October and continue to do so. I asked him what brought this on, so he told me that Derrick had proposed to you and that you turned him down.'

Mamma cut in. '*What*? You never mentioned anything of this Sofia? How could you?'

Papà turned to Mamma and continued, 'Apparently Sofia's heart belongs to someone else. When I asked him who, he was surprised I didn't know and told me to ask you, Francesca.'

Fuck! Sophie gave Stefan a panicked look. He looked equally anxious. They both turned their gaze on Mamma

She rushed into an explanation. 'I'm sorry I didn't tell you Roberto. I was trying to protect our babies. That's why I wanted him to stay in Italia for the semester. When he came home early, he promised to be-a good. With Sofia dating Derrick, I didn't think it would-a be a problem. Plus, I've kept a close eye on them and haven't seen them try anything else. I even put cameras around the house.'

Papà's eyes gradually widened as she spoke. 'You can't possibly mean…' He turned his incriminating stare on Sophie 'Am I hearing her correctly, Sofia? Does Paolo mean Stefano?'

She lowered her head, eyes swelling.

'Answer me Sofia! Did you reject Derrick because you're in love with Stefano?'

Wishing she could shrink into the floor; all she could do was nod slightly.

He gasped. 'Are her feelings reciprocated, Stefano?'

Sophie peaked up at Stefan, who appeared terrified.

'Yes, but we haven't done anything, not since Tuscany.'

Closing his eyes, Papà cursed silently. 'Do you realise what a scandal like this could do to our family? If this got out, my firm would be ruined, Mamma could lose her job. We'd be as good as bankrupt.... Sofia, you must take Derrick back. Paolo is threatening to pull the pin on his contract unless I can convince you to accept his son's offer.'

Suddenly furious, Sophie screamed, '*What*? That's blackmail. How could you agree to such corruption?'

'I wasn't planning to, but that was before I discovered the full truth of the matter. If you don't agree to marry Derrick, Paolo could take this whole incestuous affair public.'

Stefan spoke up. 'You can't manipulate Sofia like this. We haven't done anything illegal and none of them have any evidence.'

Nothing except what just happened that day. But Stefan's lie sounded convincing enough.

'That doesn't matter. It's our word against that of a state minister. Paolo Vianello has decades of experience playing dirty political games, so don't think for one second that he would hesitate to destroy us in one fell swoop.'

Mamma was hysterical by this point and Dom looked like one of those sideshow clown games with the gaping mouths as he watched the conversation unfold.

Standing up suddenly, Sophie threw her napkin on the table and ran to her room. She collapsed on the bed and let her torrent of tears flow.

A few minutes later Stefan sat beside her, placing a hand on her shoulder. She curled up in his lap and sobbed. 'I can't believe Derrick told Paolo.'

Stefan sighed. 'I'm sorry Soph. I guess I should've seen this coming. I've never trusted that slimy bastard.'

'What do we do now?'

'There's really only one option, as much as I hate the idea. You need to pretend to accept Derrick's offer. Lead him on for as long as it takes me to finish raising the funds and making our plans.'

She sat bolt upright and looked into his eyes. 'What? Are you sure about this?'

Stefan frowned. 'Not really, but I can't see any other away around it.'

'I don't like it either, but I'll try. It'll be hard to hide my anger though.'

'Just vent with lots of sex. That ought to keep him distracted enough. And whatever you do, don't tell Derrick that you know Paolo spoke to Papà because he'll grow suspicious.'

'This is a seriously fucked up plan.'

'I know. I'm sorry Soph.' With that, Stefan pulled her back into his arms.

৪৩

Standing on the threshold to Derrick's house, Sophie felt incredibly nervous. Deception had never been in her nature. The first lie came when she'd promised her parents at breakfast that she would return as Derrick's fiancée. They bought it easily enough, but the hardest part was yet to come and knowing how perceptive Derrick was didn't help. The only way this was going to work was to push her anger aside and focus on the residual feelings she still had for the man.

Opening the door, he was a little surprised to see her. 'Ciao Sofia. Is everything okay?'

She focused on all the good times they'd shared together. 'Not exactly. Mind if I come in?'

He stepped aside to let her enter. 'Please do. What's wrong?'

Once inside, she looked into his eyes. 'I've missed you, Derrick. I miss us.'

Gasping, he drew close to her, placing his hands on her shoulders. 'What are you saying, Sofia?'

'I want you back. I need your love.'

'But what about your plans with Stefan?'

'I can't go through with it. The move would be too much for me, especially since it means leaving you. I've talked him round to your idea.'

His face lit up. 'Really? That's great news.'

Their lips collided in a crazed kiss. Sophie felt her feet leaving the ground as Derrick hoisted her up and carried her to his room. At least she didn't need to fake this part of their relationship. He knew exactly how to turn her on and make her orgasm countless times.

When Sophie opened her eyes again as she regained her senses, Derrick was straddling her, a wide grin covering his face.

He held something out to her as he spoke. 'Having done the romantic proposal already, I hope you don't mind me skipping ahead this time. Will you marry me, Sofia?'

Thankful for the lack of ceremony, she forced a smile. 'Yes.'

He placed the diamond on her left ring finger, then kissed her again.

§⃝Ↄ℞

It was dinner time when Sophie returned home, slamming the front door behind her. Everyone else was already seated at the table when she walked in. She looked directly at Stefan as she spoke. 'Well, it's done.'

He gave her an apologetic expression.

Mamma jumped up and hugged her. 'Thank you, Sofia. I hope you understand that this is for the best.' As they sat down, her eye was drawn to the sparkling bling on Sophie's hand. 'Is that the engagement ring?'

Sophie replied without enthusiasm, 'Yeah,' then shoved her hand under Mamma's nose.

She gasped. 'It's magnificent. If nothing else, Derrick will give you a very comfortable life. But I do hope that you will-a be able to make the most of his love too. He is clearly besotted with you, Sofia.'

Pulling her hand back, she frowned. 'Can we drop this topic now, please?'

They ate their meal in silence, then Sophie followed Stefan up to the gaming room.

After getting comfortable on the couch, Stefan pulled her into his arms 'How'd it go? Do you think he really bought it?'

'I think so. But it's early days yet. The test will come when I try to carry on with the charade.' She sighed, then continued, 'There's another complication to this plan.'

'Oh?' He sat up to look at her.

'Derrick wants me to move in with him… like immediately. I told him I need a day to think about it.'

'What? Where?' Panic spread across his face.

'One of the Vianello penthouse apartments.

They have one available in Southbank now. He promised me that you could visit any time and he'd give us the freedom to do whatever we wanted when you do.'

Hope returned to his visage. 'Isn't that a good thing? We won't have to skirt around these security cameras anymore.' He pressed his forehead against hers.

The sudden urge to kiss him became overwhelming. 'But what happened to being careful? Especially now that Paolo knows about us. I don't know if I can trust Derrick anymore, either.'

Running his fingers through her hair, their mouths were almost touching. 'Hmm, good point. I guess we shouldn't tempt fate any further. We've already broken the law once and almost got caught by Mamma. It's just so hard to resist you, Sofia. I can still taste you on my lips and I desperately want to make you come more.'

She sucked in a sharp breath. 'I'm pretty close right now. Where the hell is Dom when we need him?'

'I think he had a date. Just remember that Mamma is essentially watching us.' Stefan's other hand slid down between her legs.

Sophie groaned, knowing their huddled shoulders would block the camera's view of his wandering hand. 'Yeah, but she won't see the footage until tomorrow. By that stage it might be too late.'

He grinned. 'I guess you'll just have to stay still and try to keep a straight face. At least she isn't recording audio.' His fingers plunged inside her.

'*Oh God*!' Sophie was amazed by the intensity of her climax. She figured the necessity of restraint must have been a factor.

'Mmm, I can't wait to become better acquainted with this part of you, Sofia.' He removed his fingers after bringing her on a few more times. Then his tone became more serious. 'I think you should move in with Derrick. It would help convince him and Paolo that you mean to go through with the wedding.'

She was surprised that he would suggest further separation. 'What? Are you sure? It'll mean less time together.'

Pulling her back into an embrace, he whispered against her ear. 'At least there won't be oceans between us. We can still visit each other often and it's only a few months. Come March, we will be free to explore our love completely.'

'The idea still seems like a dream.'

ဆာ

Sophie had settled into her temporary accommodation by Christmas and was getting ready to celebrate her fake engagement and housewarming two weeks after that. Living with

Derrick had been better than she expected, and it was great to have all the freedoms that independent living offered.

Derrick walked into the bedroom just as she finished her makeup. He gasped. 'Wow! You look stunning.'

She chose a gold and white chiffon cocktail dress for the evening. 'Thanks.'

Enfolding her in his arms, he asked, 'Are you ready? A few guests have arrived and they're waiting in the lobby.'

Why did she feel so nervous? This was just a housewarming party, she kept telling herself. The engagement wasn't real. Slipping a hand in his, she feigned a smile. 'Yeah. As ready as I'm gonna be.'

They walked out to greet their guests, many of whom were seeing the place for the first time. Derrick had insisted on getting the place in order before letting too many people in. Stefan and their parents had been the exception because they helped with the move. Then there had been Derrick's promise to let Stefan visit often, which he had only done a couple of times. They were trying to play it cool, after all.

After greeting Papà and an ecstatic Mamma, Sophie smiled as Stefan stepped forward to hug her.

He whispered in her ear, 'You are a vision of pure beauty tonight.'

'Thank you, Stefano.'

When Dominic walked in, he ran to embrace Sophie. 'Oh my God! This place looks amazing! You have to show me around!'

'Yes, of course!' She led her friends and family on a tour of the spacious two-storey apartment that was decorated in light neutral colours and modern pieces of art. One of Sophie's favourite features was the breathtaking panoramic view of the city skyline and Yarra River that its floor-to-ceiling windows offered. As the tour concluded, she found herself captivated by the vista.

Moving up close behind her, Stefan spoke softly. 'I hope you're not getting too attached to this place.'

She spun around, noticing Paolo a few metres away, watching them suspiciously. She whispered, 'Shh, Stefano… be careful what you say in present company.'

Their conversation was cut off by the sound of Derrick tapping a spoon against his champagne glass. He caught her eye across the room and summoned her with an outreached hand. 'Ladies and gentlemen, I'd like to officially introduce my bride-to-be, bella Sofia.'

There was an applause as Sophie stepped up to join Derrick, who handed her a glass. She blushed as all fifty sets of eyes in the room turned towards her.

Sensing her nerves, Derrick pulled her attention toward him, speaking directly to her as he addressed their guests. 'As some of you may know, Sofia and I have been friends for as long as we can remember. It's funny how you can spend most of your life unaware that the very person you love the most is right in front of you.' He paused a moment, smiling at her. 'But that's exactly how it was for me. After almost eighteen years of friendship, I realised that this woman standing here with me now is the only one I've ever been in love with, the only person I can see myself growing old with. And it fills my heart with joy to know that she wants to spend the rest of her life with me. So, I ask you all to raise your glasses to toast our future happiness.' He clinked his glass against Sophie's, then sipped the sparkling wine in his glass.

Oh God, Derrick! Tears were trickling down her cheeks as she imbibed the zesty bubbles. His speech was so heartfelt that it stung to think of how much she was about to hurt him.

Wiping the droplets from her face, he whispered, 'Judging by these, I guess I nailed that speech.' Then he pressed his mouth to hers and kissed her gently.

Sophie could hear the throng roaring. When their lips parted, she chanced a glance at Stefan, who was doing a good job of maintaining his composure. He gave her an encouraging smile.

'Come on, Soph. I'll introduce you to some of my extended family.' Derrick dragged her through groups of aunties, uncles and cousins from both sides of his family.

One of Derrick's aunties asked, 'So when's the big date?'

Sophie had dreaded this question, but at least she was prepared for it. 'We plan to graduate from uni before we start planning the wedding.'

After a little more mingling, Derrick pulled her aside. 'You know I was thinking that we don't need to graduate first. We're already living together, so why wait? We could get married next month if we complete the paperwork next week.'

Suddenly filled with dread, Sophie panicked. 'What? That's too soon!'

'What's wrong, Soph?' He tried to reassure her by stroking her hair.

Shit! Think quick. 'I can't possibly plan a wedding in a month.'

'It doesn't have to be a big wedding. We could just go to the registry office with a couple of witnesses. I don't want to put too much stress on you. The important thing is that we become husband and wife and I'd like to do that as soon as possible.'

Her tears returned. 'But… I want a big Italian wedding.'

He pulled her into his arms. 'Oh, Sofia, I'm

sorry. I didn't mean to upset you. I just didn't think you'd want anything large and formal. Especially with how nervous you've been about tonight.'

He wasn't wrong. A huge, traditional wedding was the last thing she wanted, but it was the best excuse she could think of.

'I'll see what strings I can pull to get you that dream wedding sooner then. But I still think we should sign the notice of intent to marry next week. That gives us eighteen months to organise something and I'm sure we can pull that off. How does that sound?'

She breathed a sigh of relief. 'I think I can manage that.'

He beamed. 'Excellent. I love you, Sofia.'

೩೦ೞ

After walking through the door placarded 'Paolo Vianello', Derrick took a seat in the plush leather seat in front of the solid oak desk. 'Ciao Papà. You wanted to see me?' It was strange being summoned to the man's office.

'Ciao Derrick. Yes, thank you for coming here. I thought this was too important to wait until our next family dinner. Besides, I'd rather talk of this matter in private.'

His curiosity was piqued. 'Go on.'

'I have reason to suspect that the Pacini twins are plotting something and I fear that you are being played. I don't have any evidence yet, but with your permission I could put some of my men on the case for you.'

'You've got to be kidding me! Look, I thank you for your concern, but I don't think there's anything to worry about. I've already given them permission to screw around so long as they do so behind closed doors. That's always been part of the deal. Not that they've really taken me up on it yet.'

Papà looked shocked. 'I honestly don't know how you could be okay with sharing your woman. But that's beside the point. I don't think they're just fooling around. I overheard something yesterday, at your engagement party. Have you got Sofia to commit to signing the notice of intent this week?'

His pulse started racing. 'Yes, why? What did you hear?'

'Stefano said something about not getting attached to the place.'

Shit! Were they still thinking of leaving the country? It could explain Sophie's hesitation about getting married soon. 'I'm sure it's nothing, but if you're worried, I don't mind if you want to look into it.'

He gave Derrick a sly smile. 'Very well. And if you can convince them that your apartment is a safe place to play, it could work in our favour.'

Raising one eyebrow, Derrick inquired, 'Why, what are you planning?'

'Don't worry about the particulars, son. Just rest assured that I will do everything in my power to fulfil my promise. In the meantime, make sure you get that paperwork done this week and don't let Sofia know about our suspicions.'

Chapter Twenty

Stefan felt a slight pang of remorse looking at the poster on the door of The Old Bar in Fitzroy. The bands playing on that early February night were Infernal Sceptre, Raven Emblem and his own, Mobius Wing. Walking into his favourite live music venue, he stopped for a moment to take in the atmosphere. The décor was simple, with the dominant feature being the plethora of band posters covering the red walls.

Luke was already on the stage, setting up his kit. 'Hey man.'

After putting his gear down, Stefan shook his friend's hand. 'Can you help with the cab?'

'Of course.' Luke followed him out to the loading bay where they both lifted the Marshall amplifier from Stefan's car.

Chris and Silas arrived as they were carrying the gear inside. Once they were all settled in and ready to start sound check, Stefan looked at the other guys and sighed. He was definitely gonna miss them all: Chris with his anarchistic attitudes and bold behaviour; Silas, whose altruistic views and prodigious creativity were the perfect mix for his provocative song writing; then there was his best mate, Luke, who'd stuck by him since their first year of primary school.

Sensing his mood, Luke asked, 'You alright dude?'

'Not entirely. There's something I need to tell you all.' He put his Ibanez back on its stand. 'This will be my last gig with you guys.'

They all looked at him in shock. It was Luke who voiced their questions: 'What? Why?'

'I'll be leaving the country next month. But you guys have to promise not tell anyone.'

Chris piped up then, 'You ain't running from the law are ya?'

'No, not exactly.' *Not yet anyway.* And he'd like to keep it that way.

Luke appeared to understand. 'This is for her, isn't it?'

He nodded. 'Yeah.'

Chris became alarmed. 'Wait, who? Don't tell me you found some foreign chick on the Internet. I've heard horror stories about those hook-ups.'

'No, nothing like that. I know this girl very well.' Stefan started fidgeting with the capo he was holding.

Luke smiled. 'Did you guys find somewhere

more accepting of your love? That's awesome.'

A confused Silas finally joined in the questioning. 'This sounds like something that's been going on a while. Why haven't we met the woman, or even heard about her before?'

Stefan decided he could trust them. 'You have met her. She comes to most of our rehearsals.'

It took them a moment, but then the lights flicked on in both of their eyes.

Chris was the first to respond. 'Shit don't tell me you're boning your sister! That's seriously fucked up.'

Stefan frowned. 'Come on man, I didn't think you of all people would be opposed to the unconventional.'

Then Silas added, in his soft, drifty voice, 'Well I don't have a problem with it. What you guys do in your bedroom is no one else's business and I don't see why a bunch of stuck up politicians should dictate who you spend your life with.'

Chris was shaking his head in disbelief. 'Sorry dude, but the thought of sex with my sister is repulsive. I guess I just don't understand siblings being attracted to each other. And what about the risk of deformed babies?'

'Well Sophie and I don't really want kids, but if we change our minds in the future we would probably adopt.'

'Whatever man. Just don't go sucking her

face in front of me.' Chris chuckled, then threw a guitar pick at Stefan. 'You dirty bastard.'

After catching the projectile, Stefan laughed. 'We'll just send you our first homemade porn vid instead.'

They all roared loudly. Then Luke slapped Stefan on the back. 'Good luck, mate.'

'Thanks. It's just a shame that I can't stick around to help you all realise your dreams with this band. I've had a blast working with you all and I hope you continue making sweet tunes.' Stefan picked up his guitar. 'Now let's play some music.'

ഈൽ

Standing on the threshold to his sister's abode, Stefan's mind raced with anticipation and trepidation. He longed to hold her in his arms, to kiss her and touch her in all the places he knew would bring her pleasure. But he also feared the consequences of doing so before they made it to the safety of Spain. He still couldn't believe they would be on their way in just a few weeks. With that in mind, he rang the bell.

The door swung open to reveal an excited Sophie. 'Ciao Stefano.' She grabbed his hands and pulled him inside. Once the door was closed, she pressed him against it to give him a proper greeting.

As their fiery kiss concluded, he grinned.

'Mmm, that's what I call a warm welcome.' He scanned the room briefly. 'Am I the first to arrive?'

'No. Dom and his new boyfriend, Patrick, are here already. We're setting up in the upstairs lounge.' She led him through the living area to the spiral staircase.

Stefan decided to hang back a little and watch her ascend the steps. That short skirt did little to hide her white lace G-string as she climbed, which in turn revealed most of the soft skin on her curvaceous backside. The sight made his blood rush.

Halfway up, Sophie turned, likely wondering what was keeping him. When she caught his lascivious gaze, she grinned. 'I see you're already getting into the spirit of tonight.'

He caught up to her, pressing his aroused body against her back as he whispered, 'If this is just a taste of what's to come, I can't wait to see what else you have planned.'

She gasped, then turned to look into his eyes. 'Just remember we have new company tonight.'

When they reached the upper level, Stefan found the others seated around a large table. He frowned briefly when he caught Derrick's eye but moved his gaze away quickly. There were several stacks of party games on one end and bottles of spirits at the other.

Dom smiled as he approached. 'Hi Stefan.

This is Patrick.'

Patrick stood up and offered his hand. 'Hi Stefan. Good to meet you.'

'Yes, likewise.' He took the man's hand and received a firm shake. From a quick glance, Stefan discerned that Patrick was quite buff and probably a few years older than the rest of them. As they took their seats, he inquired politely, 'So, Patrick, do you work or study?'

He smiled warmly. 'I'm a retail business manager. What about yourself, Stefan?'

'Nice. I'm studying commerce. I plan to major in accounting.' Stefan decided he already liked Patrick.

'Smart move. There's always plenty of work in that area.'

The doorbell rang. Stefan watched as Sophie jumped up to answer it. Once she was out of sight, he turned his attention back to Patrick and Dom. 'So, how'd you guys meet?'

Dom blush a little as Patrick replied, 'Dominic became a regular customer at my store. How about you, Stefan? How do you know everyone here?'

'We all went to the same schools, although we didn't meet Dominic until high school.'

At this point Derrick leaned forward. 'Stefan is also Sophie's twin brother.'

Damn him! Stefan was hoping to omit that

detail.

'Oh really?' There was a curious expression on his face. He must have seen the way Stefan was perving on Sophie.

Shit! 'Yes, that's true. Although we're more like best friends than siblings.'

'Indeed. I've heard that's often the case with twins. Who's the oldest of you, out of interest?'

'I am. By about twenty minutes,' Stefan explained.

Sophie returned with Luke and his girlfriend, Emma. After another round of introductions, they all settled in for a game of King's Cup to break the ice. This was followed by The Game of Things.

As Things wrapped up, Stefan looked more closely at the other game options. There was a pile of games he didn't recognise, but their 18+ age ranges suggested a common theme. 'Who brought these curiosities?'

'That'd be me. I'm a bit of a collector. I guess it comes with the territory where I work,' Patrick replied.

Stefan raised one eyebrow in the man's direction. 'What area of retail do you work in?'

Patrick grinned proudly. 'The adult sector. I own and manage the Bedroom Delights emporium.'

'Good to know,' Stefan was a little relieved by the revelation, imagining that Patrick was probably quite open-minded.

Derrick was inspecting the pile of adult games and pulled out one entitled Let's Get Personal. He held it up for the group to see. 'This one looks interesting. Who wants to give it a go?'

'That one is specifically for couples, so it might be difficult with an odd number of players,' Patrick suggested.

Derrick put an arm around Stefan's shoulders. 'I'm sure we can make it work if Stefan here forms a threesome with Sofia and me. It could be fun to see who knows her better. Don't you think Stefan?'

He glared at Derrick. 'You're kidding right?'

'Not at all. Come on, Stefano, don't tell me you're afraid of a little friendly competition.'

'Oh, I'm not worried at all. I'm confident that I know her better than anyone.'

Amused, Sophie sat back and crossed her arms. 'I'm keen to see how this plays out.'

'Right. It's settled then,' Derrick declared as he put the game box in the middle of the table.

Patrick started setting up the game. 'Well to make things fair for the rest of us, I'm gonna rule that both Derrick and Stefan have to correctly guess Sophie's answers in order to advance. But Sophie can alternate her guess for each of them.'

'Good idea,' Luke agreed. 'Then they can tally their own points separately to work out who knows Sophie better.'

'Fair call.' Derrick stood up to grab some paper and pencils.

The game was progressing well, with Team Sophie in the lead. When the final round was upon them, Stefan was impressed that Derrick had managed to keep up with him.

As soon as the question was revealed, Derrick smirked. Of course, it had to relate to sexual gratification. 'Sorry Stefan—looks like I'll probably have this one in the bag. I mean, it's not like you'd know anything about pleasuring your sister, would you?'

Sophie bit her lip as she looked at Stefan.

He gave Sophie a cheeky grin. Perhaps it was the alcohol, but in that moment he didn't care what the others thought. 'That's rather presumptuous of you, Derrick. Have you chosen your response, Sofia?'

'Yes.' She put her answer card face down.

Stefan studied the options carefully. He may not have gone all the way with her yet, but he was confident that he understood her sex drive. She needed 'frequency,' that much was certain. It was harder to determine what meant less to her between her 'partner's figure' and 'time of day.' Given that both he and Derrick were well-toned, he decided that option was more important than 'time of day.' They all revealed their responses at the same time. As soon as Stefan saw that he chose correctly, he slapped the table. '*Yes!*' But then he saw that Derrick was also right.

Derrick's eyes narrowed on him. 'Looks like we'll need a tiebreaker round.' Then he looked at Patrick. 'What do you say, Patrick? Do you think you could come up with a bunch of adult questions for us? First man to answer incorrectly loses.'

Patrick laughed. 'Yeah, sure. And since you seem so confident, Derrick, you can go first. When did Sophie lose her virginity?'

'That's too easy. It was with me during Swot Vac in June last year.'

'Is that true, Sophie?' Patrick asked.

'Yes,' she replied.

'Okay, Stefan: does Sophie masturbate? And if so, how?'

Jesus! He wasn't holding back on the personal questions. 'Yes, she does. I'm quite certain she uses a vibrator among other toys, but she also enjoys using her fingers, given the right stimulation.'

Derrick looked surprised by his detailed answer. He wasn't alone.

Sophie giggled. 'Stefan nailed that one.'

Amusement was painted all over Patrick's face. 'Alright Derrick: has Sophie ever committed incest?'

He closed his eyes for a moment. Then looked at Stefan when they opened. 'Technically no—not to my knowledge.'

Sophie blushed. 'Sorry Derrick, but you're wrong.'

What the fuck, Sofia! Stefan looked at her wide eyed, heart racing as he began to panic.

'*What*? When?' Derrick cried.

The poor girl looked embarrassed. 'December last year, before we got engaged. But it didn't go all the way.'

Derrick shot a look at the others. 'The rest of you better not go blabbing to anyone else about this.'

'All secrets are safe with me,' Patrick assured them.

Luke gestured to Emma then Dom. 'The three of us already knew and haven't told anyone else. Nor will we ever.'

Derrick appeared to relax. 'Well now that we've cleared the air, I think it's time for another round of drinks.' He stood up and took a shot of whisky before refilling everyone's glasses.

'What's next?' Luke asked.

Sophie held up 7 Deadly Sins. 'This one has me intrigued. It looks like Trivial Pursuit meets Truth or Dare.'

'A pretty accurate way to sum it up and a fine choice,' said Patrick.

They all agreed to give it a go.

Stefan had to admit the game was a lot of fun, especially since his super competitive sister had to lose an item of clothing for every step closer to victory she got. It didn't matter so much to him that everyone else had to strip too.

As the game drew towards its conclusion, Derrick pulled Sophie into his lap, grinning as his hands moved to enclose her naked breasts. 'Looks like you just need a Lust token to win, my dear.'

'This should be good.' Sophie drew a Sin card and blushed. 'So, this is an all-play. Who else wants a Lust token?'

Patrick looked at the state of play. 'Well, so far only Emma and I have that one, so the rest of you still need it.'

'To claim this one, you'll have to subject yourselves to a French kiss from moi.'

'Oh damn,' Derrick jested. Then they kissed passionately.

Stefan figured he should get a bonus Envy token when he watched them.

Dom shook his head. 'You can count me out. No offence Soph, but Tegan put me off kissing other girls.'

Luke sighed. 'We can't make this too easy for her. I'll step up to the challenge. Sophie will have to pucker up to me if she wants to taste triumph.'

Stefan's eyes narrowed on his mate. 'Are you sure about this dude? Don't underestimate Sofia's ambition when it comes to boardgames.'

'Perhaps you undervalue mine,' Luke

grinned.

'Fine.' Sophie stood up and made her way over to Luke's lap. 'Just keep your hands to yourself.'

It was surprising to Stefan that rather than jealousy, he felt turned on by the sight of Sophie kissing his best mate. Maybe that was because he knew there were no genuine feelings involved — and because Luke wasn't Derrick.

Sophie kept the kiss brief. After standing up, she moved close to Stefan and looked deep into his eyes. 'Will you take part in this all-play?'

He sucked in a breath. Sophie stood before him in nothing but that white lace G-string. The tactical — prudent — play would have been denying her; but there were parts of his body that screamed out for her embrace. And they were louder than his logical thoughts. He gave her a lewd grin. 'Let's tie for first.'

She straddled him and brought her lips down on his mouth.

In a flash, Stefan forgot that everyone else was watching them. His body was on fire despite the chill of the air conditioning on his bare chest. Blood surged between his legs. His erection pressed against Sophie, trying to escape the satin boxers, his only remaining garment. Their kiss was fervent and incredibly erotic. She was thrusting against him, her own moist arousal evident. He was vaguely aware of some people leaving the room.

But Derrick remained. Kneeling on the floor, he pressed his body against Sophie's back and started kissing her neck. Then his fingers moved to her erect nipples.

Sophie jerked her head up as she cried, *'Oh God.'*

'Let's take this to a bed,' Derrick suggested as he tore her from Stefan's lap.

He felt a pang of disappointment as she broke away from him.

But then Sophie grabbed Stefan's hands and pulled him up. 'You're coming too.'

Stefan was dragged into one of the upstairs guest rooms where Sophie gently shoved him onto the bed.

Derrick grabbed her before she could join Stefan. His hands moved to the triangle of fabric that attempted to cover her pubis. Kissing her neck and shoulders, he let his fingers linger a moment beneath the white lace. Then he removed it and pushed her into Stefan's lap.

They kissed ardently for a few minutes, then Sophie propelled them both back into the bed and their bodies frantically entwined as they continued to make out. When they rolled onto their sides, Stefan plunged his fingers deep inside her.

Derrick, who was also naked by this point, took the opportunity to lay down and sandwich

Sophie between himself and Stefan.

Stefan sensed Derrick's hands on her backside, then realised they were reaming her. She convulsed, groaned, and growled as both men penetrated her with their fingers.

Then Derrick pressed his mouth against Sophie's ear. 'What do you want now, Sofia?'

'I want to be fucked. *I need to be fucked*!' she cried.

Derrick looked at him. 'Stefan?'

He suddenly froze. As much as Stefan wanted Sophie in that moment, something felt wrong. 'I… I can't. Not like this, not for our first time.'

'Suit yourself.' Derrick flipped Sophie onto her back, then drove himself inside her.

It was too much for Stefan to watch, so he made his way to the bathroom where he cooled off in the shower.

ഇന്ദ്ര

It was the twenty-fifth of February and the Docklands were alive with the spirit of Carnevale. Flamboyant floats and a full spectrum of glittering costumes were accompanied by music and dancing through the streets. It was a warm, clear night as Sophie passed through the crowds, among the food vans and gift stalls. She wore an intricate black lace butterfly mask and classic little black dress.

Two men walked alongside her. Derrick wore the traditional *Comedia dell'arte* costume of Il Dottore, while Stefan wore a Venetian Harlequin outfit.

As they neared a jewellery seller, Derrick commented, 'Hey Soph, that necklace looks like yours.'

Stefan stopped and looked the place over. 'That's because this is where I bought it.' He turned to Sophie, pressing his body against hers, then reached for the pendant around her neck. 'This is like our six-year anniversary, in a way.'

She giggled, thanks in part to all the Lambrusco she'd indulged in. 'Yes, I guess it is.'

Derrick moved in close behind Sophie. 'Why? What happened six years ago?'

'That's when I realised how much I wanted Sofia. So, I bought this,' Stefan replied, still holding the tiny gold mask.

'And when I started dreaming of you,' Sophie looked directly into Stefan's eyes as she spoke.

'And yet you guys still haven't fucked, despite having free run of the apartment.' Derrick's fingers glided along Sophie's neck. 'I don't think even I'd have the willpower to resist Sofia after all that time.'

Being flanked by the two of them sent an exhilarating rush through Sophie's body. She was reminded of their hot gaming night earlier that month.

Stefan's eyes remained fixed on her. 'Geez, Derrick, I knew you'd resigned yourself to accepting my relationship with Sophie, but it sounds like you want us to do it.'

'I just want her to be happy.' Running his other hand down her side, Derrick lowered his voice. 'Tell us Sofia, do you still want Stefano? Do you need your brother to fulfil your desires?'

Even for the middle of an Australian summer, the heat rising in Sophie's body felt unreal. 'By God, yes.'

There was a fire in Stefan's eyes.

'Then what are you waiting for, Stefan? Let's get out of here.' Derrick led Sophie toward a taxi. He even took the front seat so the twins could sit together.

As soon as the car was moving, Stefan grabbed Sophie's hand. Throwing his mask aside, he pulled her in as close as their seatbelts would allow. 'Are you sure about this?'

Ignoring the faint warnings that sounded in her subconscious, Sophie let her carnal cravings reply, 'Yes.' She pushed her own mask on top of her head, then leaned in and kissed him. There was a strong taste of wine on his breath too. Closing her eyes, she focused on the incredible feeling of Stefan's mouth colliding frantically with hers, the sensations coursing through her body wherever his fingers met her skin.

It was just as well the drive home to Southbank was a short one because Sophie didn't know how much longer she could wait. Their lips parted just long enough to walk through the lobby and ascend the lift.

As soon as the apartment door closed, Stefan was upon her again, pinning her against the wall in the open-plan living area. Their hands worked manically to undress each other.

Sophie was only vaguely aware of Derrick watching them from the lounge. She was glad that he left the two of them to it this time. When the last of Stefan's costume fell to the floor, she whispered, 'I want you to take me to bed.'

The only reply Stefan gave her was a wide grin as he picked her up and carried her to the bedroom.

Sophie was naked except for the butterfly mask that was still on her head somehow. As he lowered her to the bed, she tossed the mask to the floor and let Stefan overwhelm her senses. Then the moment they'd been waiting for came at last.

℘℺

Sophie lay in bed listening to the approaching storm. A sudden clap of thunder and the room lit up, then the sound of rain bucketing down. As she looked at the clock, she saw someone opening her balcony door, letting the chill air touch her hot skin. Her heart started racing. Stefan locked the door behind him, then rushed to her. She pulled him down upon her and their lips came together. He smelled of sandalwood cologne, layered with the familiar scent of his spicy shower gel. Sophie loved the feel of his stubble scratching her skin; welcomed the caress of his calloused fingers as they explored her body, starting from her face and gradually working their way down. When they reached their destination, Sophie cried out as she convulsed with pleasure. 'Oh God, Stefan!' He brought her to climax repeatedly until darkness overcame her…

It was Derrick's familiar voice that woke Sophie. Rolling over to face him, she was partially blinded by the light streaming in through the cracks in the shutters. She felt extremely hot and sticky. Given the amount of moisture between her legs, she wondered if her fingers had been busy during her dream.

He was kneeling beside the bed. 'Hey Soph. I'm just heading out to meet some friends for brunch. Feel free to stay and play or rest more if you need.' He kissed her on the forehead, then walked out.

She turned back to face Stefan, who still slumbered. Even though she'd seen him sleep countless times over the years, there was something altogether different about the sight of him. Quite aside from the fact he was completely naked beneath the sheets—a detail she delighted in checking—there was the memory of the night they'd just shared.

'I can feel you watching me,' Stefan spoke without opening his eyes. It startled her every time he did that. 'Come here you.' Opening his eyes, he pulled her into his arms.

Sophie giggled with delight. 'We have the house to ourselves for a bit.'

Grinning, Stefan's hand started working its way down her back. 'I know, I heard Derrick.'

She gasped. 'You've been awake this whole time? Why didn't you speak up sooner?'

'And deprive you of your voyeuristic pleasures? That'd be quite insensitive of me.'

'Stefan! You scoundrel!' She giggled, then attempted to wrestle him. But it had been years since she could overpower her brother.

Pinning her to the bed, Stefan's expression became more serious. 'God, I love you Sofia.' He kissed her briefly, then spoke softly in her ear: 'Last night was incredible, but our senses would have been dulled by all that wine. Now I'm gonna make love to you with all my faculties.'

Sophie groaned loudly as their bodies melded, then she cried out her brother's name as he brought her to climax. Sex with Stefan was beyond amazing. It was like he knew all her pleasure points and gave each of them his attention. Perhaps this was because they were two halves of a whole. Another term occurred to her just before she lost access to her higher brain functions entirely: soulmates.

They snuggled together for a few minutes after. When Sophie could fathom walking again, she made her way to the ensuite bathroom. Upon returning she asked, 'Are you hungry? I definitely need food.'

Stefan just grinned widely.

'What?' she asked.

Standing up, he put his arms around her, his hands on her bare backside. 'I passed the third challenge for real this time.'

After a minute of thought, she realised he was right. She could recall crying 'yes' as well as his name a few times. Smiling at him, Sophie replied, 'You must have unlocked a secret part of me.'

He raised one eyebrow. 'You mean *another* secret part of you. As for your question, yes, I'm famished. You go on, I'll join you in a sec.' Then he kissed her forehead gently before heading into the ensuite.

Sophie slipped into her silk robe, then practically floated out to the living area. But her blissful reverie was cut short when she found Paolo Vianello sitting at the dining table. Panic took over.

'Um, hi Paolo, what… how did you…'

He took a full minute to look her up and down, apparently pleased by the sight of her scantily clad figure. 'Hello Sofia. I have my own set of keys for this place, so I let myself in.'

Woah talk about creepy! Sophie shivered. 'I'm afraid Derrick is busy just now.'

He advanced on her. 'Oh, I know. I saw him leaving for brunch. But that's okay, because I'm here to see you, Sofia.'

Shit! 'So, you've been here the whole time.' Sophie gulped. 'Did you… uh… hear?'

A sly grin spread across his face. 'I didn't just *hear* you and your brother. It was quite the arousing show.'

Subconsciously stepping back as Paolo moved toward her, Sophie suddenly found her back against the wall beside the bedroom door. 'What… what do you want?'

Catching up to her in a flash, he pressed his body against her. 'That's a very good question. Because what I desire most this moment is directly at odds with the purpose of my visit. I'm beginning to understand how you could have my son so enthralled.' He moved one of his hands to her thigh while the other stroked her face.

'Get the hell away from her!' Stefan cried the moment he stepped through the door. His hands flew to the man's neck.

Paolo shrugged Stefan away. Then he made Sophie shriek as he grabbed her violently. 'Or you'll what? Call the police? I'm sure they'd be interested in the photos on the dining table. Why don't you look for yourself, Stefano?'

Sinking into a dining chair, Stefan examined the evidence. *'Jesus Christ!'*

The villain gave Sophie a victorious smirk. 'Oh, I don't think our dear Lord will be saving either of you now.' The brute of a man dragged Sophie over to the table and pulled her into his lap as he took a seat. He then proceeded to open her robe and fondle her breasts.

Sophie could see the pained, horrified look in Stefan's eyes, and she couldn't tell if the tears streaming down her face were more for him or herself. She glanced at the photos just long enough to confirm her fears. They must have been taken the previous night.

Paolo adopted more of an officious tone as he continued, 'It has come to my attention that the two of you don't intend to stick around much longer. Is that true?'

They both replied in unison, 'What? No.'

He dug his long fingernails into Sophie's right nipple, which made her scream in agony. 'I find that hard to believe, but just to be sure, I'm going to have to insist that Sofia marry Derrick immediately. I can't understand why he'd want to be wed to such a defiant whore, but apparently there is nothing he wants more in this world. And I've always given my son whatever he wanted.'

There were tears in Stefan's pleading eyes. 'Please stop hurting her.'

Paolo stopped touching her breasts, but he maintained a hold of her. 'Sofia, you will marry Derrick tomorrow. It has been at least a month since the notice of intent was signed, so it can be done. And I will be watching you closely. If you ever make any moves to leave Derrick, the police will be hearing from me.'

Stefan glared at him. 'And how is that going to help Derrick's cause? His bride will be locked away too.'

'You forget who you're talking to, Stefano. With some selective photo choices, I can convince my friends in the force that Sofia did not consent to your advances. You'll be the only one going to prison and for more than just incest.'

The thought filled Sophie with dread. *What? I'd never testify to that!*

'You won't need to.' He stood up and threw Sophie to the floor. 'Now, have I made myself clear? Do you both understand my terms?'

'Perfectly,' Stefan replied coldly.

Sophie responded between sobs, 'Yes.'

'Good. I'll see you at the registry office tomorrow, Sofia.' With that, Paolo left the apartment.

'That bastard!' Stefan flew to her, picking her up in his arms and taking her to the couch. His own tears joined Sophie's as he pressed his forehead to hers. 'I'm so, so, sorry Sofia. I never should have trusted Derrick. I should have waited.'

'Don't blame yourself, my love. We both wanted it. We needed last night and this morning. If anyone's to blame, it's me. I never should have returned to Derrick's arms. Now we are both doomed.' The impact of her realisation hit her hard. It was like being punched in the gut and winded. She curled up in Stefan's lap and wept uncontrollably.

Once she was able to calm down a little, Sophie sat up and pressed her mouth to Stefan's ear. 'You should go on ahead without me. We've gotta get you out of Australia before Paolo gets the cops involved.'

'What? No! I can't leave you again.' He looked extremely distressed.

'Please Stefan. I can't bear the thought of you being imprisoned. It would break me beyond repair. I promise I'll catch up with you.' She just hoped it would be possible.

'I don't like it, but you're right. They won't be able to catch me if I'm gone when you trigger the alarm.' Stefan looked up when the front door opened.

When Derrick entered, he rushed to her. 'Oh God, Sofia. What's wrong?'

She tensed when his hand touched her back. How much of Paolo's scheme did Derrick know about? Was he complicit in the whole horrid plan to trap her in a loveless marriage? She decided he was no longer worthy of the truth. 'Mamma is sending Stefan away again. And this time it's for good.'

Derrick sat beside her and Stefan and put his arms around her. 'I'm so sorry, Sofia. I didn't think she would find out. I just wanted for all of us to be happy together.' There was a hint of guilt in his voice.

If their plan was going to work, Sophie needed to be convincing. Sitting up, she climbed out of Stefan's lap and embraced Derrick. 'I've decided I want to get married tomorrow. Before Stefan is sent packing. Having my brother present is more important than a big elaborate party.'

Derrick gasped. 'Are you sure?'
She looked into his eyes. 'Yes.'

Chapter Twenty-One

Mamma sat with Sophie in the waiting room, shaking her head. It was fortunate that Sophie was able to find an off-the rack-satin bridal gown that fit in such short notice else the woman might have had a heart attack. 'This is not-a how I pictured your wedding day turning out.'

She even felt a pang of pity for her. 'I'm sorry, Mamma.'

Mamma almost fainted when Sophie and Stefan explained that they had been caught in the ultimate act of incest by Paolo Vianello and that Stefan had to flee the country. Then Sophie told her about the urgency of the wedding ceremony, and she broke down in conniptions.

It was the looks of disapproval Mamma kept giving her that day which cut the hardest. Sophie could shrug off the words; had spent her life learning to ignore the woman's rants. But at the end of the day, she knew Mamma loved both her and

Stefan more than anything in the world and she hated being such a disappointment.

Papà entered the room. 'They're ready and waiting. You can make your entrances, Francesca and Stefano.'

Her brother, who had been quietly supportive all day, stood up. 'Can you just give us moment?'

Papà sighed. 'Make it quick.' Then he escorted Mamma out.

Sophie stood up and adjusted her layers of skirts.

'You look beautiful, Sofia.' Stefan moved close to her and drew a hand up to her face. 'I know you were never one to fantasise about fairy-tale weddings, but I'm still sorry that this day isn't even close to what you might have imagined; what I'd hope this day would be for you.' Leaning in, he pressed his forehead against hers. 'I just wish this could've been us on a Spanish island.' It sounded like he was choking back tears.

'This still could be us one day.' It felt strange having to be the strong one for Stefan, especially on her supposed wedding day. But if the last few months had taught her anything, it was that true love didn't need rules or conventions. There were no roles for couples to adopt. What really mattered was the opening of one's heart. Letting your partner in and being completely honest with each other.

With a foundation of trust, lovers can cling to each other through the maelstrom of life.

He kissed her gently on the lips, then stood back and lowered her veil. He tried to put on a brave face. 'Just as well Papà's the one giving you away because I don't think I'd be able to let you go.'

'Could make for an awkward ceremony.'

There was a knock on the door, then Papà entered. 'It's time.'

The small gathering of friends and family rose to their feet and looked at her as Sophie entered the modest, yet elegant room fitted out with Georgian décor. Two men dressed in tuxedos were playing a tune that Sophie had come to recognise as Pachelbel's Canon in D on piano and violin. It reminded her of the debutante ball. *Wow! That was only ten months ago. So much had happened since then!*

Sophie tried to focus her attention on Derrick's huge grin as she walked down the aisle. But she kept glancing at Stefan who also stood up front. She had chosen him as her attendant and witness. It was too hard to organise bridesmaids with such short notice. Besides, he was the best person to be supporting her through this charade.

When they reached the front, Papà stood beside her a moment as the civil celebrant, a blonde middle-aged woman in a business suit, asked, 'Who brings this woman to be married to this man?'

'I do,' he replied, then released her arm and

took his seat.

Derrick took her hands and whispered, 'You look breathtaking, my dear.'

Then the celebrant introduced herself as Deborah and began babbling words about commitment. A minute later she asked the two of them if they came voluntarily, without reservation, etc.

Wishing she could cross her fingers, Sophie just squeezed Derrick's hands as she lied through her teeth. 'Yes, we do.'

After some more legal nonsense, it was time for the vows. Derrick went first, reciting the words fed to him by the officiant as he looked lovingly into her veiled eyes. Then it was Sophie's turn to make her false promises of a life filled with love and devotion. The words burned her throat like acid as she spoke them.

Deborah addressed Derrick's cousin, who was there as the Best Man: 'Marcus, can you please bring the rings forward?'

He stepped forward and handed a ring to Derrick.

As Derrick slipped the gold band on her finger, he repeated, 'Accept this ring with all my love.'

Then Marcus handed the other ring to Sophie. Her hand shook as she tried to bring it to Derrick's left hand.

As if sensing her anxiety, Derrick steadied her hand and helped direct her aim.

'Accept this ring with all my love.' She breathed a sigh of relief as the words and the ring met their mark.

A brief conclusion was followed by Deborah inviting the couple to kiss.

Derrick lifted her veil, then pulled her into a tight embrace as he pressed his lips to hers without restraint.

Sophie felt sickened by his passion and wondered how she would cope with consummating their marriage.

After signing the certificates, Sophie was ushered out to a cocktail reception at the Vianello mansion.

A few speeches and formalities later, Sophie was free to mingle.

Dom bee-lined for her. 'Oh my God, Soph! I can't believe you're a married woman! Congratulations.' He threw his arms around her. 'I'm amazed at how quickly this all happened.'

'Thanks Dom. I still can't believe it either.' She bit her lip before letting anything slip. It killed her that she couldn't even tell her best friend about Paolo's blackmail.

'So why the sudden rush?'

She grabbed his arm and pulled him into an empty office. 'Stefan and I couldn't resist each other any longer. But the wrong people found out and now he needs to leave the country.'

'Dear Lord! That's horrible! I'm so, sorry.' He hugged her. 'But I'm confused. Why the sudden wedding?'

'I wanted Stefan to be here for it before leaving.' She started tearing up.

He offered her a compassionate look. 'But if you love Stefan so much, why aren't you going with him?'

'Because I can't, okay? I just can't. Please don't ask any more questions.' She started crying.

A gentle tap at the door was followed by Stefan entering. He rushed to take Sophie from Dom's arms. 'Did she tell you?'

Dom heaved a huge sigh. 'Only a fraction of it. I know you're leaving and that there's something sinister going on, but she couldn't tell me what. Now I'm seriously worried for you guys. How much trouble are you in?'

Sophie clung to Stefan for dear life.

His grip was strong and reassuring, unlike his words. 'Well I'm not a fugitive yet, but a lot of planets will need to align for things to remain that way.'

The door suddenly flew open and Derrick stepped inside. 'So, this is where the party's at. Mind if I...' He froze, noticing Sophie's tears.

She felt his hands on her shoulders, trying to

encourage her into his arms. But she resisted, clutching Stefan tighter.

'Sofia?' Derrick's tone was tender. 'Did you want to go home?'

'Only if Stefan comes with us.'

Stefan gasped. 'Is that such a good idea? After everything that's happened, I mean.'

'I know a way to sneak out here, if that's what you're worried about,' Derrick assured them. 'Come on.'

He led them to the window, which opened onto a private courtyard. Beyond the gate there was a small path lined with tall hedges. From this, they reached the service road where they found a four-door ute. 'I used to sneak out of the house this way during our high school years,' Derrick explained at they all piled into the vehicle. 'Papà still doesn't know that I have the keys to this thing.'

Derrick dropped Dom home first, then made haste for their Southbank apartment.

Stefan was holding Sophie in the back seat. 'I'm still not sure about staying for your wedding night, Soph.'

She looked at him with imploring eyes as she whispered, 'Please Stefan. I need you. Besides, it's not like we could make things any worse.'

He kissed her forehead. 'Okay.'

₧⁂ℂℛ

Dread and sorrow prevailed in the sea of emotions Sophie felt as she entered Terminal 1 of Tullamarine airport. She didn't know how long it would be before she had to opportunity to follow Stefan. With Paolo constantly breathing down her neck, it had been hard enough getting away just to see him off.

As they approached the check-in desk, Stefan leaned in close to whisper, 'You know I booked these flights ages ago. There is still a ticket with your name on it. You could just collect a boarding pass with me, and we could be on our way to freedom together.'

Hope surged through the storm. 'What? Really?' Sophie froze to think things through. Then the obvious occurred to her: 'Shit! I wish I had my passport!'

Stefan smiled. 'You do. I put it in your handbag just before we left. I also threw a few of your old clothes from home in my luggage.'

Barely able to contain her excitement, Sophie threw her arms around him. But paranoia kicked in just in time to hush her voice as she replied, 'You're a fucking genius Stefan!'

He held her close, his lips touching her earlobe. 'I don't know if Paolo has anyone watching us, so just keep playing it cool and let me take your boarding pass.'

'Okay.' She couldn't believe it. Just when she thought all was lost for them. It suddenly felt like there were springs in her heels.

৯০৫

Derrick was surprised to see his old man waiting for him as he pulled up in the parking lot beneath his apartment. 'Papà?'

A worried expression crossed the man's face. 'What are you doing home, son? Shouldn't you be comforting your wife in her moment of need?'

'What do you mean?'

'She's at the airport saying goodbye to her beloved brother.' He spat the last two words with disgust.

Panic rose, his heart pounding. 'Shit! I thought that was tomorrow.'

Papà opened the driver's door of his black Mercedes. 'Quickly then. I'll take you.'

Derrick jumped into the passenger seat and buckled in as the car sped out of the building. They made record time. Within twenty-five minutes Derrick was walking through the large glass doors of Melbourne's airport. He figured Papà would know how to get out of any speeding fines he might have incurred on the way. Then confusion set in when he noticed that they were in the domestic departures area. 'Shouldn't we be heading to Terminal 2?'

'My sources tell me that Stefan is going to Sydney first.'

'Hmm, that's odd. Why would Francesca do that?'

'Because she didn't book the flights. Apparently, Stefan arranged this months ago.'

'What? But then....' Realisation suddenly hit him like a kick in the balls. They reached the security check. He went to join the queue, but Papà walked straight on up to the guards.

One of them smiled at the Vianellos. 'Good evening, Minister. Please step right on through.'

As they ran toward the gate, a woman's voice boomed over the PA. 'This is the last call for passengers boarding flight QF 494 to Sydney...'

Then he saw Sophie standing in line with Stefan.

෪ඊ

Sophie was keen to get on the plane as soon as they reached the departure lounge, but Stefan advised against it. They needed to wait until the last minute. That would hold suspicions at bay and give Paolo's goons less time to react.

But then the final boarding call came, and her heart almost leaped out of her chest. There was still no sign of trouble. The moment of truth was upon them. They joined the small line of late commuters. She just hoped her feeble attempts to act bereaved as she held Stefan were convincing enough.

'Shit!' Stefan's whole body stiffened.

When Sophie looked at him, his expression was one of pure terror. She turned to face the direction of his gaze and understood why. Derrick and Paolo were approaching them. *Fuck!*

'Boarding passes please.' A woman in a black and red Qantas uniform extended her hand toward them.

Stefan looked at her urgently, his eyes pleading with her.

But she knew what she had to do. Paolo had discovered Stefan was going to Sydney first. He probably had men over there waiting for them. Tears filled her eyes as she kissed him one last time. 'Just go, Stefan. I'll distract them.' Then she ran to Derrick, fleeing her dear brother's arms, towards the man she had come to hate and resent in a matter of weeks; away from the man she loved — the only soul that could make her truly happy.

When she crashed into Derrick's arms, Sophie turned to watch Stefan embark. Sobbing violently, she no longer needed to fake her grief.

But then Paolo's hands seized her. 'Were you about to go with him, Sofia?'

'No.' She shook her head vigorously.

He grabbed her handbag and retrieved her passport. 'Then what's this doing here? Derrick, check her pockets and whatnot for a boarding pass.' He continued to rifle through her bag.

'I always carry that in my handbag,' Sophie protested.

Derrick looked at her apologetically. 'I'm sorry Soph.' Then he started patting her down. As soon as he'd finished, he embraced her again. 'She's clean.' He pressed his mouth to her ear. 'I'm so, so sorry. I panicked when I saw you in that line. I thought Stefan was leaving tomorrow. Why didn't you bring me along to support you?'

'I... I wanted to be alone with him. For a proper goodbye. I... I didn't realise how hard this would be. Thank you for coming just in time.' It was getting a lot easier to lie to him.

'Let's get you home then. Is your car here?'
She nodded.

'I'll drive.' He turned to Paolo. 'It's okay Papà. I can take it from here.' He grabbed her bag from him and handed it to Sophie.

Sinking back into the leather upholstery of her Maserati, she closed her eyes and tried to think of how she was going to make her plan work. Stefan had always been the practical twin. She had the book smarts and game logic. He had the common sense and creativity. Her thoughts were interrupted when a text came through. She hoped it wasn't Stefan. His phone should still be in flight mode. Relief filled her for moment when she saw the unknown number. But then she read the message:

I BET YOU AND YOUR BROTHER THINK YOU'RE CLEVER. BUT YOU FORGET WHO YOU'RE DEALING WITH. THE EVIDENCE IS WITH THE POLICE NOW, SO IF STEFAN RETURNS TO MELBOURNE, HE WILL BE ARRESTED. AND IF YOU SO MUCH AS SET FOOT ON FOREIGN SOIL WITHOUT DERRICK I WILL HAVE STEFAN EXTRADITED. AND DON'T THINK FOR ONE SECOND THAT I WON'T KNOW WHERE TO FIND HIM. I HAVE TAPS ON ALL YOUR PHONES FOR ONE THING.

No! Sophie doubled over in pain. It felt like someone had winded her. Then the contents of her stomach violently tore themselves up through her oesophagus and dropped to the floor of the car.

'Shit! Oh God Sofia!' Derrick swerved for a moment, distracted by Sophie's reaction. Then he pulled over on the nearest side street. He lifted her out the car and nursed her as she continued throwing up all over the verge. 'I'm calling an ambulance.'

After wiping her mouth with her arm, she turned to Derrick. 'Don't. I think that's all of it.'

'I guess you're in shock.' There was genuine worry in his expression. *How can such a villain still show empathy?* He helped her back to the car, putting her in the back seat to avoid the mess.

When they got home, he took her straight to the shower. After washing her hair and scrubbing her body, he just held her as the water cascaded over them. His own body shook with her convulsions. 'I love you Sofia. I love you so much. It breaks my heart to see how much this separation hurts you. But I need you to be honest with me. Why did Stefan leave? I know your mamma had nothing to do with it.'

Glaring at him in disgust, she spat her response. 'Don't pretend like you don't know.'

He staggered in response to her hateful outburst. 'What am I supposed to know, Sofia?'

Her bitter eyes remained fixed on him. 'Oh, so you didn't know that your papà had surveillance on Stefano and me?'

His eyes widened. 'By God! What did he do, Sofia?'

'Did you, or did you not know that he was watching me?'

'I knew he was investigating you, but…'

Sophie stormed out of the bathroom and made her way to one of the guest rooms where she slammed the door. It was a warm night, so she just collapsed on top of the covers and curled up in sobbing ball. There really was no hope left for her and Stefan. And she was destined to a life of misery with a deceitful husband.

‎⁖⁗

Derrick was furious. As soon as he'd put some clothes on, he grabbed his phone and rang Papà.

'Ciao Derick.'

'What the fuck have you done?'

'Woah. Watch your tone with me, son. You should be thanking me right now. There is no way Sofia can leave you now—and as a bonus, you get her all to yourself.' He had adopted his authoritative tone.

'Don't give me that bullshit! You've broken her! I wanted her to be happy with me. Now she's a shattered husk and she hates me. So, you better tell me exactly what you did.'

Derrick became gobsmacked and appalled as the man explained the blackmail. 'Fucking unbelievable! You don't understand matters of the heart at all, do you? You better fix this.'

'What's done can't be undone. The police are compiling Stefano's profile as we speak, and it will go public tomorrow.'

'Jesus! Did you even stop to think about how this would affect my relationship with Sofia?' He was shaking his head in disbelief.

'She's the one to blame here, not me. I warned her and I'm a man of my word.'

'Well I guess there's only one thing for it then. I hope you have a decent amount of savings set aside because I'm gonna need all of it.'

છ૭ભ

When Sophie awoke, she found that she was still in the guest room. Derrick hadn't disturbed her at all during the night. She got up and made her way to the kitchen for a coffee. That was where she found Derrick's note.

> *Sofia,*
> *I'm so sorry for what Papà has done. I*
> *honestly didn't know what he was up to.*
> *I just thought he was going to find out if*
> *you were planning to leave me. I'm now*
> *trying to clean up the mess he made and I*
> *promise to find a way to make things*
> *right.*
>
> *I truly love you,*
> *Derrick.*

She screwed up the note and threw it in the bin. *More damn lies!* Sophie slumped onto the couch and turned on the television. She didn't really want to watch anything that was on. Daytime scheduling was usually boring, but she didn't feel up to much else. The thought that she may never see Stefan again was painful beyond compare. How would she go on without him? Life without her soulmate seemed meaningless, especially if she had to live the rest of it with such a vile husband.

She continued flicking through the channels, hoping to find a distraction. But then something on the midday news caught her attention: ' —hunt now on for wanted rapist, Stefan Pacini of Toorak Gardens. Eyewitnesses have given evidence linking this man to several counts of sexually abusing his twin sister…'

Sophie stared at the screen in horror. *Paolo — you wretched man!* She quickly took a photo of the screen, then sent it to Stefan with the message, DON'T COME BACK TO MELBOURNE! YOU SHOULD ALSO DISCARD YOUR PHONE BEFORE REACHING YOUR DESTINATION. PAOLO IS MONITORING OUR DEVICES. She knew it was unlikely that he would see it for a while yet, but at least she was able to warn him.

As soon as she put her phone down, she jumped as the message tone beeped. *Surely not!* But it wasn't Stefan.

The text was from Derrick. START PACKING. TONIGHT, WE LEAVE FOR OUR HONEYMOON IN ITALY.

℠℣

There were butterflies in Sophie's stomach as she approached the Hotel Mediterráneo in Valencia. This was one of three places that Stefan had suggested as short-term accommodation options for their initial stay in Spain. And there was no guarantee he would be here. She cursed the fact that she had told him to ditch his phone because it made finding him difficult.

'Did you want me to wait outside?' Derrick asked.

She had been dubious when Derrick first explained his plans to take her to Stefan. Their flights to Italy had been torturous as he constantly begged her forgiveness and made promises to do everything in his power to reunite Sophie with her twin. But she remained silent, ignoring him the whole time.

When they had entered their Bolognian hotel room and he asked her where Stefan was staying, she burst into tears and screamed at him. 'He isn't even in Italy! He figured you'd try to track us down; so, he planned on covering our tracks.'

Exasperated, Derrick replied, 'Where is he then?'

'Nice try! There's no way I'm telling you that. I'd rather put up with a life of misery with you than risk Stefan's safety.'

Derrick gasped pain evident in his expression. 'Is that really how you feel about us now?'

She glared at him bitterly. 'Yes. What you and Paolo did to Stefan and me is unforgivable. I hate you, Derrick, and I could never trust you again.'

His face turned ashen, then he walked over to his luggage and retrieved a manila folder. He dropped it on the bed in front of her. 'Open it.'

Sophie couldn't believe her eyes when she found the forms within.

'I told you I would do anything to ensure your happiness, Sofia. Even if it means letting you go.' Derrick's voice was shaking as he spoke.

After reading the word 'Divorce' in the heading several times, the meaning finally sunk in. 'You would really do this for me? I thought...' her words trailed off. She didn't really know what she thought anymore.

'Well you thought wrong. I'm not my Papà. I don't like deceiving people and I don't just take what I want despite other people. I made a mistake, Sofia, and I'm sorry. I brought you here because I was hoping to repair our relationship and continue living with both you and Stefan; but if you only want to be with your brother, I won't stop you.'

After hours of talking things through, Sophie's trust in Derrick was restored—but not her love. She agreed to let Derrick accompany her to Spain and assist with her search, but only after completing the divorce papers and on the condition they both replaced their phones.

'You may as well sit inside at least,' Sophie replied as she walked in. She left her luggage with Derrick as he sat on the couch in the postmodern lobby.

When Sophie reached the reception desk, an elegant woman with straightened brown hair and a pristine French manicure looked up and smiled warmly. *'Hola. ¿Puedo ayudarte?'* Her name tag identified her as Valeria.

Sophie returned her smile to the best of her ability. Her anxiety had reached new heights as she stumbled over her Spanish. '*Hola. ¿Hablas inglés o italiano?*'

'I can speak some English, yes.' Valeria was still smiling.

She breathed a sigh of relief. 'Thank you. Can you please tell me if Stefano Pacini has checked in yet?'

The woman stiffened. 'Sorry, but we do not give out those details.'

Sophie started to panic. 'But my brother is expecting me.'

'Can I see your passport please?' After sighting Sophie's identification, Valeria relaxed. 'Thank you, Sofia. I apologise for the precautions, but Stefano didn't want us revealing his location to anyone but you.' She looked at the room listings then looked at Sophie with a curious expression. 'Did you say Stefano was your brother?'

'Yes, why?'

'It's just that we have him in a room with only one double bed. Will you be wanting separate sleeping arrangements? We could move you both to a larger suite if you like.'

Sophie blushed. 'Is there anything wrong with me sharing his bed?'

It was Valeria's turn to be embarrassed.

'Well, technically no. It's just that…'

'What?' Sophie cut her off, her anger was rising. 'This is Spain, isn't it? My brother and I have just travelled to the other side of the world so that we can be free to love each other openly. And is it really any of your business what I do in the privacy of a bedroom? Please just let me know what room he is in and I'll be on my way.'

The woman's jaw dropped. 'Oh, I'm sorry. You're right. It isn't any of my business. He is in room 215. Here is your key. Please enjoy your stay.'

She took the key and stormed off to the elevator. Sophie was still fuming as she rode the lift. Even in a country where incest was completely legal, there were people who considered their relationship taboo. But as soon as she found herself standing in front of the door to room 215, her rage vanished, replaced by some much stronger feelings. Her heart was pounding furiously as she knocked. But no answer came. Shit! Was he out? Then she tried the key.

Upon entering, she discovered that Stefan was sleeping, half naked with the bed covers tossed aside. The sight filled her with desire. He lay on his back, wearing nothing but a pair of red satin boxers. His olive skin was covered in perspiration despite the temperate weather. And he was aroused. Sophie grinned, knowing exactly who and what he was dreaming about. She quietly undressed, then snuck across the room.

She eased herself onto the bed, then carefully straddled him. As soon as the rest of her weight pressed against him, his eyes flicked opened.

He suddenly grabbed her, then flipped her onto her back. Pinning her down, he asked, 'Am I still dreaming?'

Sophie giggled. 'Would you like me to pinch you?'

'Only if you do it hard.' The moment she grabbed both his nipples, the lust in his eyes intensified. He pressed his lips to hers and pushed his tongue inside her mouth.

Sophie groaned with pleasure as Stefan's calloused fingers explored her body, welcoming his familial touch. She tugged at the hem of his boxer shorts, releasing his erection from its satin prison.

Stefan moved to the side of the bed to remove the shorts properly, then he lay on his back. He looked at her, his dark brown bedroom eyes drawing her closer. 'I want you on top this time.'

There was no hesitation in her response. She jumped on him and they kissed passionately. Hovering above him a moment, she enjoyed the feel of him being on the verge of penetration. 'I love you, Stefano—my dear brother. You are my one true love, my soulmate, all that I want and need.'

He gasped. 'I love you, Sofia. I always have and always will.'

With that, their bodies merged completely, and two halves became whole.

Epilogue

Sophie's heart was swelling with excitement as she sat by the window of her rustic suite, looking out at the stunning Mediterranean gardens set amidst the rolling hills of Cadiz.

When Dominic entered, she squealed and ran to embrace him. 'I can't believe this day has finally come!'

'Oh my God, I know right! It's unreal.' He stood back and admired her a moment. 'You look a-mazing.'

She beamed with delight. 'And you look simply dashing in that Armani. You know, I had a feeling Patrick was right for you when I first met him. I'm so thrilled to be celebrating this day with you. And the weather is absolutely perfect for a wedding.'

Dom grinned. 'Don't you mean weddings!'

Sophie squealed and hugged him again. It had been ten years since she moved to Spain, with Dom and Patrick following them a year later. Stefan had finished his commerce degree and landed himself a cushy job as a financial accountant. This allowed him to support Sophie's postgraduate studies in Immunology, from which she obtained a research assistant position at the University of Valencia.

There was a knock at the door. Dom and Sophie looked at each speculatively.

'Who is it?' Sophie cried. She wasn't about to let either of their grooms sneak a peek before the ceremony.

'It's Derrick. Don't worry, Stefan and Patrick aren't with me.'

Having remained friends, Sophie had invited him to the wedding. It took some time, but he eventually moved on and found new love with Maya, a fellow doctor working with him at the Valencian hospital. 'Okay. Come in.'

Dom opened the door. 'Hey man.' They shook hands.

Then when Derrick entered the room properly, he gasped at the sight of Sophie in all her finery. Sophie wore a light gold-toned ballgown that was covered in Swarovski crystals.

As they embraced, Derrick whispered in her ear, 'I fear that I might start falling for you all over again. You're the hottest and most beautiful bride I've ever seen.'

She punched him on the arm. 'Derrick, you

fiend!'

'Ow! Okay, hint taken.' He gave her a mischievous grin. 'I have a couple of surprises for you.'

'They'd better be good because I don't think my nerves could handle much going wrong right now.' After all the difficulties she had gone through to get this far, she couldn't help but worry that something might pull them apart at the last minute.

He gave her a look of trepidation. 'Well I don't think you'll mind the first, but I hope you'll be okay with the second.'

'What's the first thing then?' she asked.

'I have news from Australia concerning Paolo.' Derrick stopped referring to him as Papà ever since Sophie had mentioned being manhandled by him. His tone was bitter as he continued. 'The vile man is about to face life in prison for multiple charges of sexual assault and a long string of corrupt business dealings. He's finally getting his just desserts.'

She looked at him with sympathy. 'Oh God, I'm sorry Derrick. That can't be easy for you and the rest of your family.'

'Nah, it's okay. I broke my ties with him long ago. At least he can't hurt you or anyone else again.'

It was satisfying to think of that man behind bars after all the pain and suffering he had caused. 'So, what's the second surprise?'

He smiled. 'A couple of special guests would like to see you.' Derrick walked over to the door and admitted them.

She panicked the moment she saw her parents enter. *Please God, no!*

As if sensing her fear, Mamma spoke, 'It's okay Sofia. We may not like-a what you're doing, but we love you both so much that we are willing to overlook your sinful lifestyle. We are here to-a support you, not stop you.'

Relief washed over her. She flew into Mamma's arms and let the tears of joy flow. 'I've missed you so much!'

'Me too. You've always been-a precious to me.' She held Sophie at arm's length and smiled. 'You look like a princess.' Then her eye caught the pendant around Sophie's neck. She picked up the dainty little mask. 'I think I understand now why you never took this off.'

After Mamma released her grip, Sophie looked to Papà. He was smiling. Such a rare sight! She squeezed him in a tight embrace. 'I love you, Papà.'

His arms hesitated at first, but then they encircled her. 'I love you too, Sofia. It is good to see you happy again.'

The wedding planner summoned them a few minutes later. Derrick and Sophie's parents hurried out to take their seats.

Then Sophie and Dominic linked arms and made their way to the beautiful rose garden that was about to play host to a most unconventional wedding. When they reached their starting point, Sophie gasped. She was struck by how stunning Stefan looked standing in his tailored suit under the Spanish sun. They both locked eyes and grinned. Then 'New Day' by Karnivool started playing and she walked with her best friend down the aisle towards her twin brother: her lover and soon-to-be husband.

What's Next?

Thank you for reading *From Prying Eyes*. I would be most grateful if you could show your support by leaving a rating or even a review.

While Sophie and Stefan's story ends here, Phoebe's books continue with *Crystal's Crucible*, coming August 2021. In the meantime, you can read where it all began in *I Heart Mr. Collins*.

I Heart Mr. Collins

Phoebe Braddock's Love Story

Is it possible to find love without boundaries?

I might have described myself as innocent a few months ago, but that was before my schoolgirl crush turned into something real and passionate beyond my wildest imagination. Now my lustful appetite has awoken and there is no going back.

The problem is, no one else can know what I do when alone with Mr. Collins because it would jeopardise his career. Other people wouldn't understand what we have.

At least graduation is just around the corner and I will strike off lying and deception from my current list of sins. That is my hope, but will I find the courage to be completely honest with everyone?

AVAILABLE NOW

Keep reading for a sample…

Chapter One

Diary extract dated Thursday 12th April 2001

'You are eighteen years of age now, yes?'

'Yes I am.'

'Would you object to me taking this any further?'
He asked this last question while gliding his hand
under my school dress and up along my inner thigh.
Smiling I replied, 'I would not object.'

That happened on the last day of term one, during my final year of high school. Because I had repeated a year in my early schooling, I was already eighteen years old, a legal adult in Australia.

The morning started out much as any other at the breakfast bar with my Mum, Laura Braddock. 'Morning Mum.'

'Morning Phoebe.' She kissed me on the cheek, then handed me the milk. 'You were up late last night. How'd you go with that media studies project?'

'Finished, thank God. It's due in first period. We focus on TV media next term.'

'Ah good.' Smiling she added, 'Perhaps I'll get a chance to read a fresh paper again, and not dig them out of your room days later.'

I just gave her a guilty smile in response before plunging into my bowl of cereal.

'I spoke to your dad last night by the way. Plans are set for your stay there.'

'Thanks Mum. I was getting worried.' For as long as I could remember it had just been Mum and me. Dad left when I was a toddler and Mum had never remarried, claiming that she wanted to focus on motherhood rather than stepping back into the dating realm. I suspected that this had more to do with her fear of being hurt again than she ever admitted. She chose not to divulge the nature of her breakup with Dad to me because she did not want to sabotage my relationship with him. I typically only saw Dad for a few days during school holidays when time allowed for me to take a trip out to the country where he lived. Half the time he would even cancel those visits because he would decide to take-off on some wild voyage at the last minute, using the excuse of conducting important research for his writing. He was Tobias K. Braddock, successful fantasy adventure author; something I could admire him for at least.

When I was able to see him, we had a lot of fun

and I loved that he indulged my own passion for books. Some of my fondest childhood memories were of Dad reading me the works of Enid Blyton as bedtime stories. In my early teens I began compiling my own library of rare edition books from across a range of genres, but my most prized pieces were the paperbacks that I had folded over and read to bits. In more recent years my reading tastes had changed, shifting into the realms of classic and gothic romance. Jane Austen, Anne Radcliffe, and the Brontë sisters stood out as favourites to me at this time. Something about the plight of their heroines struck chords with me and gave me the vicarious means I needed to experience passionate love.

Mum handed over my lunch bag then kissed me farewell on the cheek before heading off to work. I gave the contents of the bag a quick glance and sure enough she had loaded it with a selection of my favourite healthy foods, including sushi, carrot sticks, yoghurt, and fruit salad.

ૹ૰

When I boarded the bus, my best friend Denise stood up and waved for me to join her. She gave me a hug when I reached her, then as we sat, she remarked, 'Oh my god I love your hair Phoebs! It's so straight and shiny. And is that a Gucci fragrance you're wearing?'

I carefully placed my school bag down to ensure

that it would not fall over before replying, 'Spot on hun, it's Gucci—my new fave! Thanks for noticing my hair—I straightened it today.' While I don't consider myself particularly vain, I do take some care to ensure my appearance is neat. Placing my head on Denise's shoulder I added, 'Let me guess, you're wearing a Dior today?'

'Hole-in-one babe! You are getting good at this. Oh wow—school break is about to start. I am way-excited! The gang have got some pretty wild parties planned for the next two weeks and—'

'Well H-E-L-L-O ladies!'

Her thread of conversation was broken off by a couple of guys taking their seats across from us. They wore the unmistakable uniform of St. Mark's College, the posh Catholic school down the road from our own. They both wore black dress pants, white shirts, black blazers with red trim, and black and red striped ties.

The boy who greeted us, a very attractive looking jock with spiked up hair, turned to his friend briefly to add, 'See Nick, catching the bus isn't so bad.'

Returning to smile at us both he made the introductions, 'So, I'm Curtis and this here is my mate Nick. You'll have to excuse his mood today; he's just been grounded and misses his beloved car.' He gave Nick a friendly nudge, which had the strange effect of easing the guy's mood.

Grinning and returning the nudge Nick replied,

'Hi ladies. You'll have to excuse my mate Curtis; he can be quite rude at times.'

Denise, obviously flattered by the attention and unable to take her eyes off Curtis, introduced us both in her usual fashion, using exaggerated hand gestures. 'Well it's a pleasure to meet you both. I'm Denise.' She placed both hands against her chest, ensuring attention was adequately drawn to where she thought it ought to go. 'And this is Phoebe.' She finished, placing both hands on my shoulder.

I loved Denise, she had always been a kind, loyal, and generous friend ever since I was seven years old, but her attention-seeking behaviour and model-like body meant that most boys overlooked me. My own physique was quite petite, being only five-foot-three with an A cup bra, and I chose to keep my natural dark brown hair colour rather than bleaching it blonde like Denise.

Denise leaned slightly forward towards Curtis and continued, 'Judging by your black and red uniforms I'm guessing you both go to St. Mark's?'

Curtis responded by leaning towards Denise. 'A most accurate observation, but now you have me at a disadvantage because I can't guess what school you go to.'

It was Nick who replied to this, sitting back casually and smiling at me. 'You must be blind, Curtis! The logo on their blazers and bags is from St. Teresa's.'

The focus of Nick's attention was not lost on me and I felt compelled to return his smile. It was a captivating look thanks to his deep ocean-blue eyes that made me feel lost at sea. The effect was such that I was only vaguely aware that Denise and Curtis continued to converse. I took in all of Nick's facial features, from his honey-blond hair in a classic pompadour style, to his full lips and chiselled jawline, but it was those attentive eyes that drew me back into my trance. I was not lifted from my reverie until the boys reached their stop, but Curtis had made a point of giving us both his mobile number before parting; a gesture that Denise was all too happy to reciprocate.

೫ೕ೫

St. Teresa's was a relatively large girls' Catholic college on the East side of the city that adjoined the grand old cathedral sharing the same name—a favourite feature of mine. I was never devoutly religious, but I loved attending school mass in this Baroque-revival building, complete with a colonnade of columns decorated with gilded scrolls, intricate stain-glass windows, and a ceiling that seemed as high as the sky. It was such a contrast to the little suburban church that Mum took me to on Sundays.

Every school day started with home group and this year we had Mr. Collins supervising us for this fifteen-minute period; a bonus for me because he was my favourite teacher. Initially, this was because he had also been my English teacher and netball coach every year since I started high school, but over the last fifteen months I had been crushing on him too. During this session Mr. Collins reminded us that our afternoon lessons will be replaced by the end of term assembly then an early dismissal. After the morning formalities were finished, he proceeded to share his news, 'Now ladies I wanted to inform you of this before it is announced in the afternoon's assembly. I will not be returning to teach at St. Teresa's next term. I am being transferred to St. Mark's college for the remainder of the year and this will likely become a permanent posting.'

An audible sigh of disappointment was heard throughout the classroom. I did not join this chorus, however, because I was sitting in stunned silence. I could almost feel tears welling up and it took all my inner strength to maintain composure. This man had been like a rock to me for so many years and he was leaving just at the pinnacle of my school education. I didn't know what to do or say; so, I just moved on to my next class despondently.

After my first lesson finally finished, I hurried to the library for my free period where I relaxed with the last of my current English reader, *Chocolat* by Joanne Harris. The movie adaptation of this book had just been released and I was looking forward to an excursion with my English class to see it in the cinema next term. As soon as I remembered this, I dropped my book at the realisation that a new English teacher might not honour this promise made by Mr. Collins. I closed my eyes in quiet contemplation and tried some deep breathing to keep my calm. I don't know how long I remained in this state of meditation, but the recess bell brought me back to reality, so I jumped up to join my friends in our usual spot.

ॐ

The following study periods and lunch passed by with little incident or time for pensiveness and then it was assembly. The whole thing dragged on in the usual fashion of presentation after presentation. Then the dreaded announcement came at the end. The Principal, Mrs. Caldwell, explained that Mr. Collins will be transferred to St Mark's and that the whole school community will greatly miss him. She then called for a round of applause to thank him for his work and to wish him well in his future endeavours. At this, the whole student body, myself included, gave him a standing ovation and as I looked around, I saw tears on a few other cheeks as well.

After the assembly Denise and I grabbed a drink from the canteen before heading back to our lockers to collect our bags. Most of the crowd had died down by this stage, so we found ourselves alone in the corridor just outside our homeroom when Denise broached the topic of Mr. Collins.

'It'll be a shame to see Mr. Collins go. He was always my fave and an awesome netball coach to boot.'

At this I replied, 'I agree wholeheartedly Denise. I'm really gonna miss him too, and his cheeky smile. I'll admit that I've had a huge crush on him for a while now.'

No sooner had these words left my mouth than Mr. Collins came walking out of the open door of our homeroom and approached us, giving me quite the surprise. I blushed, wondering if he heard what I said. 'Hello ladies. Phoebe, can I have a word please?'

He gestured for me to step inside the homeroom, which also doubled as his office. I bid Denise farewell with a coy smile, indicating that I would catch up with her soon, then promptly followed Mr. Collins' instructions. He closed and locked the door upon my entrance, and I stood blinking at him, uncomprehending. His gaze fixed on me intently with fierce longing eyes and then it dawned on me.

Gesturing to the hallway, I began to speak, 'Did you hear—'

His own words cut me off as he drew closer, 'While it saddens me to leave this school, I no longer feel the need to hold back from doing this.' At that he threw his arms around me, grabbing my backside, and kissed me deeply.

I was startled at first, but then I lifted my hands up, resting them behind his neck, and returned the kiss. I had kissed a few boys during my adolescent years, but this was altogether different. The scratchy stubble on his face, the scent of Old Spice cologne, and the way his tongue caressed my mouth, providing strong contrast to remind me that this man was much older and more experienced.

He pressed my body back toward his solid oak desk and I felt my backside resting against the edge of it. He lifted me up so that I was seated and continued to kiss me for a few more minutes.

Then it happened.

When Mr. Collins was eventually spent, we both collapsed onto the desk and I curled up in his arms. He was the first to break the silence. 'I am going to give you my home address. Will you call upon me Phoebe?'

'Yes, I'd love to Mr. Collins.'

'Please, call me Jonah when we are alone.' Mr. Collins stood up and quickly dressed and I followed suit. He wrote his mobile number and address on a scrap of paper, then handed it to me, asking me to visit him soon. 'We had best be going now. I do not want to arouse any suspicions.'

We parted with a kiss as fiery as its predecessors and I soon found myself hopping along cloud nine all the long bus ride home.

Also By L. Starla

The Phoebe Braddock Books
(Taboo romance)
I Heart Mr. Collins
From Prying Eyes
Crystal's Crucible (August 2021)

Winter's Magic Series
(Urban fantasy / paranormal romance)
Coming Soon

Acknowledgements

Many thanks to my editors Jason and Felix. This book would not be more than a draft on my computer without their efforts.

A special thanks to Brian O'Neill Photography (Australia) for designing the awesome images used during my launch campaign.

And a *huge* shout out to all my launch team members:

Sarah Taylor, Felix Staica, Adam Rau, Jason Suter, Matthew Buckley, Jennifer Hartmann, Yasmine Hamandi, Sandy Mill, Ariel Mareroa, Patricia Baker, Joseph Dalle Nogare, Emma Williams, and Sophie Rose.

About the Author

Laelia Starla is an Australian author who was often found raiding her mother's shelves for any form of fiction she could get her hands on. Her first love was the horror genre, but she owes her passionate affair with the romance novel to her high-school English teacher, who got her hooked on the classics. Given her earlier reading, urban fantasy and paranormal romance seemed like a natural progression. Along with erotic romance, these have become her favourite genres to write.

Laelia also loves spending her spare time playing tabletop and video games, paper crafting, singing, dancing, and watching anime.

Access Exclusive Content

Join my newsletter to access free stuff like short stories, deleted scenes, fan art, and invitations to future launch events.

Newsletter: www.starlaarts.com>freebies

Follow me Online:
Website & Blog: www.starlaarts.com
Goodreads: 19660804.L_Starla
BookBub: www.bookbub.com/profile/l-starla
Amazon Author Profile: author/l.starla
Instagram: lstarlaauthor
Facebook: StarlaArts